THE FIRST FIG TREE

Vivian Glover

THE FIRST FIG TREE

St. Martin's Press
New York

THE FIRST FIG TREE. Copyright © 1987 by Vivian Glover. All rights reserved. Printed in the United States of America. No part of this book may be used or reproduced in any manner whatsoever without written permission except in the case of brief quotations embodied in critical articles or reviews. For information, address St. Martin's Press, 175 Fifth Avenue, New York, N.Y. 10010.

Library of Congress Cataloging-in-Publication Data

Glover, Vivian.
    The first fig tree / by Vivian Glover.
        p.   cm.
    ISBN 0-312-01762-6 : $15.95
    I. Title.   II. Title: 1st fig tree.
PS3557.L68F5 1988
813'.54—dc19   87-36724
                                                                     CIP

First published in Great Britain by Methuen London Ltd.

First U.S. Edition

10 9 8 7 6 5 4 3 2 1

To my grandmother,
Annie Belle

Prologue

Ellen Bryanston Flood went about her daily work as if the war did not concern her.

'Yes,' she answered, patiently, without pausing in her work, when they asked her if she heard Mr Roosevelt had declared a war. But she said nothing more and whatever she was thinking, she kept to herself as she slowly and deliberately cleaned the little clapboard house that was one of so many scattered under, and shaded by, the tall South Carolina pines.

Nearby, Ellen's neighbours stood outside their doors, gathering and regathering into groups to talk about the war, and to spread their version of the continuous flow of rumours that were being brought back from the small town of Eautawville.

Ellen didn't seem to notice the congregating or hear the excited voices. She was, had she been asked, wondering about a more immediate matter – did she have the strength left in her to sweep off the front porch? The arthritis was bad. The morning air made it so, she would have said as she limped over to a corner for a straw broom. She paused there, her hand covering her hip, and asked the Lord for a little more strength before she began to brush the floor. One more step, she told herself, and kept the broom moving to the rhythm of her voice.

When she had finished she sat down on the porch and thought to herself what a fine, mild day it had become. The sun, strong in the winter sky, spread across the wooden planks of the porch floor, and Ellen, her head lifted slightly, nodded in gratitude for the warmth and because she had been able to complete the few chores that she had set for herself. Trying to ignore the aches in her joints, Ellen listened to the occasional rush of wind through the tops of the pines but the nearby voices interfered. The war; she could hear them talking about it still.

'Well,' Ellen said to herself, 'so they were having another war.' She nodded her head at this terrible truth but wasn't bothered to dwell on it. Her thoughts these days mostly drifted back to the past which offered her more comfort and company than the present. 'And anyway,' she said, distracted from her reverie by an outburst of shouting from the next house, 'seem like they always having a war. Some place or another.' Then after another thoughtful moment she added, 'Ever since I was old enough to know.' She was thinking back to the first war she could remember. The real war she had always called it, where they had seen the fighting, one man against another, and the destruction, as close as over there. She was peering across a field to where a large house had once stood. Ellen could see scenes from the battle as if it were just happening.

'Didn't seem like the war was ever goin to end.' She uttered a phrase they had repeated so often to each other after the months had grown into years. And they never did know what the end would bring. First, the Yankees was winning, then the Confederates had won. One day they were free and the next day they were slaves again. It wasn't until months after all the fighting had stopped that they'd all known for sure that they were free. For real free.

'Yes Lord,' Ellen said, unaware that she had spoken out loud or that she was rocking to and fro in her chair. She would always be affected by the memory of it though she had recounted it many times through the years. How one morning the Master had come out to the fields and said he had to tell them all that they weren't slaves no longer. And her mamma had stood there and looked after Master, as he walked back to the house. Looked till he was out of sight. Then dropped the rake and told us to come and walked right out of that field. Ellen could still see them walking across the fields, their short legs trying to keep up with their mother. They didn't go down the rows. They were stepping over the cotton stalks, taking the shortest route back to the cabins and all she was thinking about was keeping up with her mamma.

When they got back to their cabin her mamma told her to

go fetch some water in the basin and bring it so she could wash her feet. That was what she did, sitting in the doorway, her mamma washed her feet and put on her shoes. She stayed there for the rest of the day, wearing her shoes on her clean feet just like it was Sunday. Some of the others had starting celebrating, cooking up all their rations, dancing and playing music, singing all kinds of songs. Ellen had gone to watch and then came back with a plate of food someone had sent to her mother. That evening she sat with her while her mother slowly ate the food, chewing each mouthful till finally she had to swallow it. Cleaning the plate and then handing it back. That was the day that she was free and the war was over.

Ellen looked over at her neighbours. There were two young men talking about what they would do to win the war. It seemed that the news of Mr Roosevelt's war had stirred up the whole world, Ellen thought as she listened to what they were saying. 'Best to wait and see,' Ellen advised. In her great age, she had learned that war, like any other pestilence that travelled the land, had a way, when the time had come, of finding you one way or the other.

When she had rested enough to get up, Ellen began to think about her dinner. 'Otherwise the stove will go out.' The kitchen and bedroom were kept warm by it. After dinner, she said to coax herself up from the chair, she could close her eyes for a while, knowing that she would be warm and fed for the rest of the day. She gave herself another minute to sit in order to admire the polished leaves of the holly bush. The birds had picked most of the berries, but she had enjoyed watching them too.

Ellen didn't pay any mind to the car until it had just about pulled up in front of the house. She shaded her eyes to see who it was, though she knew from the shape of it, that the car belonged to her daughter and son-in-law. She told them, as she stood up in greeting, that she was just that minute about to put some dinner on.

They gave her news of the family and she listened, knowing that her time had come. She could see it in their eyes, their plans for her. They were going to take her away. Close the house down. 'Tom would run away,' the old woman said, thus admitting, after so many months, defeat, and betraying the mangy old cat who had chosen to make his home with her some years ago. Somehow, she had hoped, looking around at her few possessions, she and Tom would be left to see their remaining time out together. That's all she wanted to do, ease herself through the little bit of time that she could feel was left in her bones.

'Ain't that right Tom?' she asked, ignoring her daughter and son-in-law, since defiance seemed to be her last means of resistance.

Tom didn't respond. She stared at him hard, her lower lip pursed, the only sign of her sadness.

Her daughter spoke softly as if she too was reluctant to disturb the life that, over the years, had settled around her mother. She explained that there would be a room, down the hall, almost separated from the rest of the house, especially prepared for her. It overlooked the back garden. There was plenty of garden if she wanted a little patch to work on herself.

The old woman shifted her gaze from the cat to the stove to show these things didn't impress her, while she thought to herself how they would be putting her into loneliness. She could almost feel the isolation that would surround her. She made a sound of annoyance, sucking in her mouth in response to her daughter's soothing words. Tom opened one eye in case he was being offered some little morsel, but when the old woman remained still, turned his head to one side and dozed off again.

Her daughter had saved the surprise for last. Their youngest grandaughter, Joanne, Andrew's child . . . she interrupted and said she didn't know who that was and even when they reminded her of the time she'd seen her, she still didn't remember. How could they, she mumbled, expect her to know which one of all those grandchildren they were talking about. She was trying to remember though and blinked with concentration, but other pieces of reality were also crowding her mind and disturbing the even rhythm that had been her faith. They were saying the child would be living with them, someone to keep her company. Right then and there the thought of a child irritated her. Her hand shook with annoyance. She raised it from her lap and swept Joanne aside.

'Well there ain't go be no peace and quiet then.' She lifted her eyes to them, accusing them of already going back on a promise, then decided not to listen as they tried to reassure her that the child would be kept out of the way if that's what she wanted. She would be at school most of the time.

Her gaze fell on the stove again. How could they understand? After all these years she was tired out. The least she could expect was the odd comfort and not too much bother. It was up to her to know what was comfortable and what was trouble, to choose the few little things she had to look forward to.

Her thoughts drifted to the past again where she was still in control, but she could not escape for long the tone of determination in her daughter's voice. She looked at her daughter, wanting to ask her what all would she have to leave behind, aside from Tom and the few chickens. Everything in the house, according to what her daughter was saying. She wouldn't need these old things any more. And what about the life, the old woman added another silent question, her mouth growing stiff with resistance to what she was hearing: leave that behind too? She couldn't take that with her, even without her daughter knowing. Couldn't carry it in any way, shape or form.

No doubt her daughter supposed she was taking her to a better life. Well, she didn't believe so because it wasn't what she wanted. The old woman's mouth turned down deeply at the sides as she conjured up an image of the large white stucco house sitting behind a wide lawn that gently sloped down to the road. The house extended back under a row of tall trees that also bordered open fields, which eventually led, by the road that followed round it, to the campus of the Negro state college. There were only two other houses nearby, and none of the busy sounds of her neighbours' activities which she had so casually taken for granted that morning.

The old woman had on several occasions spent a few days at the house, being coaxed into joining some special family gathering. It had been an enjoyable time with the house full of some of the many relatives who knew her well and fussed over her. But she would always be fidgeting to get back to her own little home long before it was time to take her there, because she couldn't relax like she wanted to in the spacious rooms that her daughter had decorated to such meticulous specifications, and where it seemed like everything was standing to attention.

For her daughter and son-in-law the house represented and proved, because proof would always be needed, that a coloured person, educated and upstanding, knew how to and could live among the finery that was supposed to be the particular dominion of the white hierarchy. All the extra manners and starchy ways that went with it belonged to a life style, the old woman had told Tom when she was finally settled in her own house again, that she could quite gladly do without. All it did was tire her out.

The times when she was there visiting and needed to get away, so she could breathe more easily, the old woman, with the help of her walking stick, had made her way through to the back of the house and out away from the carefully tended lawns and shrubs on to where the vegetable garden and fruit orchard seemed willing to welcome her. And if, picking her way carefully, she continued her walking, she came upon a few chickens scratching around in the dirt behind a fenced-in area. She would stand there and watch and listen to them cackle to one another.

On her way back to the house she would circle the back garden and walk along beside the fence that bordered one of the two other houses that made up the rest of the rural suburban street. The old woman had come to know the people who lived in these houses, also very dignified and proud to be prominent members of the coloured community. The old woman would pass the time of day in conversation with them, say something about the weather or her health, but that was the extent of what they had in common.

'It wasn't like I was sick,' she grumbled. It was as if she had spoken so that only she heard. She eyed Tom, who was now half hidden in the corner behind the stove, and it seemed as if a distance already divided them. She spoke to him anyway, since she was in the habit of sharing her thoughts. 'One way or another, ole Tom, when the time has come, these things have a way of finding you.'

The Cat's Tale

At the back of the house in Orangeburg, the little girl had come upon the old woman. She was asleep in a rocking chair under the big pecan tree. For a while, the little girl stood and watched the old woman's still and sedate profile.

It was the first opportunity she'd had to study her grandmother's mother who had been brought to the house three days ago. Up until then, the old woman had remained in her room, the door closed, hardly making a sound except for a mysterious shifting noise from time to time which the little girl had been unable to identify. She had tried peering through the keyhole but the view into the room was obstructed by something hanging from the door knob.

On a few occasions, the little girl had followed her grandmother into the room and stood silently to one side, watching as her grandmother tended to the old woman. She had hardly spoken a word, but with a long eye had looked over the little girl until her own eyes started to shift from place to place under the unswerving, expressionless gaze.

Her reaction to all this was to ask her grandmother if the old woman was a witch. Her grandmother had dismissed her and the question as bonkers. But the little girl and some of her friends from school, having weighed up the evidence, remained suspicious, especially when they thought about the little girl's description of her.

She had told them, while they sat listening with their faces wide-open and all the time wondering, that the old woman had real, real, white hair, none of it was black, and it was plaited into tee-tiny braids, all joined together, and you could see her scalp and it was white like dried-up bones. They had all nodded as if they had seen a similar thing before and it confirmed their suspicions. The little girl had added that the old woman's face had so many wrinkles on it that that's all it was, just wrinkles, big ones and little ones. And her hands had wrinkles all over them too, thin hands, almost like a chicken foot. The little girl lifted her hand and bent her fingers so they could see what she meant. And her eyes, she had saved the eyes for last, it seemed like they were made up of two colours. They were brown on the inside and then they had a pale circle round the outside. One of her friends said that came from living in the dark, that's how she could see. They all nodded in agreement and remembered that witches could see in the dark.

The little girl had been warned by one of her friends, who had known a witch, to be careful. She'd told them all though that she wouldn't never be afraid of a witch and she wouldn't never be afraid of no old woman neither.

After she'd stared a good long time at the old woman who had not stirred in her sleep, the little girl had tiptoed to within a few feet of her and then stopped when she could hear her deep, short breaths. A moment later she stepped even closer and whispered in a haunting voice, 'I'm going to kill the kittens.'

The old woman continued sleeping.

'Did you hear what I said?' The little girl had raised her voice just above a whisper. 'I'm going to kill the kittens.' She kept her eyes steadily on the old woman whose head was bowed over her chest. She wheezed softly and stirred.

'Kill all the kittens,' the little girl hissed, and leaned almost into the old woman's face.

The old woman shifted, mumbled something into her chest and sank back into sleep.

Without moving the little girl turned her head and looked towards the house, then in her normal voice talked into the old woman's ear. 'That's what I'm going to do. Kill them. Now. NOW!' she shouted.

The old woman started. Her head jerked up and her hands flew off her lap. 'What?' she called out at the noise that had awakened her. She looked out from her chair, confused, not knowing where she was. 'What you say?' She raised her hands over her head as if to ward off trouble. 'What you say?' she asked again into the still-unfamiliar surroundings. Lowering her hands cautiously, she looked one way and then another until her eyes focused on the little girl whom she recognized.

'What's the matter?' the old woman asked, her hands now pressed to her chest to calm herself.

'It's me.' The little girl stepped forward as if to announce her presence.

'Seem like somebody was calling me just now.' Slowly, the old woman leaned back in her chair. 'Like somebody was right up beside me. Calling.' She pressed her hands to her eyes, shook her head and then looked around into the garden.

'There wasn't nobody calling you,' the little girl said.

'Sure seem like it. Seem like somebody was in trouble. Just a callin to me.'

'But you've been sleeping.' The little girl took another step towards the chair while she eyed the back door of the house.

'I know I was sleeping,' the old woman said, 'and that's what it was that brought me out of my sleep. That calling sound.' She thought for a moment. 'You wasn't calling me?'

The little girl shook her head. 'Nobody was calling you. I didn't hear nobody call you.'

'Seem like it was so real. Right up next to me.' The little girl didn't say anything. 'You didn't hear nothing?' The little girl shook her head again and took a step away from the chair.

The old woman shifted to make herself more comfortable and to help her remember. 'Seem like I could hear somebody calling saying something was going to happen. Musta been dreaming,' but she shook her head, unconvinced.

'I was going to tell you something when you woke up,' the little girl volunteered.

'Was you?'

The little girl nodded. 'You been sleeping for a long time.'

'And that was a good sleep I was having too,' she said, feeling cross that it had been interrupted. 'First sleep I had since I left home.'

The little girl didn't say anything.

'Just have to wait and see,' but the old woman pressed her hand to her head, still trying to remember.

'The cat had another bunch of kittens,' the little girl decided to tell her. Now that she was standing up close to the old

15

woman she didn't seem as frightening. The little girl continued talking. 'Grandma found them in the shed this morning. I been in to see them. There's four. Three white ones with spots and one all black.'

The old woman nodded. 'That's nice.'

'No it's not,' the little girl said, suddenly serious. 'Grandma says she's so mad at that ole cat always having kittens every time she turns round.'

Frowning slightly, the old woman leaned forward in her chair and studied the little girl. 'Wasn't you telling me something about some kittens just now?'

The little girl stopped talking and looked over at the old woman.

'Something about killing some kittens?'

The little girl didn't answer.

'That's what it was. I know it.' The old woman had solved her puzzle. 'I know I heard that thing.' She sat back in her chair and thought for a moment, then, connecting it all to the little girl, looked up.

The little girl took a step back. 'That's what I was going to tell you when you woke up but you . . .'

The old woman had raised her finger and aimed it at the little girl. 'Well if you was going to tell me, then how come I done heard it already?'

'I was starting to tell you,' the little girl said quietly, watching the old woman's every move.

'And you were standing right here.' The old woman pointed to the spot. 'I know I heard somebody. Scaring me like that.' She shook her head at the little girl's mischievous behaviour. 'Calling me out my sleep.'

'But I wasn't calling you,' the little girl objected.

'Yeah you did. Made me . . . I don't know what . . . think I was having some kinda crazy dream or something.'

'I didn't say you had a dream.' The little girl didn't want to be blamed for more than she had done in case the incident got back to her grandmother.

'And telling a tale on top of it.' The old woman had re-aimed her finger at the little girl.

16

'I wasn't telling a tale.' The list of crimes was mounting. 'Grandma did say I could kill the kittens. She did so.'

The old woman looked at the little girl as if she was trying to figure her out. 'Now you know your grandmamma didn't say no such a thing.'

'Yes she did! She did say I could kill them.'

The old woman shook her head as if she was wondering why the little girl persisted with her fib.

'She did!' The little girl stamped her foot.

The old woman raised her eyes and took umbrage at the little girl's disrespectful reaction.

The little girl didn't notice and continued to defend herself. 'She told me. I asked her two times and she said she didn't care what happen to them they was such a nuisance.'

The old woman was looking to one side when she spoke, still offended by the little girl's foot stomping but deciding that the matter needed sorting out. 'Well, saying that is not the same as saying you can kill them. Not the way I see it.'

'That's what she said.' The little girl's voice was rising with exasperation. 'And I told her I was going to kill them.'

The little girl shrugged again. The old woman watched her. After a while she said, 'I had a cat one time. Before I come here.' She paused, then continued, 'Used to call him Tom. He was a big ole cat. Everybody used to say, "That Tom sure is a ole ugly cat." And he used to walk around like he thought he was a lion or something. Mangy ole thing. He used to make me laugh sometimes, the way he would strut up to the house.' The old woman smiled and looked out into the garden, lost in some reminiscence about ole Tom.

The little girl made a note to remember to describe Tom to her friends. It was another sign. She was watching the old woman very closely when, still smiling, she looked back to the little girl.

'I liked Tom and he liked me. We used to get along fine, specially when I was on my own. He just wandered up to the house one day and stayed. Maybe,' she pointed over to the garden shed, 'there might be a Tom for somebody in one of those little kittens you want to get rid of. One day, somebody might be going to love it.'

For a moment the old woman looked at the little girl, then she sat up, resting her elbows on the arms of her chair. 'And what you want to go and kill some little kitten for?'

The little girl glanced at her and then down at the ground. She frowned. 'I told you. Grandma doesn't want them. And she said I could do whatever I like with them.' The little girl turned away but the old woman continued to hold her under scrutiny.

'And that's what you want to do?' the old woman asked. 'Kill them?'

The little girl nodded without looking up.

'Well,' the old woman said, and took a breath as if it pained her. 'You just can't go round killing everything people say they don't want. Whole lot a things would be dead. Wouldn't it?'

'She said I could.' The little girl's frown deepened and she continued to stare at the ground.

'And that's what you want to do?' the old woman asked again. 'Go in the shed and take the little kittens from their mother and go out and kill them?'

'Cause they're a nuisance.'

'Well what they doing to be a nuisance?'

The little girl didn't answer.

'What they doing to be a nuisance?' the old woman asked again. 'They ain't nothing but some little baby kittens. Probably can't even see yet and they can't walk and they can't look after theyself. So how they go be a nuisance?'

The little girl shrugged her shoulders. 'Grandma doesn't want them.'

'Well maybe what one person don't want another person might want real bad.' The old woman paused for a moment, then added, 'Just cause one person don't want a thing don't mean that everybody don't want it. Does it?'

The little girl glanced over at the old woman and then looked away. 'Well why doesn't Grandma want them then?'

The old woman sighed. 'I don't rightly know. Maybe if you live in a big, fine house, you don't want too many cats around. Seem like coloured folks do a lot of changin when they living in town.'

'Are you only suppose to have one cat if you live in town?'

'Maybe so. Folks in the country don't mind if they got a few cats. Help to keep the rats down. No they don't mind a few cats. They do a lot of good. Keep away vermin.' The old woman sat back in her chair, resting her head as she raised her eyes to say a few more good things about cats.

'Folks used to say a cat would even fight a snake. That's something I didn't never see, so I don't know. I heard tell of it. But folks do say that you don't have no snakes around if you keep a cat and since I had Tom, I never had no snakes. That's a fact.'

'We used to have snakes in our house,' the little girl said.

The old woman nodded. 'I know, but you can't keep snakes off a farm.'

'Maybe you have to have a whole lot of cats on a farm if you don't want any snakes.'

'Might be,' the old woman agreed, 'but most people don't want a whole lot a cats round. Not even on a farm.'

'My daddy doesn't even like one cat,' the little girl said. 'Cause he said cats are sneaky.'

'Well, I wouldn't say they was sneaky. They just got their own ways. That's why some people don't take to them. But I'll say one thing for a cat, where it's different from a dog. A cat always knows when you don't like it, while a dog don't know one way or the other. A cat always knows and it won't like that person neither.' The old woman nodded her head. 'Now that's a fact.'

The little girl inadvertently moved backwards. 'But how can a cat tell if you don't like it?'

'I don't know,' the old woman answered. 'But they got their ways and they can tell. And something else,' the old woman continued, 'if you be good to a cat, a cat a be good to you. But if you mean to a cat,' she paused for effect, 'then you better watch out.'

'How come?' The little girl decided to brave it out, at least for a little while.

'Cause' – the old woman's reply was slow and deliberate – 'that cat go do something mean back to you. When you least expecting it.'

19

'What? A cat can't do anything to you.'

'Oh yes he can. Yes sir.' She leaned forward in her chair and lowered her voice. 'Could be anything. I heard tell of whole lots of things cats done to people. A cat will bide his time till he's good and ready, then it's go take its revenge. A cat's peculiar that way.'

'But how can a cat get you back?' The little girl looked around her to make sure nothing was creeping up on her.

'Cat got plenty a way. And it's got nine lives. So, if it don't get you in the first life, then it's got eight more times left.'

'I don't believe it.' She swallowed and stood her ground.

'Suit yourself. I'm only saying what I know. When I was a young girl, there used to be a lady that work roots and she know a whole lot about cats. She used to say cats can tell when you just thinking of doing something mean to them. Cats can sense it and know what you planning to do.'

The little girl looked quickly over to the shed and then back at the old woman. 'But what can a cat do?'

'Like I said. Plenty. Just what it wants to do.'

'Well I don't believe you. You just making it up. A cat can't know what I'm thinking inside my head.'

'Oh yes it can,' the old woman nodded her head firmly. 'Yes it can.'

'I don't believe you cause you're making it all up.'

'All right. Don't believe it.' The old woman began rocking in her chair and the little girl wandered off and seemed to be interested first in one thing and then another in the garden. She kept the old woman within her vision though and was wondering if any of what she had just said was true.

The old woman carried on rocking as if she were on her own. Her mind was busy sorting out the many impressions she had of this child, so strong-minded and quick-tongued. The old woman was thinking that when she was a child, she wouldn't have dared talk that way to one of her elders. Sass them like that! She would have had a whipping to remember if she had. Got a little chip on her shoulder too, the old woman observed, a good-size chip matter of fact. She wondered if the child would take it in her mind to kill the kittens. The old woman didn't like killing things, excusing mosquitoes, and something told her the child was meaning to carry out her threat. She wondered why and knew it would take some time to figure that out.

When she saw the little girl look over her shoulder and then head in the direction of the shed, the old woman sat up in her chair and glanced around, trying to think of something to say to make the child change her mind.

'My, my,' she said, rocking and shaking her head slowly. 'Wasn't that a terrible thing.'

The little girl didn't say anything, though she was openly watching the old woman.

'I sure don't want to think about it now. No siree. But I wonder if that man is still living?' She looked towards the little girl as if she might have the answer, then answered herself. 'Believe he is. Poor critter.' She slowly shook her head in sympathy.

The little girl was still watching her. And the old woman, deciding that she had recollected enough of the details to embellish the tale, leaned forward in her chair.

'I know somebody right now that could tell you bout a cat's revenge and bout a whole bunch a cats that was in on it as well.'

'What did the cat do?' the little girl called out, not showing too much interest.

The old woman raised her hand as if preparing to take a solemn oath and then shook her head. 'Now that, it's too terrible to talk about. And the man they did it to, even he wouldn't talk about it. Matter a fact, the truth is he wasn't never able to talk about it. Used to get to stuttering real bad if somebody as much as mention it to him. But if he could,' the old woman dropped her hand, patting her lap for emphasis, 'he would tell you what a cat could do. Anyway, a whole lot a other people heard tell of it and one of them, who I happen to know got the facts straight, told it to me right after all this took place. And from what I heard, that cat sure did fix that man.'

The little girl stood very still watching the old woman, her head askance as if she was making up her mind whether or not to believe what she was hearing. 'What did the cat do?' she insisted.

'What did who do?' The old woman appeared to have lost interest in the conversation.

'The cat,' the little girl told her.

'The cat? You mean the cat I was talking about just now?'

The little girl nodded.

'Oh I couldn't tell you. Not about that.' The old woman shook her head. 'No, I couldn't tell you. It's too scary.'

'It wouldn't scare me,' the little girl said.

'No, I can't tell you. Oh that thing is just too frightening. Scare you half to death.'

'It wouldn't.' The little girl went up to the old woman's chair. 'Tell me. Please.'

'No,' the old woman shook her head. 'No, I can't do that.'

'Cause it didn't happen. You're just saying something happen and it didn't. Nothing happened.'

'It sure did happen. As sure as I'm sitting here in this chair. And it wasn't far from your grandaddy's farm neither.'

'But what was it? I won't be scared. I not scared of nothing. I won't be scared.'

'I don't know.'

'Please tell me.' The little girl pulled on the arm of the rocking chair.

The old woman looked at her. 'You sure you not going to be scared?'

'No. I won't be. I promise.'

'Well, I suppose since this thing really happened . . . Let me see if I can remember exactly how it was.' The old woman looked down and thought for a moment. 'Let me see if I can get it right.'

'What happened?' the little girl asked impatiently.

'Just a minute. Hold on. Now this was a good little while ago,' the old woman explained as she looked away to sort out the details. 'I believe it was before your daddy was born. That's right. And your grandaddy had the farm down in Bowman. Yes, that's when it was. Now, on down the road from his farm, as you heading into town, there is another farm. Used to belong to a man name of MacBrown. John MacBrown. That was his name. Folks used to call him Johnnymac. He didn't have a whole lot of sense. Wasn't what you'd call real sharp. Folks like him though. He had a wife name of Henrietta. Folks just called her Henrietta cause she wasn't the kind of person you'd give no nickname to. Folks didn't like her all that much on the count of her being stingy. She didn't like to part with nothing if she could help it. She was all right. Wouldn't never miss church, but she could make a terrible face when they was passing the plate round.

'Anyway, they had this farm. It should a been a good farm cause they land was good but with Johnnymac being a slow thinker and his wife being so tight, didn't seem like they could make nothing grow too successful. Still they got by. They didn't have no children though. But since there was one or two peculiar things about them, seem like that was probably for the better anyway. Because they didn't have no family to help out, they used to board one or two boys who work for Johnnymac on the farm. And that's how they got by.'

The little girl had settled herself on the ground near the old woman. 'And what happened?' she asked when the old woman paused.

'I'm getting to it. I got to set it up right. Get the facts straight so that you'll know that what I'm telling you is a true story. You believe what I say so far?' She looked down inquiringly at the little girl who nodded.

'All right then. Now as I was saying. While the good Lord didn't bless them with no children, for some reason nobody could ever figure out, they was blessed with plenty a cats. Now they never had much else, but they sure had a bunch a cats. They was everywhere! Everywhere you looked! Families of 'em used to live on that farm. Mother cats, father cats, sisters and brothers, cousins, second cousins. Didn't none of them go away and find another home. They all stayed right there. So everywhere you looked, a cat be staring right back at you. And everyone of 'em look like it was about a day away from starving to death. Hardly a rat got near the place before fifteen cats hadn't jumped on it. Then they'd get to fighting among theyselves bout who was going to get a little piece of rat for they supper and there used to be such a swailing and a wailing. They'd be making a terrible racket. Could hear them cats all up and down the road.

'Now, since nobody needed to have all that many cats round the place, not even on a farm, people used to wonder why Johnnymac keep all those cats. They used to say when they stopped by, "Lord have mercy Johnnymac. Can't you do something bout all them cats?" And the person would be looking round the place trying to count just how many cats there was. But they couldn't never finish counting. Some people say they got up to thirty or so and still hadn't finish counting. But they was having a hard time trying to act like they was carryin on a conversation with Johnnymac and count cats at the same time. Anyway, there was a least thirty of them.

'Johnnymac used to say when people started asking him how come he had all those cats; he used to say in this high-pitch voice, cause that's how his voice always sound. No matter what he was talking bout it always sound like somebody was pinching him. He used to say, "Oh I don't know. They ain't all that many. Sides they don't bother me." He'd answer something like that and people would scratch they head and go away wondering how come Johnnymac was so peculiar about having all them cats.

'Nobody didn't bother to ask Henrietta why they had all those cats cause when Henrietta didn't want to answer, she would look you straight in the face and say, "What that you say? My hearing get so bad sometimes. What was it you said?" Every time you said something about the cats, that's how she would answer. Same as when you went to borrow a cup of sugar or a little piece of fatback. Wasn't no point asking her nothing she didn't want to talk about.

'Now it wasn't till one a the boys, used to work for Johnnymac, left the place that folks heard the truth about them cats. And the truth was, as I heard it tell, that Johnnymac couldn't stand them cats. Couldn't stand the sight of em. Hated every living one. Hated em so much he used to go all funny acting when he come up on a mess of em. That's what was told to me. He be standing there looking at em like somebody done a hoodoo on him, and they be standing there, just the same looking back at him. After a while his head would kinda jerk forward like somebody had a string round his neck pulling at it. And when that start to happen, the cats would get to acting funny as well. They'd all start to meowing till it was a whole chorus of em, bunched up together, twining round and round, and it would get to such a pitch, till Johnnymac would break loose, and run after them like some bull that done gone mad in the barnyard.

'They couldn't stand him and he couldn't stand them. Now, it turned out that there was a reason why he couldn't get rid of nary one of them cats. Cause of this one cat. A tom. Head of the tribe. That cat was the biggest, blackest, meanest, nastiest, ugliest cat that ever was born. And this cat, it wasn't scared a nothing. He'd fight the dog just like that.' The old woman slapped the arm of her chair, startling the little girl. 'That's right,' the old woman said. 'Mean! Evil!' She leaned towards the little girl. 'One day, and I know this for a fact, cause two people come and tell me about it, that cat jump up on the mule back and started fighting the mule. The mule wasn't doing nothing. Just got on the cat's nerves. If that tom walked into the barnyard looking for a rat, wouldn't nothing move, not even the rat. That's just how mean he was. Didn't nothing want to tangle with that cat. Everything stayed out of its way. But this was a sneaky cat. It could sneak up real quiet. Used to get right up behind the dog while the dog was trying to eat its little bit a supper and hiss right in the dog's ear. Make the dog jump so bad, you declare it was part rabbit. Then that tom would sit there and take its time and eat up the dog's supper.

'Now Johnnymac hated that tomcat more than all the other cats put together. But he wouldn't go near it, not even if that cat was beating up one of his bird dogs cause that cat had given Johnnymac a bad fright. It happen one night. Johnnymac and Henrietta was getting ready for bed and he'd done had a bad day with them cats. He said to Henrietta, "I know what I go do. I go get rid of that tom. That's what I'm go do and then all them other ones a go off from round here. Every time I scat a bunch of them cats, that tomcat be right there like he guarding them. If I get rid a him, then I can get rid of all the rest." He got to thinking about a plan to do away with that tom and that was what he was thinking bout when he drop off to sleep that night. There he was sleeping in the bed till something told him to wake up and when he wake up, that tom was standing there by the side of the bed staring at Johnnymac. He hollered this real high-pitch holler, probably what make Henrietta think she had gone deaf, and the cat jump on the bed and then jump out the window. Henrietta didn't never say whether she saw the cat or not. And if the boy working there hadn't come a running to see what the matter was and near bout run into the cat, probably it would a been said that Johnnymac had dream that thing. But he swear he didn't dream it and the boy swear he see the cat jump out the window. After that, Johnnymac stayed out the cat's way, but that cat would be watching Johnnymac just like it know what he was thinking.

'That's how things was on the farm till this particular Sunday afternoon. This was late in the autumn. Just after butchering and they had smoked a nice fat hog and had some nice pieces of meat put up in the smokehouse. Johnnymac was telling people they had a good harvest and had put plenty by for the winter. But Henrietta declare they ain't had nothing t'all to put in there but a runt and she didn't know how they was going to get through the winter. That's just how that woman was. But the boy that worked there say the table be loaded down with food come time for them to eat dinner. Anyway, this Sunday afternoon, Henrietta had been to the smokehouse and had cooked up a big ole piece of pork. Been roasting it in the oven since early morning and you could smell meat cooking all over the farm. Johnnymac couldn't hardly wait to get to church and back so they could get to the table. There was all that pork, browned and juicy with a nice crackling on it. Besides that was a pan of hot cornbread and a big bowl of collard greens and another one full of rice and a dish of sweet potatoes that had been baking in the oven along with the pork. When all the food was ready, Henrietta call the boy to the back door and she give him a little scrap a meat wasn't no bigger than the spoon he had to eat it with, and a lee-little bit a rice and sweet potatoes and another little spoonful of collard greens, then break off a little side of cornbread and put that on the plate. She give him a cup to get some water off the back porch.

That's where the boy was, on the back porch, when they all heard this hollering and squealing coming from the barnyard. They went running out to see what it was and there was a fox running off into the woods with one of the pigs. Johnnymac got down the shotgun and took off after it but it was gone and they didn't never even find a trace of it. Johnnymac took the dogs and went after it but it wasn't no use. When it started to get dark, they give up the search and went back to the barnyard where Henrietta had been trying to board up the pigpen cause they know that once a fox start to raid a farm, he keep on coming back. They stayed out there making sure that fox wasn't going to be able to get back into that pigpen.

'They were pretty tired out when they went back to the house. And both of them was thinking how they was just about to enjoy all that good food when that fox had to come and mess up everything, and get away with one of the pigs. Johnnymac said he was so hungry he didn't know where to put himself. But Henrietta said it wouldn't take but a few minutes to heat everything up again. And then they walked into the kitchen. Lord have mercy! They just stood there in the doorway like they was statues. Couldn't move. Couldn't say a word. There on the kitchen table, on all the chairs, on top of the stove, under the table, was every cat that lived on that farm. And there wasn't a speck of food nowhere. The place was cleaned out. There wasn't even no sign that there had ever even been any food. There wasn't nothing but cats.

'Johnnymac couldn't believe what he was seeing. He just stood in the doorway getting so mad that his eyes had nearly popped out his head. He just stood there staring at those cats. And the cats, they were staring back at him. Henrietta said it sound like Johnnymac started growling. And then he walked into the kitchen and the cats just stood there like they was froze to the spot. Johnnymac kept on walking round in the kitchen growling. The cats know they was in trouble when Johnnymac reach out and grab one of them like he was going to strangle it. Then, before anybody could blink – that black tom had jumped in front of him. It didn't seem to come from nowhere. Just jump up on the table in front of Johnnymac. Stood there staring and Johnnymac forgot about the other cat.

He just stood there staring back at that tom. Then that cat raise his back till it had swell up to twice his size and it snarled to freeze your blood. It rise up some more, hissing worse than a snake. That cat was waiting to spring on Johnnymac if Johnnymac didn't back off and leave them other cats alone. Johnnymac step back like he was retreating, then – BAM! Fore that cat knew it, Johnnymac done thrown a ice pick. That cat flew up at Johnnymac, then fell at his feet. It drop right out the air with that ice pick in its belly.

'Nobody said a word. They just stood there staring down at that cat. It was dead. The ice pick had gone right through it. The boy that help out on the farm, he heard all this commotion and he come inside to see what it was. They was still standing there looking at that tom, lying on the floor by Johnnymac's feet. All the other cats was staring down at that tom too. That's how the boy tell it anyway. I believe they used to call him Eugene or something like that. But I know that his mother used to work roots. She live on the other side of the woods from the farm and people used to go there and get medicine and get her to work spells and things. Do hoodoo on folks. Now I don't know if that's true or not. That's just something I hear tell. Anyway I do know that the whole family was real superstitious, and this boy Eugene started getting worried cause Johnnymac done killed a black cat. He started saying something bout that was the devil's cat and all of them was going to have a whole lot of bad luck. Then he said he didn't know if he was going to stay round there after that.

'Anyway, Henrietta come to her senses first and told the boy, Eugene, there wasn't no such a thing as having bad luck after no black cat. She went into the kitchen and started shooing and swinging at those cats till they was all gone. Then she told Eugene who was still standing in the doorway to pick up that cat and take it off somewhere and bury it. But Eugene didn't want to pick up that dead cat till Henrietta said she was going to give him something to be real scared about if he didn't get on and do what she said. So the boy went and got a shovel and shovel up the cat, with the ice pick still in it, and took it outside. He kept on mumbling bout bad luck and how he didn't have nothing to do with killing that cat.

'Johnnymac sit down at the kitchen table but he was real quiet. Not that he had much chance to say anything. Henrietta was getting herself worked up about how come he had let all those cats take over the farm in the first place. And she was saying why hadn't he gone on before now and get rid of that tom stead of acting all crazy every time he see one of them cats. She went on bout how she spend all day cooking and getting everything ready and it was all for nothing. She said she wasn't never gonna understand country people. Seem like all of em was simple acting or something what with working all day on a farm that hardly gave them a living, letting cats run the place and to top it off, there was that old stupid boy Eugene talking bout black magic and devils and things. No wonder country people didn't have nothing. Henrietta said she was fed up with it all.

'After that Sunday, there wasn't never another cat to be found on the place. Not nary a one. All of em had gone and nobody ever saw not even one of Johnnymac cats. Things got back to normal except they still had to keep a eye out for the fox. Then about a month afterwards, this was another Sunday, Henrietta and Johnnymac was at the table having their dinner. Henrietta could cook now. Maybe some folks didn't like her too much but they had to admit that she could cook up a good meal. They always got her to do the church suppers and suchlike. Both her and Johnnymac like to eat. They did like they food. You could tell Johnnymac like his cause most of it stayed on him. He was a good size to look at. And Henrietta, she could do justice to a plate quick as the next man. But cause she was the nervous type, she was always kinda stringy. Some people say she never had no weight on her cause she stayed so busy nosing into other folks' business. That might a been true, but she also had bad nerves. Bad nerves and stingy. Now that's the truth and everybody know it. They would come calling to your house just when you was about to sit down to a meal. Henrietta would come in the door: "We just drop by for a minute. No we not go stay. Just come to see how you getting on." Course they sit down and stay till you offered them something to eat. Then Henrietta would say, "Oh, y'all getting ready to eat? We better be going on home then." And all the time she know you go offer them a plate. Then they'd settle down to eat till they was fit to be tied. If on the other hand you go by to visit them, well you might just as well try and get a meal from a weasel cause they wouldn't never offer you nothing. Henrietta would say, "I sure wish I know y'all was coming by, I would a cook up something nice. All I got in the kitchen is some cold hominy grits and a little piece of fatback." Starve themselves before they invite you to sit down.

'Anyway, on this particular Sunday, they had a big ole stewing hen cooking in the pot. Just for the two of them. And they had a whole pile of dumplings swimming in gravy, plus a dish of corn pudding, a big ole plate a biscuits and another dish full up with rice. And the way they told me Johnnymac face was still shining with chicken grease when he come running into town. Said he could see him bobbing down the road from a mile off, like a headlight on a car. That's the way I heard it anyway.

'So there they was munching and a chewing on this stew hen, smacking they lips and all they was thinking about was getting to the next mouthful. Then – BAM! The tom jump up on the table. First thing, they didn't even see the cat. Both of em was too busy eating, had they heads down over the plates chomping away. Then Johnnymac smell something funny. He got a whiff a something smell terrible and he look up to say something to Henrietta and the cat was right there sitting in the middle of the table. Ice pick still sticking in him. Johnnymac couldn't do nothing. Couldn't get his mouth open, couldn't get his feet moving. Nothing. Later on he said he sure know what a car feel like when the battery dead. Then Henrietta look up in order to get herself another piece of chicken and that's what she saw, Johnnymac and the cat staring each other in the face. Henrietta wouldn't never have no dead battery in her and she jump up from that table and was gone. But lo and behold, by the time she was heading for the back porch door, Johnnymac was pushing pass her. Both of em got there at the same time. Folks say they know that a terrible struggle took place cause both of them was looking real bad when they saw them running through town shouting for Jesus to help them. Somebody had to go and fetch a blanket to put over Henrietta

30

cause she must a got her dress caught on something and let it stay. And when they finally calm her down, they notice that a big ole patch a hair was missing from the back of her head. Johnnymac, he still had a mouth full a chicken and come to find out, he had three teeth missing. Folks used to wonder how he manage to holler so loud with all that chicken inside his mouth. Later on, when they used to asked him about it, he couldn't never explain the thing too clear cause his voice started getting higher and higher till it was sounding like a sireen and they'd have to talk to him real quiet to get him to calm down. None of them never got too much information outa Henrietta either cause as soon as she starting to explain she would get the hiccups and none of what she said made no sense. They said the reason she had the hiccups so bad was cause she'd swallowed her mouthful of chicken and it look just like she had a crop in her neck. She had the hiccups real bad. Somebody offered to put a piece of straw through her hair so as to get rid of them, but since she didn't have no hair on the back of her head, where you suppose to put the straw, it didn't do no good.

'Well, when folks was finally able to piece together what had happen, nobody believe it except Eugene. Eugene mamma, she was there saying it was the devil's work brought that cat back. She said they had the evil eye on them and folks starting buying up her potions to ward off evil eyes. Course Eugene mamma just happen to have a bag full of potions for warding off spells. Anyway, when the folks sat down and thought about this thing, they said there must be a way to explain what happen. They said probably it could be one of two things. It might be that the cat wasn't never dead in the first place cause the boy Eugene was too scared to bury it. So the cat had been alive the whole time. The other thing was that it might a been the boy, Eugene; if he was standing outside the window watching them eat all that food probably he throw that dead cat through the window to give them a fright. But Eugene swear up and down that he wouldn't never pick up no black cat, dead or alive.

'In the end they said the only thing to do was to go back to the farm and see if they could find the cat. So that's what they did. Some of em took down they shotguns and went out to

Johnnymac's farm. Except Johnnymac. He said he felt like staying in town for a spell. So, they got to the house and went inside and there it was. Sure enough that tom was on the table. And, it was stone dead.

'They didn't never figure out how that cat got up on that table. They all said the best thing to do was to take it outside and burn it to make sure it wasn't getting back up on no more tables. In the end they took the table and all the food and the dishes, everything, outside and set fire to it all. Some of them stood round watching the fire till there was nothing left cept some ashes and the ice pick.'

With a final nod, the old woman sat back in her chair. 'Whatever the truth was, I told it just like I heard it.'

For several moments they both sat in silence; the little girl awed and horrified by her new knowledge of the power of cats, wondering if that cat was really burned up and dead forever, and the old woman satisfied that she had remembered that old story she'd heard from her mother more than once. She reckoned she'd made it sound every bit as good.

The old woman was feeling something else though she probably wouldn't admit it to herself: enjoyment, mingled with pride. Because something from her time and place had made an impression on this modern-day little girl, cushioned by privilege and brought up away from down-home folks so as not to have to know their ways and habits which, the old woman had been told by the younger generation, were best forgotten.

Talking from her past had eased something inside her, and the old woman looked around her in the garden, thinking how the calm of the late afternoon put her in the mind, just a little bit, of the afternoon outside the home she had left near Eautawville.

A fair wind rustled the leaves on the pecan tree overhead and both the old woman and the little girl looked up and watched the swaying branches. For the first time, the old woman allowed herself to miss her home.

The little girl, gazing through the leaves up to the sky and aware of the old woman musing in her chair beside her, was for the first time, since she had come to her grandparents' house, feeling contentment.

Finally, the old woman reached down for the walking stick lying beside her chair. 'Anyway,' she said, 'if you want to go and kill those kittens . . . well then, it's up to you.'

'Is that a real story?'

'I heard it and I told it.'

'But how could that cat come back if Johnnymac killed it?'

'I already told you. A cat got nine lives.' The old woman looked over at the little girl. 'But it don't matter if it got a hundred lives, it's wrong to want to kill. It's wrong and it make you have a mean heart if you go round wanting to kill things. Your heart gets all tight and you can't love nothing and you can't enjoy no living things, not if you want to kill even one. Some people gets to be that way and it's pitiful.' She continued to look at the little girl who was thinking about what it would be like to be mean and ugly all the time. The old woman put the stick on her lap and again gazed around the garden. 'People that learn to love all the living things, they heart grows big and they feel good inside cause they can see how wonderful are all the things God made. They learn a lot about the way things are and they understand about life and they don't never want to kill nothing. They enjoy it too much and they know there is plenty a space for everything.' She leaned forward and with her walking stick touched the ground near where the little girl was sitting. 'Look here,' she said, 'I want you to think about what I been saying and then you make up your mind about how you want to be. What kind a person you go be.' She waited for an answer. The little girl didn't say anything. 'All right?' the old woman inquired.

The little girl nodded.

'All right, you do that.'

They sat quietly again, both of them reluctant to move. The little girl didn't want to get up and lose the good feeling that had come while sitting on the ground listening to her great-grandmother's voice. And the old woman was seeing in the garden, for the first time since she had come to her daughter's house, the wonderful living things that she was just talking about. After a while she leaned the stick beside her chair.

'I'll tell you what,' she said. 'I know another story. This one is bout a rabbit. Cleverest rabbit you ever did see. Couldn't nobody outwit him. If you go to the house and get me a nice, cold glass a lemonade, I'll see if I can't remember how that story goes cause he sure was a clever rabbit.'

The little girl jumped up and ran off towards the house. 'I'll be right back,' she shouted. Boy, oh boy! she was thinking as she rushed to get the lemonade, wait till I tell them about the cat!

The old woman didn't know whether she was up to another story. It would have to be a short one. Come to think of it she knew a lot of rabbit stories, but there was one in particular she was trying to remember.

'Now how did that story go?' she asked herself. 'Been a long time since I tell that one. Let me see if I can get it right.'

The First Fig Tree

'Mind you don't fall outta that tree!' The old woman thought she could hear leaves rustling in the nearby orchard. She leaned forward in her chair and listened. 'Did you hear what I say?' she called over in the direction of the trees. There was no reply. The old woman shaded her eyes against the afternoon sun, trying to see if the little girl had climbed one of the fruit trees, but the orchard appeared hazy in the vibrant summer light and she couldn't see. 'You better come down from there before you fall,' she called out again, certain now that the little girl had gone up into one of the trees. 'You hear me?' She waited, her head cocked to one side. Yes, she could definitely hear something moving about somewhere in there. 'You up there eating figs?' Still there was no reply. 'They too green,' the old woman shouted, pressing her hand to her chest with the effort. Then she said to herself, 'I bet that's why she gone up in that tree.' Once again the old woman shaded her eyes, but still unable to see, she gave up and shook her head in disapproval. 'Go give you belly ache.' She didn't bother trying to shout any more.

The rustling in the tree stopped for a while, then it started again.

'All right then. Pretending you don't hear me.' The old woman sat back in her chair but remained agitated. 'I know your grandaddy don't allow you up in his trees and soon as he get back, I'm go tell him.' The rustling stopped again. The old woman waited for the little girl to come down.

'I'm not eating figs,' a voice called from the top of one of the fig trees. 'I'm just looking at them, that's all.'

'You not suppose to be up in that tree!'

'But I'm just looking at the little figs.'

'You coming down or not?' There was no answer.

'All right,' the old woman warned, 'then you go get what's coming to you cause I'm go tell.'

'All I'm doing is looking at his old figs,' the little girl shouted in defence of herself.

'And if he finds out somebody been picking his figs and done broke off his branches, they go be in a heap a trouble.'

'I'm coming down.'

'And I think that's his car coming now,' the old woman continued as if she hadn't heard. 'Yeah, I know it. That's him coming now.'

They both stopped and listened as a car drove slowly along the road and then passed the house.

'That wasn't Grampy's car,' the little girl shouted from the tree. 'Anyway Grampy's gone to Elloree and he's not coming back till this evening.'

'Well he might get back early and if he finds you up in his tree, you go have a time trying to explain your way out of it.' The old woman picked up a fan from her lap and fanned herself to cool off. She had become hot worrying and shouting in all that heat. She told herself she was too old to be bothering about such things.

After a while, the old woman got up and pulled her chair deeper into the shade. She looked over towards the orchard, shaking her head again, then sat down. 'You not coming down out that tree?' There was only silence. 'It's your neck going to get broke, so go right ahead.' The rustling continued and so the old woman picked up her fan and slowly rocked herself back and forth in the chair. Again she told herself that she was too old to be worrying about everything and was cross with the little girl for causing her so much concern. She looked over into the orchard, pursing her lips with annoyance. 'And the trouble is,' she went on to herself, 'children don't never know when they getting themselves into trouble till it's too late. Be better off if they had something to do, stead of having all that time on they hands. That's not the way it's suppose to be. Not how we was raised. Things sure done got different. Suppose to be better. I don't know.'

Every so often the old woman could hear the little girl move around in the tree. A few times she thought she heard something like a branch snap and she would stop rocking to listen. Whenever she stopped, the snapping sound stopped too until she began to wonder if it wasn't the gravel underneath her chair that was causing the noise.

With only the occasional rustle of leaves coming from the orchard and the soft, repetitious crunch, crunch of the rockers over the sand, the old woman was gradually lulled into repose. The fan slid onto her lap as she drifted into the soporofic haze that had come over the garden.

Somewhere in the distance she thought she could hear singing. She perked up her head and listened. It was the little girl. She was singing to herself; about how lucky birds were to have homes in trees. It was a slow, winsome song, low-pitched, interspersed with hums and pauses as the little girl thought up the words to express her feelings. Her voice wavered out of tune as she told the birds to fly away because they had to find a new home.

The garden was in silence again. The old woman looked around her, wanting someone else to be there, to have heard the child's song. It disturbed her and there was nothing she could do. 'Least I had plenty of family round me,' the old woman said, reminded of her own childhood. 'And know all the folks, stead of just having strangers.'

On the day that the old woman had moved to her daughter's house she had met the child when she returned from school. It was only the second time she'd seen her. The first was at her christening. 'Don't seem to be too much to her except for a pair of long skinny legs and three thick plaits.' This was the old woman's first impression as she studied her. She had large, thoughtful eyes that would light up with curiosity, but dulled into retreat when she was asked about herself. She was a shadowy little thing, wafting alone through a house that for years had followed a set routine and remained undisturbed by her presence. She needs bringing out of herself, the old woman had concluded.

'I found a place up here to rest.' The little girl's voice floated down from the tree. The old woman wondered what she was talking about. 'I could go to sleep up here,' the little girl said in the same dreamy voice. 'I might even build me a house if I want to and live up here.'

The old woman didn't say anything. She still couldn't lend her approval to what the little girl was doing.

'Why do people live in houses anyway? They can just live up here. It's nice. Why don't people live in trees?'

The old woman couldn't help herself. ''Cause they got too much sense. Live in trees!'

'All kinda things live in trees. Squirrels and monkeys. Lions and little worms and little bugs.'

'I ain't saying nothing more to you about that tree.'

'But it's nice sitting in trees. I can see everything. I can see right over into the field and down the road. And the top of the chicken coop. It's got chicken poo-poo all on top of it. I can see into Miss Dunbar's backyard. And the dog. He's sleeping by the door. Here dog,' the little girl called. 'Look up here dog. Doggie.'

The old woman looked away from the orchard and smiled. 'I sure don't know what they go do with you,' she mumbled between chuckles. She didn't know many of her great-grand-children, especially the younger ones. Most of her daughter's family had grown up away from her after their parents had left Eautawville. Other than the occasional brief and perfunctory visit, she did not see them. She had, however, known the child's father because he had lived on a farm her son-in-law kept for a time after moving to Orangeburg. As a boy, the child's father had spent time on his own too. The old woman remembered this now. He had to be by himself a lot, tending to cattle and whatever else. It wasn't till after he was a young man and had discovered women that she began to hear more about him. He used to be something with the women. She wondered if having a wife and family had quietened him down. She seem to remember there had been some rumour about him and a married woman and then trouble with the husband. Was that why the child's mother had decided to get some more schooling in the north? She was supposed to be sending for her daughter when she got settled and had found a place to live.

The little girl began to sing again, a song about flying away in the sky and having wings like angels. When a dove began to coo, the little girl cooed as well, incorporating this into her song. The old woman leaned her head to one side. All that thinking had tired her out. She sighed and wondered why she still worried about what other people were doing. 'Never mind,' she told herself, trying to shake off her anxiety. She was tempted to sing herself. One of the great comforts of her life was singing spirituals; the old ones that her mother had sung. Whenever she needed to lighten the burden of her worries, a song rose from her chest, lifting the weight of her troubles for a little while. She would have said this was her salvation if she had been asked why she did it. Time and time again, she would have said, to sing had been her salvation. Now she was listening to the little girl. I don't know why it is, she thought to herself, feeling better for remembering that she could still sing, but there's something about a child's voice that sound like holiness. I don't know what it is, but it's something. And seems like it sweetens the air so you can breathe better. So go on and sing, child. 'Like little David,' she said after a while, 'singing for Saul.' She was reminded of how the Old Testament king was healed by the voice of the shepherd boy. You can always learn something from the Bible. She nodded at this old truth which gave her solace and with renewed faith resumed her rocking. Gradually, however, the rocking slowed down and then, joining in the hush that had fallen over the garden, it ceased.

'How did Adam and Eve put on fig leaves?'

The old woman heard the voice but didn't know where it had come from. She blinked, trying to focus her eyes on the figure in front of her.

'Adam and Eve? How did they dress in fig leaves?' The little girl stood before her clutching an armful of fig leaves.

'I want to make me a dress,' the little girl continued. She dropped the leaves on the ground where there was already a pile. 'They sure needed a lot.'

The old woman stared at the leaves. Slowly she reached down and picked up one as if to confirm that it was real, then put it back down again. 'Whatever done come over you?' she asked in wonderment. The old woman looked over towards the orchard to see if any leaves were left on the tree. It didn't seem possible that there were. 'You tear off all them leaves?'

'I told you. So I can make a dress. How come they used fig leaves?'

'You sure gone and done it now. Didn't I tell you to leave those figs alone?'

'I did leave the figs alone. I just got some of the leaves.' The little girl stooped down and began to spread them about on the ground. 'I'm going to make a dress,' she confirmed again.

The old woman sat back in her chair. 'Well, if this don't take the rag off the bush!'

'Adam and Eve did it,' the little girl told her as she continued to spread the leaves around.

'Well I know one thing, Adam and Eve didn't get they leaves off your grandaddy tree and if they had to, they'd be walking round buck-naked till this day.'

'But God didn't mind. Did He?'

'If this don't take the rag off the bush then I don't know what!'

'How did they get them to stay together?'

'I'm sure I don't know.'

'Didn't you read it in the Bible?'

'Read what?'

'How they got all the leaves to stay together.'

'I don't know,' the old woman replied.

'Cause you didn't read it?'

'Cause it don't say.'

'Did they have needles?' Undeterred, the little girl continued to arrange the fig leaves. She crawled around on her knees under the disapproving gaze of the old woman. 'I could probably make two dresses,' she said, after looking at the mound of leaves that remained. 'And, I might give one to somebody.'

'Sure enough?' the old woman snorted.

'This is going to be my dress,' the little girl pointed, then leaned back to study her arrangement. 'All I need to do is sew it up. That part's the front and that's the back.' She looked around at all the leaves surrounding her and then sat back dissatisfied. 'How come they used fig leaves?'

'I don't know.' The old woman refused to be drawn into a conversation.

'They're not very big. How old was Adam and Eve? Maybe they were just standing by a fig tree. They might a been hiding in it.'

The old woman didn't say anything.

'What does the Bible say?'

'That they dressed in fig leaves,' the old woman admitted, thinking it might be unChristian to withhold knowledge from the Bible.

'Collard greens are bigger than fig leaves,' the little girl observed. 'They should a dressed up in collard green leaves.' She looked over in the direction of the vegetable garden. The old woman followed her gaze.

'Well you better be glad that they didn't cause if you had gone and pulled up your grandaddy greens, there wouldn't be nothing for you to do but leave town as fast as your feet could move.'

The little girl gave a big, frustrated sigh. 'But I want to know. How did they sew them? So they stayed together?'

'I told you I don't know. Maybe they got hold of some pine needles.'

'Pine needles? Can they sew like real needles? I'm gonna go find some so you can show me.' The little girl started to get up.

'Now you just hold on a minute.' The old woman pointed her finger warningly at her. 'If you think you gon get me twined up with these here fig leaves, then you got another think coming, cause that is your doing. You done it by yourself,' the old woman paused for effect, 'and you taking the blame by yourself.' She nodded with finality. 'So that's that.'

The little girl sat back down and, chewing on her lower lip, stared at the leaves scattered around her. Slowly she brushed a few grains of sand off them.

The old woman had something else to say. 'Plenty of times you could a just come on down out the tree. But no, you had to stay up there climbing round till something take a hold of you and tell you to tear off all those leaves. Now that wouldna happen if you'd listen.'

'I like being up in a tree,' the little girl said quietly.

'Well going up there got you into trouble. Didn't it?'

The little girl shrugged.

'Didn't it? It sure did,' the old woman answered herself. 'Those your grandaddy's trees out there' – the old woman pointed towards the orchard and then towards the house – 'and this here his land and his house. Everything you see round here belong to him. You can't just go and do what you want with it. You just asking for trouble. What you think he go do if you start acting like that?'

'Send me away.' The little girl didn't know where to look.

The old woman sank back in her chair. She had made her point sooner than she had expected and it had caused more dismay than she had intended. They sat in a heavy silence that couldn't be relieved, not even by the melodious chirping of a little bird perched on a branch of the pecan tree. The old woman raised her head to avoid seeing the drooping little figure sitting on the ground. 'Nobody said nothing bout sending you away and it ain't nothing for you to be worrying about.' She lowered her gaze and studied the little girl who was fingering the sand, then looked past her, catching sight of a bunch of flowers growing along the fence in front of the vegetable garden. Her daughter used these flowers to make bouquets for the living and dining rooms. The old woman had often wished that she had a few flowers in her own room, but did not feel comfortable about picking them and couldn't bring herself to ask her daughter. 'You just have to learn about how other people like to have their things and how they do things and what not. That's having respect and you have to learn it while you growing up. That's what it is. Wasn't nobody talking about sending you away for nothing like no fig leaves.'

The little girl's sigh ended with a quiver and she continued to play absently in the sand. After a while she said, 'But God sent Adam and Eve away and my momma and daddy wanted to send me away.'

'They want to send you away?'

The little girl nodded.

'Now what make you think they was go send you away?'

'They didn't want me cause I'm too bad.'

'Well I don't know what make you think your momma and daddy don't want you cause they do. Course they want you.'

'No they don't.' The little girl shook her head.

'Course they do want you,' the old woman repeated.

'Nope. Daddy said I'm too bad to be with.'

'Well they just say that so you'll try and be a good girl. That don't mean they don't want you. That's a bunch of stuff.'

The little girl shook her head again. 'Nope cause my daddy told me he didn't want me till I was good.'

'You know he didn't mean that. That's just something he said. All children get told that.'

'And that's why he sent me away and then he went away.'

'Now you don't believe that. You know you come up here to go to school and cause your daddy's gone off to the war and your mamma's gone back to school herself. You can't never get too much learning, specially these days. And when she come back, she'll be able to get a good job and be able to do more for you. If your daddy didn't go and fight in that war, then all those Germans a soon be over here bombing us all up. They didn't send you away. That's just how things happen. They're missing you a whole lot. They sure are. Course they didn't send you away. Don't you think they missing you?'

The little girl shrugged and then set her face so she wouldn't look bothered any more. She began to push sand away from her. 'I don't care because I'm not missing them anyway. They don't care either and that's why my daddy didn't want to kiss me goodbye cause he said I was no good. And Grampy told me to get in the back of the car so he could take me away.'

The old woman could think of no words which might remove the scowl from the tight little face. Finally, she was forced to look away, but she continued, through a wave of disconsolation, to hear the soft, swishing sound of the sand as it was pushed away. It had brought back the memory of the heavy crocus sack, which as a child she had dragged up and down endless rows of cotton. It had got heavier and heavier. Her back and arms had ached, then grown numb, but still she was forced to carry on till all that she was aware of was the swish, swish sound of the cotton sack as she pulled it over the ground.

The old woman looked back down at the little girl. Some things do change, she told herself, while some things don't.

'You know what I was thinking bout just now?' she asked the little girl, then went on to answer the question. 'Bout just how bad your daddy was when he was a little boy. I use to know your daddy before he grow up. I bet you didn't know that.'

The little girl shook her head.

'Yeah, I use to know him. Your grandaddy had a farm down near Eautawville that wasn't too far from me and your daddy stayed down there till he was up a size. And talking bout somebody full of devilment. Always wanting to play tricks on somebody. Bet he never told you about that.'

The little girl looked up from the sand and shook her head. 'No.'

The old woman chuckled softly and picked up her fan. 'Oh yes. He used to get into a lot of devilment, specially after they got that house in Bowman. I can remember this one time, just after they moved there, when he caused a bit of fracas. See, the reason your grandaddy bought this house was because your grandmomma wanted somewhere nice for her daughters to take company. They were old enough to start courting and this house had a nice-size parlour.

'When your grandaddy bought it he decided to have electricity put in. Everybody used to talk about it because in those days hardly anybody had electricity. They all thought he must be rich so quite a few young men was asking to call on your aunts. Of course this got to be expensive and your grandaddy started to complain about all the bills. He said they were using too much electricity and finally he went round the house and took out all the light bulbs except one. He said they'd just have to make do because he was tired of paying out so much money on the house. So your grandmomma used to put this one light bulb in the front parlour when the girls had company.

'Now this particular Sunday evening your Aunt Ethel was seeing her beau. It happen to be your Uncle Bill cause later on they got married. But at this time they had just started to courting. Anyway, the light bulb was in the parlour and they were in there sitting together. Everything was going along fine till your daddy, he must a been about ten or eleven at the time, decided to go in there and sit between them. He would stay there long enough to get your Aunt Ethel mad and then run off laughing. Finally Aunt Ethel got fed up and told your grandmomma. And for a while they had some peace and quiet cause your grandmomma told your daddy he better not set foot in there again. But the next thing you know, he was standing there in the doorway making funny faces every time one of them would look his way. Your Uncle Bill couldn't help laughing and your Aunt Ethel got mad at him so he said he thought he better be going. Well your aunt got worried because she figured he might not come back and she jumped up and slammed the parlour door in your daddy's face.

'Course it's not proper for a young lady to be in a room alone with a young man when the door's closed because she had to keep her reputation if she wanted to be respected and get married. Anyway closing the door didn't stop your daddy. He just started peeping through the keyhole and every time your uncle say something nice to your aunt, your daddy would start to say the same thing, just to mock them. There wasn't nothing they could do so they act like he wasn't there and sure enough that seem to do the trick and he went away. Your aunt was just beginning to relax and enjoy your uncle's attention when BAM! The parlour door flew open. Both of them jump. Your daddy come in and said, "Mamma sent me to get the light bulb." And he walk right up to the light in the middle of the room and take it out. They were left sitting there in the pitch-black and BAM! The parlour door shut.

'Your aunt didn't know what to do. It had happen so fast. She just sat there wondering what to do. Meanwhile, your daddy went to the kitchen where your grandmomma had the kerosene lamp and he told her that the light bulb had gone out in the front parlour and please could they have the kerosene lamp. Then he picked that up and was gone. So the whole house was in pitch-black and everybody sitting there thinking the other person had the light.

'After a while your aunt got so worried and she shout out from the front parlour: "Mamma we sitting here in the dark." And she started crying cause she figured her reputation was ruined. Then when your grandmomma heard her she couldn't figure out how they come to be sitting in the dark. They kept on hollering back and forth to each other till they figured out what your daddy had done. Your grandmomma nearly had a fit and was insisting that your uncle leave the house and he was falling all over the furniture and messing up the parlour trying to find his way out the door. In the end, I believe that's why they rush your uncle through the courting and marry him into the family cause they didn't want too many people to hear about what had happened.'

The old woman laughed for a good while. 'Yes siree. He sure caused a fracas that time. Little imp!' She continued to smile and rocked thoughtfully while the little girl sat and watched her with fascination. Then she stopped rocking and said, 'You think he cut out all that foolishness when he and your momma got married?' She shook her head. 'I believe it got worse.'

'What did he do?' the little girl asked.

'He did plenty a things, but I remember this one in particular. It was just after your Uncle James and your daddy start farming together. Your uncle build himself a house just down the road and they would do a lot of the work from your daddy's house where the barn was. That's where they'd store everything. Now this particular year they made a whole lot of cider and they decide to put most of it in the shed next to your daddy's house.

'One evening after it had got dark, your Uncle James decided he would like a drink of cider so he sent the three children over to the house to fetch it. These were your cousins and they were just little children at the time. Naturally they were scared about walking down the road in the dark. But your uncle told them there was nothing to be scared of and gave them the kerosene lamp so they could see where they were going.

'When they got to the house, your daddy was already in the bed like he'd been sleeping and your momma, who was playing along with him, told the children that your daddy was asleep, so to be quiet, and she went out to the shed and got the cider. So there they were tiptoeing around trying to be quiet and your daddy done take the sheet off the bed and run out the house to hide in the field by the road.

'The children had been hoping that your daddy would a walked back down the road with them. It was bad enough having to come by themselves in the dark night, but to go back seem even worse. Your momma said she was sorry but they couldn't wake him up and so they left holding on to each other, the kerosene lamp and the cider jug.

'Well by the time they got halfway down the road, they thought they heard this noise. Ooooh, it went. They told each it was just an ole owl. Ooooh, it went again and this time it sound even closer and even less like a owl. They started to walk a little faster. Ooooooh. Oooooooh. They were so scared they could hardly walk straight. Then they heard footsteps behind them and when they turn around to look there was this white thing weaving and waving about and running towards them.

'They didn't even stop when they got to your uncle's house. They just kept on running and hollering and your uncle had to go after them to make them stop. Course there wasn't nothing to see when they turn round to point to the ghost.

'They'd done dropped the jug of cider and the lamp in the middle of the road and when they got back to it the cider had just about leaked out. Your uncle was real cross because he knew it was his brother and not any ghost. He took the children back to your daddy's house so he could prove that it was him and also to get some more cider.

'Well your daddy was lying up there in the bed snoring his head off. The children nearly bout died of fright. He never did admit it was him under that sheet, but your momma took pity on the children and said that it was your daddy. Even after those children had grown up they'd still asked your momma if that was really your daddy they saw that night.'

The old woman leaned back in her chair. 'Your daddy was something. And I expect wherever he is overseas, he got somebody wondering whether they coming or going. Both your momma and your daddy used to get the devil in them every so often so I guess you come by it honest.'

'What does that mean?' the little girl asked.

'Means that you take after them cause you they child.'

'Did my daddy do that for real?'

'Sure as I'm sitting here.'

'And he was bad when he was little?'

'Bad? Times he would shame the devil himself!'

'Then how come he doesn't want me to be bad?'

'Cause that's how folks get when they grown and got children. They forget all the things they used to do. The ones that been bad children, they the worse, wanting their children to behave like angels. They don't remember how they used to behave when they say all kinda things to their children trying to get them to be a certain kind a way.'

The little girl sat quietly for a moment. She looked down at the ground and began to doodle in the sand. 'But they said they don't want any bad children. They only want good ones.'

The old woman leaned forward in her chair, suddenly impatient with the woes that burdened the little girl. 'There's no such a thing as a bad child. Sometimes they do bad things just like grown people, but that don't make them bad.'

The little girl looked up puzzled. 'Did God send Adam and Eve away cause he didn't want them?'

The old woman had to think for a while. 'God love Adam and Eve. He was just angry about what they had done. He didn't never stop loving them. He was their father and fathers and mothers love their children. Sometimes they have to punish them when they do something wrong, but they don't never stop loving them.'

The little girl sighed deeply, still bothered by unresolved questions. 'But if children think their momma and daddy don't love them, then it's the same as when they really don't love them. Isn't it?'

The old woman nodded. 'Yeah. Sometimes it seem like that's what it is. Sometimes grown people say the exact same thing about God. They say it seem like God don't love them cause they feel like He done left them and they all alone. But God hasn't left them. He just know that there come a time when a person got to find they own way. It seem like He left them, but He hasn't and it seem like He don't love them, but

He do. And grown people have to have faith so they can believe in something when they can't see how it could be so.'

The little girl began to push the sand again. 'Well I don't believe that my momma and daddy love me.'

'They'd be mighty sad if they know that's what you was thinking.'

'I'm not going to tell them anyway. When they get back, I'm not going to say nothing.'

'Is that so?'

The little girl nodded without looking up.

'Well I don't know,' the old woman said. 'Maybe I'm not going to say nothing neither. I don't know. Maybe,' she said, and paused till she had the little girl's attention, 'just maybe if you go and take those leaves and put them back there on that big pile of weeds they'll be all right. Ain't no use trying to dress up in fig leaves. The first ones couldn't a been too good else they'd still be wearing em. No I don't think the Lord made the first fig tree for Adam and Eve to make dresses from.'

The little girl began to gather up some of the leaves. 'Then why did God make fig trees?'

'I can't say why the Lord decided to create a fig tree, but I got a pretty good idea why your grandaddy got that one growing in the garden.'

'Why?'

'Well,' the old woman replied, 'if you take after your daddy side of the family, then one day you'll know.' The old woman chuckled to herself. 'Never mind,' she said to the little girl who was frowning with puzzlement. 'Just go on and do like I say.'

The little girl, with an armload of leaves, ran towards the compost heap.

The old woman chuckled again. 'I don't know,' she said to herself, 'maybe that is why he made the fig tree.'

Slavery Times

The old woman sat down on the side of the bed and looked through the opened window across the room. Outside, the air was heavy with heat. It seemed to shimmer, blending tones of light in the space above the windowsill, and if she had been nearer, the old woman would have reached out to touch the colours with her fingers. But she remained on the bed, allowing her senses to be lulled into inertia by the silent, trance-inducing vibrations outside. She blinked once and stared through the heat; her features becoming as still and quiet as the woman they had buried that morning.

A light breeze, billowing the lace curtains at the window, caught the old woman's eye and brought her back into the bedroom. She watched the curtains swaying back and forth, and when the breeze had died down, she looked slowly around the room as if to renew her acquaintance with each item in it.

After a while, the old woman shifted herself nearer the edge of the bed and, reaching up, unpinned the black straw hat from her head. She placed it on her lap and carefully brushed off the thin layer of dust with her handkerchief. When she had finished, she patted the hat into shape, then put it on the bed beside her. 'Do let me get out a these shoes,' she mumbled to herself and, grunting, bent down and untied her shoelaces. She sat up again to catch her breath and then began to move her feet from side to side until she had loosened the shoes enough to take them off. Slowly, she pushed one and then the other from her foot. The old woman sighed in relief, massaging the soles of her feet against the floor. When she was able to move her toes, she eased her feet into a pair of slippers, then sat back and rested for a moment.

'No wonder people was fainting in that church,' she said, continuing the conversation with herself. 'It's just puredee hot!'

She reached down for the shoes and, getting up from the bed, carried them and the hat to the closet. 'How many more times I got to wear you?' she asked the hat as she pushed it to the back of a shelf. She dropped the shoes on the floor, took a cotton frock off a hanger and walked back to the bed.

When she had finished changing, the old woman went to the chair by the window and sat down. She picked up a fan from the table and, leaning her head back, waved the fan back and forth in front of her. The heat and the effort of changing had sapped her of all her strength and for a while the old woman sat with her eyes closed. How she wished for rain. She felt parched just thinking about it. She couldn't remember when the heat had been so merciless. Some rain just now would cool off her body and her mind.

Every so often, she patted the beads of perspiration from her forehead and neck. And once, after she had pressed the handkerchief to her chest, the old woman dropped her head forward and for a long time stared down at the floor. When she sat up again, she seemed even more weary and tired. She shook her head regretfully. No, she couldn't think about these things, she told herself. Her mind just wouldn't let her. Overcome by weariness, she rested her head against the back of the chair and this time closed her eyes to sleep.

She dreamt she had walked to the graveyard to have one last look at Tateta's resting place. But the grave wasn't there. She searched everywhere for her sister's grave and each time she came upon a tombstone, the words on it would become senseless. Finally she gave up and, sad and dispirited, she decided to return to where the others had gathered after the funeral. As she walked past Tateta's old home, she saw the grave around the back of the house and, so glad to have found it, she began to hurry to where her sister was buried. But as she came closer, she realized she was coming upon the row of huts that used to be the old slave quarters. She stopped, distressed to discover that Tateta had been buried in such a miserable place. She raised her arms to protest and, as she did, something jerked her backwards. She saw the chains, locked around her wrists. They were tied around her legs as well and suddenly she couldn't move. She opened her mouth to cry out that she was supposed to be free, they couldn't put her in chains any more, but something weighed so heavily on her chest that she couldn't utter a word. She tried and tried to speak but no sound came out of her mouth, nor could she shift the chains that gripped her.

The old woman shook her head, struggling to get out of the dream. Grunting in distress she lurched forward in her chair, then sat there wide-eyed and still trying to catch her breath as the dream began to fade and she knew where she was. A while later, she looked around the room which seemed so quiet and undisturbed after the oppressive turmoil she had just relived. A breeze pushed the curtains away from the window and the old woman slowly raised her hands to it and felt the soft lace as it brushed over her fingers. Outside the leaves on the trees stirred gently and then quietened again as the curtains fell back to the window.

The old woman looked around the room once more. The feeling of being enslaved was still with her. It surrounded her, an aura of sensation, like the quivering heat waves just outside the window. She spread her hands protectively over her chest and brought her legs out from under the chair. They were free. Her hands and feet were free. She drew her legs back and dropped her hands into her lap.

The dream had come back to her after all these years. She sighed wearily and told herself it was because she had been thinking so much about Tateta these past few days. She looked down at her hands and arms, wondering how little they must have been, little and defenceless, when they had those chains on them. Tateta was even smaller than she was when it happened. The old woman remembered the small, trembling figure of her sister standing beside their mother, crying as they dragged her away and tied her to the tree.

She had stood, then lain, against that tree for three days and three nights and had gone on calling for her mother long after she had given up hope that she would ever come. It was Tateta who crept out of their cabin in the dead of night to sit with her, talking to the night, daring the unseen things that felt so close to harm them. As they sat facing the blackness, Tateta had told her over and over again that if their mother dared come to her, they would whip both of them, then sell their mother far away.

During the day, Tateta stood not far away and begged her not to cry and rub her eyes so. But the ants wouldn't stop biting her legs and she did cry until her eyes were sore and the flies came and caused them to fester.

The old woman blinked and had to cover her eyes. She had been staring into the distance where the sun glared down with white intensity on to the flat, dried fields beyond the garden. Nothing moved now. The leaves hung limp and dusty. Plants were bowed over the ground, fatigued and drained of colour. For one moment though the old woman thought she heard, far off, the rumble of thunder. No, she told herself, she had just imagined it, and again lost in thought she looked off into the distance.

When they removed the chains, her legs were so numb and swollen that she had immediately collapsed when they pulled her up from the ground. She had tried to get up by herself, but again she fell, back against the tree this time, carrying a slurred image of her mother who was standing nearby. She had lain there, helpless, struggling like a bird with a broken wing. Eventually, someone told her mother to come and take her away and they lifted her up and carried her inside.

She remembered how her mother, silent and grim-faced, had wiped the dirt from her body, then washed her, putting sab on the sores on her legs. Her vision had become impaired by the infection and when her mother washed her eyes, cleaning the pus from in them, they hurt too much to keep open.

Afterwards, she lay on her mat in the corner and, keeping her eyes closed, listened to her mother's laboured breathing, hearing her every step, as she moved around the room tending to other things. All day she kept her eyes closed, ashamed of herself because of the trouble she had caused. Even when Tateta came and knelt beside her and gently began to pat her legs to try to stop their uncontrollable spasms, she couldn't open her eyes. Tateta stayed beside her for a long time and she knew that evening had come because of the sounds around her. When she thought it was dusk outside and her corner of the room was in darkness, she let the tears roll from under her eyelids.

But years were to pass before she was able to open her mouth and hear herself cry again.

The fan rested on the old woman's chest. She had stopped moving it some time ago. Now she lifted it, as though curious about its use. She looked at it closely, studying a picture on one side. It was of a family standing together in church. They were harmoniously gathered in such peaceful surroundings, secure and unthreatened. Nothing distracted their family devotion. The mother and father were standing in front of a pew sharing a hymnbook and directly in front of them were their son and daughter, sharing a book as well. The parents each had a hand on a child's shoulder. The mother touching the daughter and the father, the son. All of them looked worshipfully upwards, presumably over the altar where God was, and were bathed in the light shining down from a beautiful stained-glass window behind them.

The old woman wished she could be in that picture, to stand there in that nice church and always be protected from the sorrows of the world and at the same time have showing on her face, for all eternity, how good life is.

She studied the faces on the fan, touching each one as if it helped her to learn more about them. The old woman lingered over the face of the mother, wondering what this lady thought of her daughter. Would she protect her with the hand that was resting so lightly on her shoulder? Would she pull her daughter into her arms and fight off any harm that threatened her well-being? Or would she use her hand to push her daughter away from her? Shove her towards trouble and the enemy? You never know, the old woman mused sadly, what a mother will do with her daughter.

Absently she moved the fan back and forth, still wondering about the two females. Then she thought she heard the sound of thunder. She looked out of the window. The sky seemed to have dulled to a pale yellow, but she couldn't be sure. In any event, the heat remained as intense as ever. Just have to wait and see, she told herself. Like life sometimes, nothing to do but wait and see what's go happen. Like when you leave home and go off from your momma's house to somewhere else. You don't know what lies ahead of you or how you gonna tackle it. But what you do in the end, more times than not, depends on how you was brought up and how you feel about yourself when you do leave home.

The old woman looked down at the face of the daughter on the fan. Just a child, she mused sympathetically. No way of telling what would become of her. Would she grow up and leave home ashamed of herself and ashamed of her body, wishing somehow she didn't have to take it with her? And afraid even more of the trouble she was bound to bring on herself? Knowing from her mother's warnings that somehow, and in some way she had never understood, she was doomed?

The burden of her self was so great, the old woman remembered, feeling the heaviness spread through her as she sat in her chair. It had always seemed a burden, even before the chains. There had been times when her small shoulders were weighed down by the faults she had been told she possessed and she had shrunk from within when nothing of herself was judged to be redeemable. It had saddened her to her heart whenever she realized this. How heavy was the hand on the daughter's shoulder? She shook her head, overwhelmed with weariness and unable to continue. It must be the pressure dropping, the old woman told herself. Then maybe it might rain. Since I can feel the pressure tighten round my head. Maybe.

Her legacy from her mother when she reached womanhood had been a forewarning which turned out to be as accurate as it was terrible. Her mother had said she would never amount to anything. Because somehow her mother had known through all the years of her growing up that what she was should be condemned. She used to deny these wounding pronouncements against herself and was knocked down for disputing her mother which was, as she knew it, a sin.

That was how it was. Some things her mother had to beat into her. Others she had to beat out. And if she showed disrespect or interrupted, she was slapped as reproachment for what she had done.

The old woman supposed she should have learned quickly either to duck and miss her mother's fist or to keep quiet in the first place. Because her mother was, after all, telling her about life. Not as she herself wanted it to be or thought it should be, but how, in fact, it was. But she never learned the lessons, even when her mother resorted to beating them into her. Instead, she continued to try to tell her mother what she thought and her mother continued to knock her into silence. She left home searching and hoping for somebody or something that would prove she was right. It led her down many a rough path and her mother's words followed behind her. She could till this day hear her voice. 'You hear me talkin to you?' Her mother had already raised her hand as she waited for a reply. 'Yes'm,' she muttered. 'You might think you free.' Her mother's voice was low and tight. 'But long as you in my house and livin under my roof, you ain free from me. Long as you livin in my house, you go do what I says for you to do. Ya hear me?'

The heat of her anger burned in her eyes and she dropped her head to hide them. 'Yes'm,' she murmured into her chest.

Tateta would never talk back to their mother. She had never entertained the idea. She would stand silently and say nothing, never tempted to speak or pout her face and sulk. That was because Tateta wasn't there. She had closed the door on herself and taken her mind for a walk through a green field. The old woman pursed her lips, thinking of the differences in herself and her sister. No, she would have to talk back. She couldn't help wanting to tell their mother, but never dared, because she was afraid of what she might do to her, that she and Tateta might as well still be slaves. Often she had told Tateta this when her frustrations were too much to bear. 'Ain no used in worryin bout it,' Tateta always said when she was through. 'Cause they ain nothin you kin do.'

The old woman wiped her face with her handkerchief. It was damp and left her face wet. She sat back in the chair and fanned herself but it gave her no relief. Even the occasional breeze was too warm to shift the air. It blew in through the window hot like it had just come out of the oven.

The old woman remembered how they used to pick cotton in such weather. Bent over, pulling the white balls out of the brittle claw-like hulls while the sweat rolled off their bodies. Up and down the rows they went with no shade to relieve the burning on their backs. They used to get up early in the morning and work in the same fields they had worked in slavery. She and Tateta would pick side by side, hour after hour. The dew evaporated from the cotton leaves as the sun rose overhead at the start of another sweltering day. Most of the time it was too hot to talk, too hot to move anything except your hands, pulling and picking, your feet shifting your body from one bush to the next. Sometimes though, towards the end of the day, when the sun had moved from directly overhead, she and Tateta would talk and enjoy each other's company. They would speak in low voices so the others could not hear what they were saying, but then one or both of them would burst out laughing. Or someone would try to creep up on them to eavesdrop and when caught by the two of them would call out for them to stop talking so much and get on with their work. Tateta would answer back, 'Yes'm,' while she pretended to ignore whoever it was. 'Why they got to be so mean and so nosey all the time?' she would hiss to Tateta when they were out of earshot. 'They ain got to be like that all the time! Justa frownin and watchin, tryin to see what you up to.'

'They ain't tryin to be mean,' Tateta said after a while. 'They just serious and it ain nothing you can do about the way they is. You ain go change em. Try and get along with it Ellen. That's all.'

She didn't answer Tateta and they moved to another row. She looked up to make sure no one was nearby. 'One day,' she said, as she snatched the cotton from the hull, 'One day soon, I'm gettin as far away from this place as I can git and ain't man nor beast go be able to drag me back here. You hear me?' Tateta didn't say anything so she continued, 'I mean it cause they got to be somethin bettern this. Ain no sense in livin like this, Tateta. Like a slave. I'm a go. I mean it. I got to.'

A voice called out from behind them, 'What y'all up there whisprin for? Go get you inta trouble. What y'all talkin bout?'

Tateta straightened up and shaded her eyes to see who it was. 'We ain talkin bout nothin,' she called back.

'Young gurls, whisprin so nobody can't hear, they gits inta trouble,' the voice called back again.

'Yes'm,' Tateta said and returned to picking cotton. She laughed quietly and then mimicked the voice. They both covered their mouths and laughed.

'All right,' Tateta said later on. 'If that what you go do. Go on off. It ain go be no different. They ain nowhere you can go gon be different. Lessen you goes up north and work for some white people up there. Be one of them maids and they go treat you the same as down here. Cause what else you gon do? Child they ain nothin t'all to bein free. Nothin t'all.'

'Maybe not,' she said when Tateta was through talking, 'but I'm go find out.'

They didn't speak again until they had finished picking for the day and were dumping the cotton out of their sacks to be weighed. Tateta sat down under a nearby tree and began to fan herself with the straw hat she'd been wearing. She said to no one in particular, 'This here heat today been enough to turn anybody mean. Lord it's too hot to have to pick cotton.'

Their mother had looked up from the cotton she'd been separating. 'Lest we workin for ourself and gettin paid for it. Ain nobody standin over you wid no whip and you betta thank the Lord for that.'

The old woman's palm and the handle of the fan were wet with perspiration. She wiped them with her handkerchief and then absently rolled it into a little ball which she kept in the palm of her hand. She turned the fan over and read on the back, 'McBrides's Funeral Home. In Your Hour Of Need.'

She had needed to know so many things. That's what she had discovered once she left home; just how little she knew about anything. She used to wonder whether her mother had deliberately kept her ignorant about life or whether her mother never knew any more than she did. How could she be so naïve about so many things? about people? about herself? That was the most distressing realization of all. Once she left home all her willpower seemed to wilt and she drifted and swayed whichever way she was pushed. Why? That's what she had wanted to know. So finally she had returned, wanting the answers from her mother. She had come back, prepared to challenge her mother's hold on the truth because she had found out that her truth didn't fit anywhere in the life she had known. But instead of the strong, heavy-boned woman who had stood over her, fist ready for an assault on her as she defiantly grew into adulthood, she had found a small, shrunken frame lying helpless and almost unrecognizable in her mother's bed. The shock of seeing her mother so reduced in size had taken her breath away and in disbelief she had sank to the chair by the bed, wondering what had happened.

She just sat there waiting for some sign that her mother knew who she was. Eventually her mother had lowered her gaze from the ceiling, ending, for a while, her vigil of some unseen thing. She looked over towards her daughter, causing her head to roll feebly to one side of her pillow. Her eyes rested on her daughter but remained devoid of any emotion.

For a long time she stared at her mother, trying to comprehend what had happened to her. She was unable to stop herself from watching the small bird-like chest rising and falling under the covers, the only sign of life visible to her.

Still, she told herself, feeling for the threads that tied their lives together, when her mother spoke to her, then they would talk. It wouldn't be too late for that.

She had come back to talk, to ask her mother about her childhood, though she hadn't specifically known that until she had walked into the house where it suddenly and clearly became the reason she had returned. Because somewhere along the way home, she had become desperate to know about her imprisonment and once inside her mother's house, she had to ask her what she had felt when they had locked chains on her arms and legs and dragged her off to that tree. She wanted to listen to her mother say how this thing had affected her so they could finally share the nightmare experience which had always been hers alone. She was ready and prepared to ask her mother what had gone through her mind.

The silence in the room lengthened. Neither she nor her mother had acknowledged each other as she sat beside the bed, her hands respectfully folded, knowing that as the strain on her emotions increased she was starting to drift off again, away from the link with her past. Because even though she wanted to stay there, she had no idea how to grasp whatever it was that would keep her there. What should she hold on to? That's what she had come to find out. It was like being out in the world on her own again. The chair seemed a hundred miles from nowhere.

She had had to stand up, ready to leave the room, but not knowing how. Later when she thought back on it, she supposed her mother had sensed she was about to go because she had opened her mouth in an effort to speak.

'You know,' her mother eventually whispered in a dry, gravelled voice, the words so slow in forming that she had to repeat them to herself to understand what her mother was trying to say, 'they didn't never sell nary one of my children.' Her head, as if of its own accord, had turned away from her daughter and with an effort she spoke again. 'Not nary a one. All of em stay wid me till they was grown.'

She continued to stand by the bed, waiting until she realized her mother had forgotten she was there. She gave up for the last time and walked over to the window. She stood there looking out but a growing tightness in her chest made it hard for her to see.

After a while she wiped the water from her eyes and tried to focus on something outside the window, and because she had to grab hold of something she asked, 'Didn't you never love us. Didn't you care about us, Mamma? Cause I don't believe it.'

The tears rolled down her face as she stood facing the window, having bluntly and ineptly said everything her emotions contained, waiting now for an answer she knew was not forthcoming.

'That you over there crying?' Her mother's voice seemed strickened with weariness. 'What you cryin for?'

Tears tumbled out of her eyes. She wiped her face but did not answer. After a while she turned and looked over towards the bed. Her mother was watching her but a moment later her gaze shifted to the ceiling. Unable to answer, she turned back to the window.

'What you crying for?' Her mother's voice came from far away.

She shook her head. There was nothing she could say. She

wouldn't know where to begin. This was what her mother had always denied her. There had never been a way to come to her. No path to her bosom. They had no special words or signal to let one another know they had some intimate thought or concern they needed to share. She shook her head again. There was nothing to say and so she stood by the window and cried in the knowledge that she cried alone and that her reasons for doing so would never be known.

'You know,' her mother's voice was as weak as it was thoughtful, 'I never know you to cry since that time they tie you to that tree. You wan't nothing but a little thing. You don remember. Wasn't nothin but a poor little thing when they done that.'

'I do remember.' She leaned against the window and mumbled the words into her chest. 'I didn't never forget what happen.' When she was able, she straightened up, sniffing back the tears. 'No. I always remembered.'

'I don know.' She tried to listen to the faraway voice, wondering whose weariness coloured the words. 'I ain got much longer. I git so tired all the time. This ole body done bout worn out.' Her mother grunted softly as confirmation. 'Different kinda tired from what I use ta know. I just don't feel like carryin on no more. Cain carry on.' She moaned a little, almost as if she was beginning to sing a hymn, but the sound faded and the silent presence of the two women, both waiting, filled the room.

'John use ta say in the evening . . .' The words seemed amplified in the quietness of the room, after the long expanse of waiting. She found herself straining to hear what it was her mother had decided to talk about.

'Sometimes they used to work him real hard. Real hard. So he couldn't hardly make it. Use ta say: "Lord I'm so tired." Sound like the words was aching when they come out his mouth. "Lord I'm so tired." That's how I am, tired like John.'

She heard but did not understand what her mother was remembering. There seemed no point in asking, so she stood and listened, more to hear her mother's voice than what she was saying. When her mother had been quiet for a while, she turned from the window and found her watching her again.

This time her mother's eyes dropped to the chair beside the bed.

'Can I have a glass a water? I git so thirsty.'

She went to the bed and slowly lifted her mother's head and held the glass for her. When she had finished and pushed the glass away, she gently lowered her back on to the pillow. She wanted to sit down on the side of the bed, next to her mother, and knew this was the moment to do it. She pictured herself there, where she should be. But the hope of it happening was a flicker and was gone, and whatever had taken its place wouldn't let her sit on the bed.

She stood with her hands folded. 'Can I get you something to eat, Mamma?'

Her mother didn't answer.

'If not, then I think I'm go step outside for a little bit of fresh air.' She went towards the door and noiselessly opened it.

'John was a good man to me.' Her mother's voice was clear. 'He was a good father to his children. Times he get quiet and go off by heself. That was all. He always love his children.'

She stood by the door. 'John? What John you talking about?'

'John.' Her mother repeated the name. 'My John. You know my John.'

'No,' she answered. 'I don't know who he is.'

'If'n he was feeling all right, he would go and sit outside and whittle on a piece of wood. I use ta sit there next to him. That's how I know he was sick. The heat was comin outta his body. That night he say to me, "Every night I pray to the Lord to look after my children and if it his will, let them be raise together, wid their mother. I pray that every night." Then he stop talking for a while and whittle away on that stick till he was ready to talk some more. "Seem like last night I done got a answer. Lyin in the bed, seem like the Lord tell me they was all go be raise together wid they mother. Seem like he say he go look after my children." Neither one a us could sleep that night cause the fever start to burnin John and I know he wan't go be wid me for much longer. Next day they come and got me out the field. Said he had the sunstroke. I already know. John know it too. But they done make him work anyway. Brought him to the house and he died next day in the bed. Fever burn him up fore my eyes. Master come to the cabin after the funeral. Say. John sure been a good worker. He sorry to lose him. Look down at my babies standing there sides me. Say. They fine-looking children. Look for a long time. Say. He don know how he can afford to get another worker like John. I say. Master. Look Master in the eye. When my children git grown, they go work just as hard as they pappy done. He look at my children for a long time. Then say. That's right. Raise em to be hard-working like they pappy.'

Her mother's eyes moved over towards the door as if to see if she was still there, but she did not look directly at her. Her breathing had quickened but she continued to talk in the same slow, quiet voice.

'That's what he pray for. For all of em to be raise together. Lord see to it. They didn't take my children from me.'

She walked back over to the bed and looked down at her mother who was still gazing at the spot by the door where she had been standing.

'Momma. My pappy's name was John. That's who you talking about. Was that my pappy? Momma?'

Her mother wiped her hand over dried eyes and then began to stroke the covers on the bed. Her eyes followed her hand moving slowly back and forth as she gently touched the quilt with her fingertips. She pressed her mouth down firmly and no other words passed her lips.

The air didn't seem any fresher outside than in her mother's room. She walked over to a tree and sat down on a bench in the shade. Across the road and in the field on the other side, she could see the figures of a man and a mule ploughing up the damp, red earth. She leaned forward, resting her elbows on her knees, and watched their slow, even progress as the man shifted the plough and reined the mule at the same time.

Her mother was inside on her deathbed. She had come home, pulled by something, to find her there and now she did not know what to do. She couldn't explain any of it to herself. Her head was buzzing. It was like a beehive inside.

She knew she had come searching for something. It had made her wander through the house trying to conjure up the past. She lingered there fingering objects that belonged to her mother, recalling something that her mother had said or done, trying to revive the stir of life that was fading from the rooms. She couldn't explain what she was looking for. If it had met her at the door or stood waiting for her in one of the rooms, she would have recognized it instantly and could have made sense of her search. But it hadn't been waiting and she knew, as she continually roamed through her mother's house, that she wasn't going to find it.

She had gone outside and sat down under the tree because she wasn't looking any more. She had, she now realized, lost hope of finding whatever it was when she walked out of her mother's bedroom. This confusion she was facing now was tightening her chest. She looked across the road for the sight of the man and the mule, but they had ploughed their way to the other end of the field and were little specks in the distance.

What had led her to believe that the moment she walked through her mother's door, to be surrounded once more by all the things that she had missed and thought about over the years, she would be fulfilled? She'd had some idea that she was coming full circle, when in fact she had missed her mark. Because she had somehow persuaded herself that her mother would be different. Or maybe she believed that she was different. Something here had eluded her or, worse, she had deluded herself and had been found out. The chains are still on me, she told herself. She was shackled. The hope within her was dying a painful death. Just like the time she had waited for her mother to come to the tree.

She felt so very weary thinking about it all. 'Which one is the worse?' she asked herself as her throat contracted and caught her voice, 'being chained to that tree or this here now?' For all the times her mother had warned her, with one of her fierce omens, of the suffering that awaited her in life, nothing she had ever known had hurt more than what she was feeling now. She dropped her head into her hands.

The old woman was startled by the loud crackle of thunder. For a moment, she wasn't sure where she was then she leaned forward and looked out of the window. The wind was blowing. It rose then swept down through the garden, swirling dust and sand, swishing the leaves back and forth before it dropped down again and went off somewhere else. The light over the fields had grown duller. The thunder did not return and it wasn't dark enough to convince the old woman it might rain. She was grateful, however, for the breeze. It had dispelled the heat waves and the air was cooler. Nowadays she couldn't take the heat the way she used to. Some things, she reckoned, a person could take better when they got old. While other things seemed easier to take when a person was young. Then there was those things that a person never got used to, young or old. But these things had to be accepted. The old woman's eyes softened. That was the kind of thing Tateta would have said. And now Tateta was gone too. She picked up the fan, but immediately forgot she was holding it. She stared out of the window, seeing the image of her sister's coffin.

She had had to let Tateta go. When they came to tell her her sister had passed away, she heard what she had been waiting to hear. Sooner or later one of them had to hear it about the other. At least now she knew Tateta was all right, beyond any further tribulations. If she had died first, she'd have gone to her grave worrying about her sister. At least she had that comfort. Anyway, death didn't separate them. She had known it and Tateta too well. Both had been a part of her life for as long as she could remember.

From the time they were young, she and her sister had seen each other through so many hard times. It seemed as if something had always plagued one or the other of them. Even though for many years they had lived away from each other, they had remained close and held steadfast ever since coming together again when they were trying to come to terms with their mother's death.

She remembered how in the evening after their mother's burial the two of them had left the others and gone to sit out on the front porch. They sat for a long time without talking, just being together. Finally she had said, 'I don't even know if she was suffering.' She had thought this so often she might as well tell Tateta. 'I came and when I got here I tried to tend to her. But all the time I kept on thinking about what Mamma didn't never do for me. That's what was on my mind.'

Once she had begun her confession she continued, needing to unload these troubling thoughts from her mind. 'I didn't want her to die. Not cause she was my mother and I would miss her. I just kept on hoping that somehow or nother we might be able to talk things through. Even after she stop making sense. I was thinking if she goes now, I won't never know my mother. I won't never know if she love me and I won't never know if I love her.' She had wept quietly in the dark remembering how she had tried to the last to discover her mother's feelings about her.

After a while, Tateta began to talk. Whatever she had been thinking during their long silence when they first came out on to the porch, she kept to herself. But as with so many times in the past, she seemed to know when her sister had come upon an impasse and needed to be given some reason or explanation to help her get through.

'Sometimes we just don't know the reason why we feel certain things. Sometimes though we see the reason later on in life. Cause maybe later, we understand something about ourself that we didn't know before. Then again we might not never understand why we feel a certain way. But there always be a reason for it and if you want to, you can think and think on it till that's all you got on your mind. Now me, I think it be better to let the thing go. Accept it and then let it go. Cause Ellen you can't understand everything. You can't understand everything about Mamma. She just had her ways. When I was little, seem to me that half the time she was possessed by something and I used to wonder if she was our real momma. Other times seem like she was just scared, afraid like something was going to hurt her. She act like she was frighten inside, like a child that know it go get a beatin. Then when I was grown, I told myself that something had always bothered Momma. But she never let on what it was and whatever it was, she take it to her grave. We just got to carry on Ellen. I don't see nothin else to do but carry on from here.'

When Tateta had finished they sat in a silent aftermath, unburdened and relieved. She had listened and drawn comfort from the sound of Tateta's chair rocking over the wooden planks of their mother's porch. Neither of them wanted to move, though they could hear the others inside getting ready for bed.

'I suppose,' Tateta had said, after someone had come to the door and said good night, 'when you think about it, all the ones that was brought up in slavery, they didn't think about living in freedom. I mean to say, they might a wished for freedom and talk about what they want to do. But all they know about was slavery. All they thinkin and talkin was slavery way. They didn't know nothin else. And when freedom come, what was they suppose to do? Ain nobody tell them how to be free. Ain nobody give them nothin cept they children. They ain had nothin. Didn't know how to do nothin cept what they was doin in the slavery times. They had to get on and make a living for theyselves and they children. So they take the slavery ways and they become the freedom ways. Wasn't nobody there for them to talk to about how things out to be done and just like we learn how to do things by watching them, that's how they had learn. And it go on back, slave to slave, learnin from the one before.'

Tateta paused and looked up at the stars as if they would tell her what to say next.

'I don't know. Probably we still doing things the way they did in slavery times. We was born into slavery. I remember when they said all a us was free. Everybody jumpin and shoutin, talkin bout what they gonna do. But after a while we all know nothin much had change. We wasn't change. Was we? I didn't feel no different. Nobody treat me no different. And that's how it is. People just the same. Acting just the same. I don't know, maybe when we get old our children be tryin to figure us out and wishing we could a been different, been kinder somehow. And be wondering if we ever love them while we be thinkin that they don know how hard life been, that they didn't appreciate all the sacrifices we made for them. I expect some of em be sittin here on this front porch cause they can't get to sleep for trying to figure us out. Lordy. Lordy.' Tateta laughed softly then stood up and stretched. 'Yes sir. One day we be old and tired. Old and tired. Shoot! That's how I'm feelin right now. Let me get on in this house.'

They walked quietly off the front porch and into the house which was dark and sleeping.

The old woman rocked in her chair, grateful for the drop in temperature. She knew it didn't make any sense but she thought that somehow the cooler weather was Tateta's doing. Outside in the garden a breeze blew steadily and sometimes with strength through the trees. They swayed vigorously with their leaves turned upwards to a paler colour. The colour of rain, the old woman told herself, as the curtains rippled in the wind which brought the faint but growing sound of thunder through the window. While she watched, the rumbling came over the horizon embedded in balls of thick dark clouds. For a while the sound of it dominated the area as it rummaged ominously inside the clouds, and then it rolled away echoing occasionally from somewhere else.

The old woman nodded wisely. There would be rain. She was content to listen to the sounds of its forecast in the garden but she was soon drifting into sleep.

Once more she was sitting on the front porch in the dark. It was her house this time. The children were inside, asleep, oblivious to the loud voices and the music that blared from the house on the corner. From where she sat the lights inside the house outlined the figures dancing back and forth in front of the windows. She sat there and stared into the house, not caring if she never moved again.

Tateta was almost on the porch before she saw her.

'Hey,' she said as she came up the steps. 'I didn't know if that was you or not. How come you ain got no light on inside?' Without waiting for an answer, Tateta sat down on the edge of the porch and stretched her legs over the steps. She continued to talk. 'She got a bunch of them over there tonight. Fire start, go be a bunch a fried niggers to go along with that fried fish.' She laughed and watched a couple who were dancing close together glide past the window. 'Well, they gettin what they pay for. Where Charles?' Tateta asked and glanced round behind her. When there was no answer she carried on talking. 'Least he don't let the children see him acting like that. Some of them be so drunk up round here, they can't even see how to get home. Be lyin round here tomorrow morning sick as a dog and stinkin of lickka. That's what I can't stand.'

'He gone out a town,' she answered Tateta.

'Who? Charles? Say he gone out a town?' Tateta turned around. 'For what? Where he gone to?'

'They gone off together.'

'He didn't go off with that woman?'

She didn't answer.

'Gone!' Tateta turned back round to think about what she had just heard.

'That's what I said. They gone somewhere. I don't know. Come and got his clothes while I was working this morning. When I got home the children told me Poppa come and took all his clothes. He told them he was going to send for us in a few days.'

'No!' Tateta said. 'He ain go leave like that and go to that woman.'

But she knew it had happened whether Tateta was prepared to believe it or not. 'Lord I'm so tired of that man. I can't take no more. I mean it. I just can't take no more. If I could lay my hands on him right now, I think I'd kill him.'

'No. You just sayin that. You got them children to think of. He ain gone nowhere outta town. You know he up to that woman house and if I was you, I go right on up there and have it out. Get him back. You got the children.'

'No, Tateta. I don't want him. She can have him. I know I got the children. Don't you think I don't know?'

'How you think you go make do, Ellen? On your own?'

'Just like all the rest of them ain got no husband. No. I had enough. That's where he wants to be and I don't want him back. My bed ain't good enough. And it ain't never been. I know that now. I don't want him in it no more. I'm through with him.'

'You talk like that now. Go ahead and get it off your chest.' Tateta sighed. 'You know they all like that. They all like that.' She emphasized each word. 'They can't help it. Child they's so much temptation. They get out there and they forgit about everything. Wife, children, they home. All they can think about is that little bit a money in they pocket and those women

69

smiling cause they want the money spent on them. You know they all the same. Just some worse than others. You just got to put up with it that's all. He'll be back.'

'No Tateta. Not this time. I'm not lettin him back in this house. Cause I been taking it from the start. Even before the children was born and you know it. No, I brought it on myself and I got to live with it. I see it now what Momma was tellin me. She said he wasn't no man. She told me, but all I wanted was to listen to him tellin me how much he love me and care about me. Cryin in my lap about how he ain never had nobody. Didn't have no parents and all he wanted was a family to love. How he needed me. I believe it cause that's what I wanted to believe. I shoulda known better. But I listen to all that and wouldn't listen to nobodys else and that's why I sittin here now. Ain nobody to blame but me.'

'It's not your fault Ellen,' Tateta said quietly. 'And it's not they fault either. Not all the time. They has it hard out there. The men have it harder than the women. I see em out there sometime and the white man be on their back, gittin at them bout everything. There something between em cause they men. Something that bother the white man and he make it harder for them and I see em out there and I think that something inside them bout to explode. They keep it all inside. I don't know what's goin on in they heads. They don't never talk about it. It must be terrible though cause it make em do terrible things sometime. That's why they got to go out there and git rid of it. They got to.' Tateta was looking at the house on the corner as she talked.

'I'm go explode,' she told Tateta. 'I'm go explode or I'm go lay down and die cause I done take too much. They ain't nothin left. There ain't nothin left Tateta. If it wasn't for my two babies sleeping in there, I'd go off somewhere and keep on going till I drop. That's the truth. That's how I feel.'

'You can't be thinkin like that,' Tateta mumbled to hide her concern.

'But that's how I feel,' she repeated, frustration and hurt taking control of her voice. 'When I'm sittin here bone tired, cause I work too. Hard. Cleaning and cooking in that woman's house every day except Sunday, then trying to get the strength to get up and go inside and cook some supper for my family and that hussy come walking down the street and ask me if I know where Charles is. And my children can hear her talking to me and she know it. Then say, I know where he is. Sleeping on my bed and I'm going to get him something good to eat and fix it for him when he wake up. Then wave his money in front of my face and gone on down the street laughing. No. I can't take that. I'm a do just like our momma did, raise my children by myself. And I'm not go ever say one word about they father cause as far as I'm concern they ain't got one.' She wept silently, covering her face with her hands, not even wanting Tateta to be there. She heard her speak though.

'It don't never get easy do it? No, it don't never get easy. You born cryin, and ain't that the first thing you got to learn how to do. Never mind,' Tateta said, knowing that was all the comfort she could offer. 'Never mind Ellen.'

Across the road, at the house on the corner, they heard a woman cry out. They watched as she tried to pull away from a man who had grabbed both her arms. He pulled her to him and slapped her face. She fell against a post and he slapped her a second time. They heard him call her a whore. The woman sank to her knees and the man punched her in the back, calling her a whore again. Then he stepped away from her, turned and walked back into the house. When she could, the woman pulled herself up from the ground, holding on to the post. Still crying, she began to straighten her dress and pull her hair back in place. Then she brushed the sand off her arms and legs and wiped her face with her hands. Moving slowly, she walked over to the steps, went up them and back into the house.

They didn't say any more until Tateta got ready to leave.

'You comin to church tomorrow?' Tateta asked her.

'Yeah. I'ma try and make it to Sunday school with the children.'

'All right then.'

'All right. I'll see you tomorrow.'

Afterwards, she lay awake hearing the noise of the people at the house on the corner. It got louder until just before the dawning of the new day they made their way, a few at a time, back to their own homes.

★

The old woman smelled the rain in the air. She lifted her head and looked out of the window. It was even cooler. The breeze felt good against her skin. She inhaled deeply, wishing the weather had changed before the funeral. It had been too hot for her to go to the grave and see Tateta laid to rest. Instead, she had been taken to the house of a relative and waited there for the rest of them to return for something to eat. That was how she had known that her sister was buried.

The old woman watched as the sky changed colour. The light from the sun, hidden now from view, tinted the colour of the garden. She looked pensively into it, drawn by its peacefulness. When she finally turned back into the room, she found the little girl standing in the doorway watching her.

'Hey. You home from school?' The old woman cleared her throat and picked up the fan from her lap.

'I been home. You were sleeping all the time. You always sleeping.'

'That so.' She cleared her throat again. 'How long you been home then?'

'A long time.' The little girl stepped inside the room. 'You been sleeping and sleeping.'

'Sure enough?'

The little girl nodded. 'You know what? You were talking when you were sleeping.' She watched the old woman for her reaction. She didn't seem to hear. 'You were talking while you were sleeping, just like there was somebody here for you to talk to.'

'That so?'

The little girl nodded again and walked over to the bed and sat down. 'You had your eyes closed and your head was like this.' She leaned over and dropped her chin on her chest, then closed her eyes and started mumbling. 'Just like that,' she said, peeping up at the old woman.

'I musta been talking in my sleep.'

'I know. That's what Grandmamma said you were doing.'

'That must be what it was,' the old woman conceded.

'Who were you talking to? Grandmamma said you must be thinking you were talking to somebody.'

The old woman shook her head. 'Old people be dreaming all the time. Sometimes they dream they talking.'

'Did you dream you were scared of something? Cause sometimes you sound like you were scared.'

'No. I can't remember nothin scaring me.'

'I had a scary dream one time,' the little girl admitted. 'And I started crying and calling for my mamma cause I was scared the devil was after me and I was running from him and he was trying to get me cause I broke the eggs in the bird's nest.'

'That's what you dream?'

'Yep. And when the devil tried to grab me, my mamma heard me and she woke me up.'

'So you know it wasn't nothing but a dream.'

'You were calling your mamma in your dream.'

The old woman didn't say anything.

'That's what I heard you saying sometimes,' the little girl continued. 'Did you dream the devil was chasing you?'

The old woman put the fan back on her lap. 'No. There wasn't no devil chasing me.' A moment later she said, 'There wasn't no devils. All the devils I know are through chasing me.'

'Well what were you calling your mamma for? Cause she can't come and wake you up.'

'No.' The old woman looked out of the window as if she had lost interest in the conversation. 'Oh, I expect I must a been dreaming about something a long time ago. That must be what it was.' Her attention was on the weather outside.

'And you were dreaming about your mamma?' the little girl asked.

The old woman nodded.

'And there wasn't any devil in your dream?'

'No. I done told you. I'm too old to run from any devils and I believe them devils is too tired to be chasing me. Just every so often, I get to thinking about one, that's all.' The old woman looked at the little girl. 'And all you got to be scared of is breaking birds' eggs. Anyway, you shouldn't go round bothering birds' nests.'

'I didn't mean to. When I was climbing up the tree, it fell down and they all broke.'

'Well,' the old woman said, 'if that's the only bad dream you have then you mighty lucky.' She pulled herself up from her chair. 'Come on here and help me put down this window.'

'You know what?' the little girl said. 'I'm not scared of bad dreams any more cause I'm growing up.'

'That's right,' the old woman agreed.

'I'm not scared of anything.'

'Sure enough?'

'Nope.'

Lightning flashed across the sky and the thunder crackled, then rolled over the house. They pulled the window down and saw the first rain drops pelt the ground outside.

'I'm not even scared a thunder,' the little girl shouted over the loud rumble that seemed to envelop the house.

'I'm not scared a no thunder neither,' the old woman added. She sat back down in her chair. The little girl stood beside her and they watched the rain together.

Oh Henry!

The little girl stood by the fence and called across Miss Dunbar's back garden and into the next where the new boy was playing with a puppy. The boy stopped playing and looked over towards her. She looked back at him, ready to smile. The boy, about to speak, hesitated, then without saying anything turned away and continued to play with the puppy.

Disappointed, but undeterred, the little girl watched them. She stepped up to the fence and leaned against it, trying to think of something to say that would catch the little boy's attention. He had begun to tease the dog with a stick. A few times he glanced over at her, and as she watched him he held the stick higher and higher, while the dog jumped up after it. The boy laughed loudly, apparently enjoying the puppy's antics, and this made the little girl even more eager to be a part of their play.

The little girl stood on her toes and shouted that her dog in Bowman could jump as high as that too. The boy ignored her, but the puppy, distracted by her voice, ran barking towards their side of Miss Dunbar's fence.

Smiling at her success, the little girl bent down and called to the puppy as it reached the fence and tried to get over. The boy shouted for the dog to come back. When it didn't, he ran after it, picked it up and, without a glance in the little girl's direction, took the puppy back to where they had been playing.

The little girl stood up, taken aback by the rebuff; her smile gone, she stepped back from the fence.

Once the boy looked over at her while he carried on playing with the puppy. But he quickly looked away when the little girl found him staring at her.

The boy began to run frantically in zig zags across the garden, while the puppy tried to keep up with him, barking in excitement. The boy stopped suddenly and looked at her. 'Go away!' he shouted. 'Go away!' Then he ran out of her view calling for the puppy to come after him.

For a while, the little girl stayed where she was, perplexed and embarrassed by the boy's outburst, then she moved away from the fence and wandered, without much purpose, around her own garden, until eventually she decided to go into the house.

'Henry won't play with me.' The little girl entered the old woman's room and walked over to where she was sitting by the window reading. 'I told him he can come over here,' the little girl continued, 'but he won't come.' She sighed in exasperation, dropping her hands to her sides.

The old woman looked up at her and then continued reading. It was her Sunday School lesson. She read a little of it each afternoon, patiently mouthing each word, as her finger underlined the sentences she was studying.

The little girl was determined to interrupt her, something she was not allowed to do. In an even louder voice she said, 'And he won't talk to me neither. So I don't have nobody to play with.' She looked down at the floor.

The old woman read on and, when she had finished she marked her place with a card and looked up at the little girl. 'Now how come you couldn't let me read for a little bit without carrying on so?'

The little girl frowned and didn't say anything, annoyed that instead of getting sympathy over her problem, she was being scolded.

'Where is your manners? That you come in here and see me trying to read my lesson and you don't say excuse me or nothing. Just rummaging on. You can see I'm trying to get through with what I'm doing.'

The little girl looked away from the old woman who was shaking her head at her as if she were beyond redemption. 'I'm sorry,' the little girl mumbled, looking down at the floor again.

'You should be sorry cause you certainly know better. And the next time you do that, I'm going to shoo you right out of this room and you go have to stay out.'

The little girl nodded her head. 'I won't do it again.'

'Well I'm go wait to see about that. Never mind now you in here.' She put her Sunday School book on her lap. 'What Henry this is you talking about?'

'Henry's who's staying over at Mrs Dansler's house.'

'I didn't know there was no children staying over there, lessen they come for a visit.'

'Yes he is. He's staying over there. I saw him when he came yesterday morning. In a taxi. And he had a suitcase and his mamma brought him to stay with Mrs Dansler.'

'Well, I haven't heard nothing about it. I reckon he might be one of her grans.'

The little girl nodded. 'Yes. He's one of her grans and he's come to stay with her cause his mamma's on her way to Florida with a no-count man and she left his daddy in New York. And he's running a nightclub up there and doesn't want to be bothered with him.'

'Now hold on a minute!' The old woman was nearly breathless from trying to listen to and understand everything the little girl was telling her. 'I don't know what in the world you talking about. So just hold on a minute. I thought you come in here to tell me that you wanted to play with this child staying at Mrs Dansler's. How you got to talking about nightclubs and people running off?'

The little girl was shaking her head at the old woman's confused interpretation of Henry's circumstances. She tried to explain further. 'But that's why he's got to stay here at Mrs Dansler's cause she's his grandmamma and he hasn't got not another soul to look after him.'

'Well, I don't know what you talking about and I don't know where you got it from. But you must a got it all twisted, somehow or nother.'

'No I didn't!' The little girl had become excited in her attempt to explain why Henry was staying with his grandmother. 'You don't understand. But it's true. That's what Grandma was saying on the telephone. She said it was because Henry's mamma shouldna never married Mrs Dansler's son, but it was just as much his fault because he was always following after girls he picked up in the honky-tonk.'

'Now hold on and stop right there.' The old woman was

waving her hands in the air, horrified at what she was hearing. 'You don't know what you talking about. You done got two or three things tied up together. And you don't understand it no better than me. And besides it don't concern you and you know you not suppose to go round repeating things you hear other people saying. That's the first thing. And the second thing, you shouldn't be listening to your grandmamma talking on the telephone.'

'I wasn't listening,' the little girl protested, 'I was in the kitchen getting a glass of water and I just heard.'

'Well it wasn't meant for your ears and I don't want to talk about it no more. Cause you don't understand what you heard and on top of that, it's none of your business.'

'But I was just trying to tell you about Henry, that's all.' The little girl felt she was back to where she started when she first came into the room.

'Well that ain't got nothing to do with whether or not you play with this Henry.'

'But he won't play with me. I told him he could come over and he won't even say anything and I want to play with him.'

'I see,' the old woman said, then went on to inform the little girl, 'But you know you can't make nobody play with you if they don't want to. That's up to them.'

'But I don't have anybody to play with and I want to play with him.'

The old woman looked at the little girl, seeing the undisguised longing in her face. She said quietly, as if this would help the little girl to understand what she meant, 'Still, you can't make a person do something if they don't want to. Maybe he just don't feel like playing right now.'

'He keeps playing with his dog all the time,' the little girl quickly retorted, unwilling as before to accept the old woman's opinion.

'Then I don't know,' the old woman said. 'I expect he might need some time to get use to being in a different place. New York is awful different from here. Awful different.'

'How come it's different? Cause it's got all those big ole tall buildings?'

'That's one thing. Cause it sure is stacked full of buildings.

Even when I was there. All of em bunched up together and no space between.'

'Is that what it's like?' the little girl asked.

The old woman nodded. 'And the streets is full of cars, going this way and that way, honking their horns all the time. And you never seen so many people, pushing and shoving and rushing everywhere. And the noise. Everything is making some kind a noise. It don't never get quiet. Not even at night-time.' The old woman paused, thinking about the city she had visited so many years ago. 'And besides people act different up there. They not the same as the people down here.'

'But Aunt Agatha lives in New York,' the little girl said.

'Well she don't live right in New York. And besides she comes from down here. So she knows how things are here. I believe Mrs Dansler's gran, that you talking about, was born up there in New York and he live there all his life. So he don't know what it's like down here. He got to adjust and that take time.'

'How long is it going to take?'

'Now that I don't know. But I don't suppose it'll take him too long. Children get use to things faster than grown people.'

'But how long?'

'I told you, I don't know. It all depends on the boy. Maybe if he likes it, it won't take too long. And you got to remember that he don't know his grandmother. They are strangers to each other. He got to get use to her as well. That's a lot for a little boy, specially when his mamma and daddy not with him. He's probably missing them and feeling lonely down here on his own.'

'I don't feel lonely for my mamma and daddy.'

'Well you sure use to. When I first got here, you were dragging yourself round like a sick cat. Didn't want nothing to eat. Didn't want to talk to nobody. And you just come from a few miles down the road. And you known your grandparents since the day you were born. Still the least little thing anybody say to you set you off wailing like a sireen. And couldn't nobody make you stop till you was good and ready. Now I remember that. Saddest little critter you ever want to look at.'

The little girl laughed. 'No I wasn't.'

'Yes you was. I know it and you know it.'

The little girl leaned away from the old woman's chair, feeling bashful in front of her. She continued to laugh and shake her head. 'No I wasn't.'

'You was too.'

A thought occurred to the little girl. 'If Henry came over and played with me, then he wouldn't be lonely and I wouldn't be lonely either.'

The old woman sighed. 'I don't believe you heard nothing I said.'

'But then he wouldn't be lonely!' The little girl spread open her arms to emphasize how obvious this seemed to her.

'Just you remember what I told you. You can't make people do like you want. And anyway, I know that before too long, your grandmamma and Mrs Dansler see to it that you and this Henry meet each other. Now, I got to get on with my lesson. So if you don't mind that's what I'm gon do. You can sit here and be quiet or go back outside and play. Suit yourself.'

The little girl looked around the room, her face dropping with boredom. 'I might as well go back outside and play by myself.'

'That's right. Go on and play.'

After the little girl had left the room, the old woman picked up the book and found her page, but for a long time she sat staring out of the window.

It was a clear, warm afternoon. The sky, which seemed higher than usual, was a deep, penetrating blue. Enough leaves had fallen from the trees that bordered the other side of the garden to allow the old woman to see well across the field that lay beyond the house. Flat, yellowish grass stretched over the land which looked desolate and bare in the late autumn, despite the brightness of the day. Along a narrow path that divided the field diagonally, there was a scattering of wild flowers, gone dry and leaning stiffly over the path that led one way to a small wood and thicket, while the other way was the only route to a dreary group of grey, washed-out clapboard houses that collectively made up the local shantytown, Sunnyside.

80

Although the old woman had never seen it, from the descriptions she had heard she recognized Sunnyside as one more of the many places dotted throughout the south, so much alike and still home for the majority of the coloured people. Up until she had moved in with her daughter, the old woman had lived in one and then another of these shantytowns herself. They were once the only place for her people, even if they had become educated and prosperous.

While she wondered whether to go outside and enjoy some of the afternoon sun, the old woman spotted the figure of a small boy walking over the field. He was huddled inside a jacket that seemed too big for him and was making his way along the path that led to Sunnyside. She sat watching as the boy hurriedly stepped over the tall weeds and grass hanging over the path, while his puppy ran alongside. The boy seemed almost as thin as the weeds, the old woman told herself. But then they didn't have such good, wholesome food and no fresh air in New York. And he wasn't used to walking in fields, she could tell that. The little dog wanted to stop occasionally to sniff something in the grass, but the little boy was impatient to keep going and wouldn't wait. With his head down and his hands deep in his pockets, as if he were confronting a gale wind, the boy ploughed on until he had gone out of sight.

When Henry came to the little girl's house, he carried his puppy in his arms. Mrs Dansler introduced him as 'her fine grandson from New York, come to stay with her for a little while.' Henry wouldn't talk and Mrs Dansler told him that if he didn't say anything, they might think he was dumb and he wasn't dumb was he? Henry wouldn't answer her either. Mrs Dansler shook her head and looked, with some despair, over at the little girl's grandmother. Then she took a deep breath and attempting a smile said to Henry, 'They sure will think the cat's got your tongue, won't they? Never mind.' She patted Henry on the back of his head while smiling down at the little girl. 'Y'all play nicely together. Go on now.'

The two women then went into the house for some tea and a piece of pound cake and to have a talk.

The little girl took Henry to her swing in the back garden and offered to let him ride first. Henry shook his head.

'Don't you know how to swing?' the little girl asked.

Henry didn't say anything.

'I been know how to swing,' the little girl said and got up on the seat, 'ever since I was little.' She began to push herself backwards and forwards. 'My daddy build me a big ole swing down on the farm, in Bowman. Even bigger than this one. And it can go right up to the top of the tree. Higher than this one.'

Henry still didn't say anything. He held onto the puppy which was struggling to get down.

'Don't they have swings in New York? Do they have trees? Is that why you don't have swings, cause you don't have trees.'

'Course we have trees,' Henry said.

'But you don't have no swings?' the little girl asked.

'Course we have swings. We have all kinds of swings.'

'What kind of swings do you have?'

'I told you. All kinds. Better than that old thing.'

'It's not old. Grampy just made it.'

'Well it looks old.'

'No it doesn't.'

Henry shrugged his shoulders and walked a few steps away.

'I bet you don't have no swings in New York neither,' the little girl shouted after him.

'Course we do. We have hundreds,' Henry shouted back, not bothering to look round.

'No you don't.'

'We do.' He turned around, annoyed. 'All kinds of things, merry-go-rounds, sliding boards. Hundreds.'

'What kinds of things?' the little girl copied the annoyance in his voice.

'I told you. Everything. All kinds. Climbing frames, ropes.'

'Can you go for free? I bet you can't.'

'Course we can. It's free all the time. Course it is.'

'We got a playground,' the little girl suddenly remembered.

'No you don't.'

'Yes we do. We do too have a playground.'

'Then where is it?'

'It's on Broughton Street.'

'Where's that.'

'Broughton Street? On the way downtown. And it's got a whole bunch of swings, all in a row. And swings for the little children and two sliding boards. One's a big one and one is not so big. And there's a merry-go-round and a sandbox.'

'I don't believe you. Cause Nana said there wasn't any playground round here.'

'Yes there is but you just can't go to it.'

'How come you can't go to it then?'

'Cause you can't. Cause it's only for the white children. But you can go and stand by the fence and watch,' the little girl added.

'You made that up.'

'No I didn't make it up neither!'

'I don't believe you.'

'It's true. There is a playground on Broughton Street. You just can't go play in it, that's all.'

'How come it's only for white children then?'

'I don't know. But it is. There's a sign on the gate and it says, For. White. Children. Only.'

'Well I can go there anyway.'

'No you can't!'

'Course I can. Cause I'm from New York and we're allowed in playgrounds.'

'No you can't. The policeman a come and get you and put you in the jailhouse.'

'Course he won't.'

The little girl nodded her head vigorously. 'Yes they will! If you go to the white playground and play on the swings, they'll put you in jail.'

'Course they won't.'

The little girl stopped the swing. 'They do cause I know it.'

'They don't put kids in jail.'

'Yes they do. They put you in the back of the police car and take you to the jailhouse.'

'Course they don't.'

'Yes they will. Cause I saw them put a boy in there once and they tied up his hands behind his back and put him in the car and took him to the jailhouse.'

'Why? What did he do?'

'He didn't do nothing.'

'Then why did they arrest him?'

The little girl nodded. 'They arrest him and he wasn't doing nothing. They just said he look like somebody they was looking for and they arrest him and took him to the jailhouse.'

Henry looked around the garden, trying to think of something to say. The little girl, satisfied that she had impressed Henry more than he had her, started to swing again. Then she thought of something else to tell him.

'You better watch out if the policeman comes. Cause he might take you away and your mamma and daddy can't even do nothing.' Henry was watching her and she nodded her head solemnly. 'They get people all the time. Especially men. They come driving round real slow in the car and if you don't get out of their way, they'll tell you to come up to the car and they ask you what your name is and what you doing. And if they don't like you, you have to go to the jailhouse, even if you haven't done nothing. Sometimes, even if you're driving a car, they'll make you stop driving and start to ask you questions and you have to tell them what you doing driving the car. Sometimes if we go driving somewhere, they stop Grampy and ask him if that's his Cadillac he's driving and they ask him where did he get the money to buy a Cadillac. One time we just had to sit in the car for a long time till they said it was all right for us to go. I don't like no policeman!' She shook her head from side to side, still swinging. 'They so mean. That's why you can't play in the playground cause somebody'll tell on you and they'll come round and get you.' The little girl looked at Henry to see what his reaction was to what she'd been saying.

He was wandering aimlessly, nearby, one hand in his pocket. The expression on his face did not betray what he was thinking.

'Do you have any policemen in New York?' the little girl asked.

'Course we do,' Henry answered.

'Are they mean?'

'Sometimes they are and sometimes they're not. Course they have to shoot gangsters.'

The little girl nodded in agreement. 'Do they let you play in the playgrounds?'

'Course,' Henry said, and began to wander a little further away from the swing.

'You can have a swing if you want to,' the little girl offered.

Henry stopped and turned around, considering her offer. 'All right.' He put down the puppy, which had by then become content to be carried around.

The little girl jumped off the seat and ran to the little dog. 'Can I play with him?' She was already picking the puppy up.

'Just for a little bit. While I'm swinging.'

They took turns on the swing, then played with the puppy and ran about the garden chasing each other. They raced to the orchard and played hide-and-seek, while the puppy ran after them among the trees. They called out to it, and then covering their mouths so as not to laugh they hid, waiting for the little dog to find them. Finally, when they had become exhausted from running and laughing, they went back to the house and sat on the back steps to catch their breath.

The little girl's grandmother came to the door with cake and milk, and they sat opposite each other, eating quickly without talking, suddenly aware of their hunger. The puppy wandered between them, licking up the crumbs of cake they dropped.

When they had finished eating, they became self-conscious, so sat watching the puppy as it sniffed around them, still looking for fallen crumbs. After a while the puppy gave up and, tired, it climbed up beside Henry's feet and fell asleep.

Henry put his chin on his knees and looked down at the puppy whose fat, round tummy rose and fell in even, rhythmic breathing. He reached down and stroked the side of the sleeping dog while the little girl watched him. She studied his hand as it slowly and gently caressed the sleeping puppy, realizing that Henry's fingers were thin and longer than her own. The skin over his knuckles was dark brown and his fingernails were very short and, unlike her own, very clean. When Henry glanced up at her, she looked away.

He stopped stroking the dog and sat up, turning away from

her. Squinting, with his hands shading his eyes, he stared up at the sky. The little girl looked up. She didn't see anything, so she looked over at him again. She could see his shoulder blades through his sweater as he moved his head about searching the sky. He held his shoulders high and rigid and she wondered if he were cold. The old woman had told her that it was warmer here than in New York, so that must be the way he held his shoulders. His hair was a mass of thick, shiny curls that came down nearly to his shoulders and curled over his ears. The little girl wondered if he brushed it himself. Sometimes she brushed her own hair after her grandmother had braided it for her. She knew that his eyes were light brown and that his brows and lashes were thick and soft-looking like his hair. His skin was smooth and creamy like chocolate. She liked being on the steps with him. She was aware of his closeness and breathed quietly, something within her content, as she watched him silently studying the sky.

'Call him Bongo,' Henry said thoughtfully. He looked down at the sleeping dog. 'Hey Bongo,' he nearly whispered, putting his chin back on his knees, 'Bongo? Are you sleeping?'

The little girl leaned over towards the dog too. 'Why you calling him Bongo?' she asked in a whisper.

'Cause,' Henry said after a pause while he continued to look at the dog, 'his stomach makes me think about a drum.' He sat up and began to slap his knees with the palms of his hands.

The little girl watched him.

After a while he stopped. 'There's a man who plays bongos at my daddy's club in New York. He came all the way from Jamaica. He can play so fast!' Henry slapped his thighs harder and faster than before. It roused the puppy. 'Hey Bongo,' Henry called down to the puppy. 'You hear me Bongo?' He jumped up and ran down the steps. 'Come on Bongo.'

The puppy ran down to him.

'Come on Bongo,' Henry called as he ran towards the bottom of the garden.

The little girl stood up, watching. She hesitated for a moment, then ran down the steps after them.

★

'What's a bongo?' the little girl asked.

The old woman stood at her dresser rummaging through one of the drawers. 'What's a what?' she asked, bending over to have a closer look for whatever she was trying to find.

'A bongo,' the little girl repeated.

'Bongo? I never heard of nothing call no Bongo. Sound like some kinda crazy person. Bongo. Don't sound like it can do you too much good.'

'A bongo!' the little girl said again, repeating the word as if that would help the old woman to know what it was. 'It's like a drum.'

'A drum?' the old woman asked, and looked briefly at the little girl. 'I don't know nothing bout no drums.'

'You play it in the nightclub.' The little girl offered another clue.

'In the nightclub? How you know what they be playing in the nightclubs?' The old woman pulled a pair of thick cotton stockings from the drawer.

'Henry said that somebody played the bongo in his daddy's nightclub in New York.'

The old woman picked up her sewing box from the top of the dresser, went over to her chair by the window and sat down. 'Well I wouldn't know nothing t'all about that.'

'But you used to live in New York. I want to know if it's a drum.'

'Well you asking the wrong person.' The old woman lifted the lid of the sewing box. 'Come on over here and see if you can't thread me this needle. Something told me this stocking had a hole in it. Been nagging at the back of my mind all week.'

The little girl went over to her, took the needle and began to thread it, while the old woman picked up the other stocking and examined it for holes.

'What else you and this Henry talk about?' the old woman asked her as she scrutinized the stocking.

'Oh nothing.' The little girl knotted the thread and returned it.

'Nothing! After all that time you were in here aggawaiting

me about this Henry. And y'all ain had nothing to say to one another except about some bongos and nightclubs and suchlike.'

'Well we just talked about things,' the little girl said shyly. 'He was telling me all about New York.'

'Then you ought to know what a bongo is. Ain't that right?'

The little girl didn't answer. She strolled over to the bed.

'So what you know about New York?' the old woman asked her as she began to mend the stocking.

'You know what Henry said?' The little girl asked, but didn't wait for an answer. 'He said they got hundreds of playgrounds in New York. I thought you said they didn't have nothing but big ole buildings.'

'Well that's all I see when I was up there. Didn't see nothing look like no playground.'

'Henry said they got hundreds with all kinds of things to play on. And it doesn't cost anything and he said they got plenty of trees too.'

'Then they must have been busy planting them since I left.'

'When were you up there?'

'Too long ago to even talk about it.'

'But when? Was it before I was born?'

'Yeah. It was when your grandmamma was a young girl.'

'Did you used to live up there?'

'No, I wasn't living up there. I just went up there for a spell. Like for a visit.'

'Who did you visit?'

The old woman leaned over her sewing.

'Who did you visit up there?' the little girl asked again. 'Was it somebody I know?'

'No. It wasn't nobody you know. I had some business to tend to, that's all.'

'In New York?'

'That's right.'

'You went to visit somebody in New York to tend to some business?'

The old woman nodded.

'But who did you visit?' the little girl asked. 'What's their name?'

The old woman placed the stocking in her lap. 'Your

grandmamma's sister that you never met. She took sick up there one time and I went up to see about her.'

'Was she real sick?'

'Yes, she was.'

'Did she die?'

'No she didn't die. But she was real sick.'

'Is she still up there?'

'I believe so. I don't hear from her too much nowadays.'

The little girl stared at the old woman who had taken off her spectacles and was rubbing them with a handkerchief.

'How come I never met her?'

'Because, like I told you, she stayed in New York.'

'After she got better?'

'That's right.'

'Oh,' the little girl said quietly. 'Didn't she like it down here?'

'Not too much. No, she like it better living in New York.'

'Why?'

'I suppose cause she didn't have no prejudice against her up there.'

'What's prejudice?'

'What I mean to say is she figure folks didn't mind too much about her colour.'

'Why? What colour was she?'

'Well, she turn out to be real fair. Then when she went up to New York she had something done to her hair to make it all yellow. I don't know. She took after her daddy side more than she did mine. Anyway she got herself so changed till I didn't hardly recognize her. And by the time I got up there and saw her, she'd done lost a good deal of weight cause she hadn't been eating too well. No, she didn't look like herself. Not with that yellow hair. Anyway, she got herself a life up there and that's what she want. So that was that. As far as I know that's where she stayed. I heard one time she had a hairdressing shop and was doing well.'

'Why did Henry's daddy go up there?'

The old woman put her spectacles back on and picked up her sewing.

'Was he real fair too?' the little girl asked.

'No. He's brown-skinned, just like Henry.'

'Then why did he go up there?'

'That I couldn't tell you. I don't believe nobody know where he was heading when he left here. That was some time ago. He was going with the boy's mother. When she left, he left. That's all I know.'

'Henry said he had a nightclub.'

'So I hear tell.'

'And at night-time, people get all dressed up and they come there and dance and drink whiskey. And ladies and men sing and then all the people clap for them.'

'How Henry get to know all what goes on in this nightclub?'

'Cause sometimes his daddy takes him there.'

'To the nightclub?'

'Yes. That's where the man is who plays the bongo. Henry can play it if he wants to.'

'Well I don't know if that's no place to be taking a child.'

'Why?'

'Cause it just ain't. I don't believe that no mother or father who cares about how their child is growing up would take them to no place like that, specially at night.'

'Why? Doesn't Henry's mamma and daddy care about him?'

'I can't see how they can let him go to no nightclub. That's all I'm saying.'

'Is that how come Henry's mamma left him here and went to Florida?'

'I can't tell you why she did it.'

'Why won't his daddy come and get him?'

'I can't tell you that either. I never did know his daddy that well and I didn't know his mamma a'tall. Anyway that's nothing for you to be asking about. Come here and cut this thread if you want to.'

The little girl got up, went over and cut the thread from the stocking then stood watching as the old woman returned her sewing implements to their basket. Her expression had become downcast. The old woman noticed but decided not to say anything.

'I'll wash these out tonight so I can wear them tomorrow,'

she said as she folded the stockings on her lap. 'Maybe my legs'll feel better than they did today.'

'I feel sad about Henry,' the little girl told her.

'What you feeling sad about?' The old woman got up from the chair and put the sewing basket on top of the chest of drawers.

'I don't know,' the little girl shrugged. 'I'm just feeling sad.'

'Well there ain't nothing to be feeling sad about. He seem to be doing all right down here. He made friends with you, didn't he?'

The little girl didn't answer.

'He's a nice boy. He'll be all right,' the old woman said. 'I don't know, maybe I'll get on in there and wash out these stockings now while I still feel like it. Make sure they be dry for tomorrow.'

After the old woman had left, the little girl got up from the bed and slowly wandered around the room, fingering one thing then another. It was something she enjoyed doing, looking about the room which was decorated with some of the few possessions the old woman had brought with her. There was a story behind each item and sometimes, when the old woman related how she had come by a particular thing, the little girl was allowed to pick it up and hold it.

One of these was the big coral seashell. Every time the little girl put it to her ear and listened, it roared of the sea. She would sit for a long time, her eyes closed, imagining what the sea looked like as it rushed on to the shore.

There was also a wonderful little round glass case that contained a tiny red-and-white house with windows and shutters, a door and a chimney. Around the house stood little evergreen trees and the ground was covered with snow. To the little girl, it was a world enclosed in a bubble. When she shook it, the snow rose into the air then slowly and silently fell over the house and trees.

In the corner, on a little wooden stand, there was a silver tray on which stood six burgundy goblets with clear glass stems that spread like flower petals at the base. When the little girl flicked the rims with her finger, they rang musically, like a bell.

On this occasion, the little girl didn't care to hear the sea or watch the snow fall or tinkle the glasses. None of these things could hold her attention or rouse her sense of imagination. She continued to wander about, a little sad-faced and bored. Eventually she ended up standing at the dresser, staring at the china figures that were arranged just in front of the mirror.

The little girl's grandmother had brought these into the room just before the old woman was due to arrive. They were delicately moulded and painted with creamy pastels, and had been admired by the old woman when she was shown her room. But neither she nor the little girl had paid them much attention once the old woman had put out and arranged her own treasured keepsakes.

The little girl picked up one of the figures. It was of a man, dressed in pale blue breeches and a jacket of a darker blue. In one hand he held a hat up against his chest; his other arm was gracefully outstretched. Near him stood a lady in a long pink dress with a petticoat underneath. The dress billowed with laces and frills and the little girl felt it would almost sway back and forth. The lady had on little pink slippers that peeped from under her hems and over her head she held a parasol, edged in lace, with pink and white ribbons on top.

The little girl walked the man over to the lady. He bowed and offered her his hat which had turned into a beautiful bouquet of flowers. The lady put down her parasol and took the flowers from the man. He asked her if she would like to dance. She said yes. And they stood together and danced and danced.

On Monday, Henry started school. The little girl saw him sitting with his grandmother in the principal's office. She stood in the hallway waiting for him to see her so she could wave to him, but Henry didn't look her way. As she watched him, he nodded his head while his grandmother or the principal spoke to him, but he kept his eyes downcast. His head, which had been covered in curls when the little girl first saw him, had been shorn. His hair was now parted and held in place with brilliantine. She noticed that his shoes were polished to a shine. Henry had told her that all the men who came to his daddy's club had real shiny shoes, that just outside the door of the nightclub was a shoeshine man, who would sing and dance while he polished your shoes for you.

She waited for him in class. Miss Funchess said Henry could sit next to her since she knew him and the little girl had already prepared his desk with books and paper. But Henry was sent up to the next class. The principal came to their room and explained that he was ahead for his age. Throughout the day, the little girl would look over at the empty seat next to her.

After school the little girl waited outside. As Henry's class came out she overheard two girls talking about the new boy. One was telling the other that he came all the way from New York.

'I like the way he talks,' the second girl said.

'I'm going to go over and talk to him,' the first girl revealed.

'I dare you.' Her friend pushed her towards Henry. 'I double-dee dare you.'

'You don't believe me?' The first girl stood her ground but continued to look over in Henry's direction.

'No. Go ahead. I dare you. Go ahead.'

'All right. You'll see. Come on. You'll see.'

They started giggling and, pushing each other forward, went over to speak to Henry.

The little girl didn't wait for Henry or walk with any of the other children. She hurried on ahead and when she got home stood outside, near the front of the house, and watched as the children went past. Henry was walking in a group with the two girls. She watched till he was out of sight then turned and went into the back garden where she stomped about, not knowing how and with what to vent her anger. Finally she came back to the house, dropped her books on the back steps, then sat down beside them and cried.

Saturday was a mild, luminous day, warmed by a sun that highlighted all the rich burning colours of the season while luring from the earth the damp, poignant smells of the field after harvest.

The old woman had settled in her chair as soon as it was

warm enough for her to be outside. She had buttoned her sweater to the top and covered her lap with her shawl. She told a cat that had come to share her sunny spot that the cold weather was certainly on the way. And if her leg stopped aching, she would have one final walk around the garden to see how things had changed. The cat patiently cleaned itself as she talked then curled its tail around its bottom and closed its eyes. The old woman looked away from the cat and around at the garden. She nodded at what she could see. But for the time being, she was content, like the cat, to sit with her eyes closed and feel the sun on her head.

She was roused from her nap by the smell of smoke. The old woman sat up and looked around, waving away the grey haze that was drifting over her. She guessed that someone had started a bonfire in their backyard. She thought she would have to move if the smoke continued to blow her way and got up to see where it was coming from.

The old woman walked over towards Miss Dunbar's fence, suspecting that it was somewhere in her garden. It was. She could see it at the bottom, and when the wind shifted the smoke trailed off over the orchard. She thought that whoever it was should have made a better bonfire than that. Smoke was pouring from it and blowing everywhere.

As she made her way back along the fence, having decided she'd have to go inside, she heard voices and, looking over into the next garden, saw Mrs Dansler and Miss Dunbar walking side by side away from the fire. Both women had their heads down and their arms folded across their chests. They didn't seem to be bothered by the billowing smoke and were unaware of the old woman standing by the fence. As they came nearer, their voices floated over to her.

'I've already told him.' Mrs Dansler was talking. She stopped walking so as not to detract from what she was saying. 'I said to him the first time I found out. I said, Henry I don't want you going over there to Sunnyside. Suppose something should happen to you. There's some very rough people over there.'

'Aint that the truth.' Miss Dunbar had stopped as well. 'No, it's not a t'all safe. Somebody's always being cut up over there. No, it's not safe. Not even for a grown person.'

'He still went over there yesterday. I thought he'd gone to the store. Then when he didn't come back, something told me he had gone on to Sunnyside. I don't know what to do about it.'

'Well, he can't keep on going over there. You got to put a stop to that.'

'I know. But he's got this idea that he's going to find his mother's people.'

'Lord have mercy.'

'And you know none of them ever stay in the same place for long.'

'They sure don't.'

'I told him and he ask me to take him over there.'

'That's out the question.'

'I know. Of course I'm not going to take him over there looking for those people.'

'No! No. You can't be expected to do that. You can't bother with those people. Not for a minute.'

'But he thinks that somehow they're going to know where his mother is.'

'And how would they know? Lord have mercy.'

'Of course they don't know. Even if he did find one of them.'

The old woman's leg had started to ache and, holding on to the fence, she made her way along it and then back to her chair where she sat down heavily. Fortunately the smoke was drifting in another direction. She had forgotten about the smoke though. She was also unaware that the cat had come up to her chair and was rubbing itself against her fallen shawl.

She shook herself out of her thoughts and at the same time reached down for her shawl. It startled the cat who sprang away from the chair.

'Go on cat,' the old woman said, once she had seen what had frightened her. 'That's what you get for being where you not suppose to.'

She was rocking and humming to herself when the little girl came out of the back door and called to her. She lifted her hand in a wave, continuing to rock back and forth. The little girl walked down the steps and came over, then stood by the chair with her hands behind her back.

'What you got there?' the old woman asked, appearing to look behind the little girl's back.

'How do you know I've got something?' the little girl asked.

'Oh I know,' the old woman said, nodding. 'I might be old but I can still figure out one or two things.'

'But how did you know?'

'Well, the way you walking. And your hands behind your back.'

'Then guess what it is,' the little girl said, stepping back from the chair.

'Oh, I don't know. A big, ole watermelon.'

'Nope.' The little girl shook her head. 'That's not even like it.'

'Is it bigger or smaller?'

'Smaller.'

'Well it must be a peanut then.'

'A peanut! Nope. It's bigger than a peanut.'

'It's bigger than a peanut and littler than a watermelon.' The old woman shook her head. 'You got me foxed.'

'But try and guess. Grampy gave it to me.'

'Well it can't be no money.'

'Nope. It's not money.'

'Well that's my three gone. You have to tell me what it is.'

'Look,' the little girl said, holding a tangerine in each hand.

'What's that you got there?'

'Tangerines. Grampy gave them to me. He's got a whole crate full.'

'Is that so?'

The little girl nodded. 'There's one for me and one for you.'

'Well that's a nice surprise. You go peel it for me?'

The little girl nodded and sat down on the ground by the old woman's chair to peel the tangerines.

'Try to get all that white string off a mine,' said the old woman, pointing to the fruit.

'I know,' the little girl said.

'So where your grandaddy get all these tangerines?'

'A nice man brought them. He came in a truck full of

tangerines. He's driving them up north. And he gave some to Grampy.'

The little girl finished peeling the tangerine and handed it up to the old woman who began to separate it into pieces.

'So that's where you been all morning. Looking at tangerines.'

'And I was helping Grampy.'

'This morning I thought you'd be outside somewhere playing.'

The little girl shook her head after she'd put a piece of tangerine in her mouth. 'I like helping Grampy.' She chewed and swallowed, 'And I don't like playing any more.' She broke off another piece of tangerine and popped it in her mouth while the old woman watched her.

'You say you don't like playing?'

The little girl shook her head again and continued chewing.

'Oh,' the old woman said quietly. 'And when did you stop liking to play?'

The little girl shrugged. 'I don't know. I just don't want to any more. I must be growing up.'

For a moment the old woman didn't say anything. She picked up a piece of tangerine and studied it. 'Well I thought all little children was growing up?'

'But I'm nearly grown up.' She put the last piece of the tangerine in her mouth.

'I see,' the old woman said.

'I might be going to college soon.'

'Going to college?'

'Yep. Instead of that ole baby school.'

'Baby school? You talking about Dunton?'

The little girl nodded. 'I'm tired of going there.' She took a deep breath. 'So, I'm going to college.'

'Well that's news to me. I thought you like going to your school.'

'Nope.'

'Well I thought you did. Specially since your little friend started to go there. What's his name. Henry?'

'I don't like Henry any more,' the little girl announced.

'Say you don't like him?'

The little girl shook her head. 'Huh-uh.'

'Well I thought you like him.'

'Nope. I don't like him.'

'I see,' the old woman said. They sat silently for a while. The old woman chewed thoughtfully on a piece of tangerine. 'I thought you was friends,' she said when she'd finished.

'No. I told you. I don't like him.'

'Well the last I know you wanted to be Henry's friend so much and seem to me Henry was being your friend and y'all was getting along just fine.'

'He doesn't want to be my friend,' the little girl said. She had begun to trail a piece of tangerine skin in the sand. 'So I don't want to be his friend either.'

'Is that what he said? That he didn't want to be friends?'

'He said I keep on following him all the time.'

'Oh I see. Well little boys can be that way sometimes. One minute they want to play and the next minute they don't. I wouldn't pay it no mind. I bet by tomorrow, he'll be out here wanting to play again.'

'No he won't,' the little girl shook her bowed head. 'He doesn't want to play with me any more. He said he hated me and to go away and leave him alone.'

'Oh I don't think he mean that.'

'Yes he did. He said, I hate you. I hate you. Then he pushed me back and said, Go away and leave me alone. I hate you.'

The old woman put the tangerine down. 'Well I tell you what. Probably he was just upset. Something must be bothering him for him to say that. He didn't mean it.'

'But I didn't do anything,' the little girl said, digging her finger into the tangerine skin. 'I just asked him where he was going and he wouldn't answer me. He just kept on walking and he wouldn't say anything when I talked to him. Then he just said, I hate you.'

The old woman shook her head. 'No it's not easy to understand.'

'But why doesn't he like me any more?'

'Oh. I expect he's just feeling all mixed up inside. He still likes you. He's just not settled about being down here. That's what it is.'

The little girl looked up at her. The old woman picked up a piece of tangerine, then said, 'You just going to have to be patient till he gets his mind settled and can understand about being down here with his grandmother. And when he's feeling better y'all be able to be friends again.'

The little girl turned to look over towards Henry's house.

'That sure was a big tangerine,' the old woman said, lifting up the two pieces she had left in her lap. 'I don't know if I can eat both of these.'

'I'll eat one,' the little girl offered.

'Well that'll sure help me out. You say your grandaddy got a whole crate of them?'

'Yep,' the little girl answered. 'I sure love to eat tangerines.'

'Then this your lucky day. Come on,' the old woman said, 'hand me my walking stick so I can get up from here. My leg sure know winter just round the corner. That's for certain.'

The little girl gave her her stick and the old woman pulled herself up from the chair.

'Come on and give me a hand to the house 'fore this leg give out on me. I ought to go and get me a new one.'

'You can't get a new leg,' the little girl told her, almost laughing.

'Why can't I?' the old woman said, huffing at the challenge of finding a new leg.

'Cause you can't get new legs anywhere,' the little girl said, her voice rising incredulously.

'At the five and ten cent store,' the old woman announced with finality as they reached the back steps.

The little girl was jumping up and down. 'You can't buy legs.'

The old woman paused to think. 'Well I know they got em in Belk's Department Store. All them dummies in the window. I can get a leg off a one of them.'

'Those legs don't work!' the little girl exclaimed, wondering how she was ever going to explain about things to the old woman.

The Hanging

The little girl was sitting on the steps that led up to the front door of the house. From there, she could watch, without being noticed, the few passers-by out for a quiet stroll in the warm spring evening.

The day was nearly over, and as the little girl sat with her arms wrapped round her legs and her knees tucked under her chin, birds fluttered overhead and scampered across the lawn in the lively stillness that lingered in the air. The sun grew big and round and luminous then began to slip down behind the fields.

In the distance, the little girl could hear a voice shooing in chickens, followed by the worried cackle of the hens as they set about roosting for the night. A dog barked over the other side of the road where through the trees lights glowed from the small wooden houses.

The sky was streaked with colours, and for a few moments, the little girl's house and the garden glowed warmly in the mellow light. The little girl leaned against the front door, her eyes shaded, as she watched the sunset on the horizon. Daylight receded and faded, the birds gathered to their trees and the house gradually turned to a shade of darkness.

Inside, the sharp sounds of the kitchen echoed from the back and after a while the smells of cooking floated through the opened windows to mingle with the odour of fertilizer dust that lay in a haze over the newly ploughed fields. The little girl stood up, ready for supper, then tarried to watch a young couple walking hand in hand down the road. She turned to go inside just as someone called her to come to the table.

Later in the evening the little girl returned to the front steps, this time to watch for cars. On the screened-in porch behind her, her grandfather sat pensively smoking a cigar. The little girl had decided that he was in a serious mood and so she would have to identify the cars by herself. Only two had come by so far, a rattling old Model T Ford and a slightly better-running, but still old, Buick. Neither of them really counted in car spotting and the little girl was hoping a fast, new car would come by before she had to go in and get ready for bed. She mumbled this out loud and wondered if her grandfather heard her. She doubted it since earlier he had said he was coming outside to sit on the front porch and think, which was what he had done all through supper.

The little girl had watched him at the table as he absently chewed his food while studying first one and then another of the pictures hanging on the dining room wall. Her grandmother, who sat opposite him, had chatted idly about what she had done that day. But he hadn't responded to her either and had continued to stare, over her head, at the pictures.

The little girl looked round behind her on to the porch and saw the red glow of her grandfather's cigar which outlined his face when he drew on it. When the smoke drifted her way, she inhaled it. She liked the smell of cigar smoke and thought that one day she would smoke one. For the moment though she had to be content with wearing cigar bands. Her grandfather had given her the one off the cigar he was smoking but wasn't so deep in thought that he would agree to let her have a puff.

Finally a car was coming up the road. It sped towards them, its powerful headlights beaming across the road and spreading on to the houses. As the car slowed down the little girl recognized it. It belonged to Dr Green who must be coming to visit her grandfather. She sighed and wished it could have been somebody other than Dr Green coming to the house. She didn't like him, even though he had a fast car. She found his manner too brusque and unpredictable. Invariably he approached her asking short, snappy questions which she could hardly think of the answer to before he was asking her something else. Normally she stayed well away from him, but when she wasn't fast enough he'd cup her head in his hand and turn her head from side to side as if he was looking for something. She would squiggle uncooperatively underneath, but he held her in place until he was finished, when he'd tell her she was too skinny and to wash behind her ears. It seemed nothing about her physical appearance escaped his attention which she resented. She would tell him she liked being skinny, that it was better than being fat. Which she thought he was.

Dr Green would have been considered portly since his waistcoat fitted snugly over his middle. He had short legs which made him seem broader than he was. He was, however, a smart dresser. Even the little girl, who had an eye for fashionable clothes, always noticed what he was wearing as she made a beeline in the opposite direction. He had several well-cut suits and as many pairs of shoes and beautifully starched collars and shirts. The little girl often remarked to the old woman about his clothes but said it was all a waste because he had pop-eyes like a toad. She was often tempted to say this to him too when he was telling her she was too skinny. The old woman said she was being disrespectful and the little girl retorted that she wasn't calling him a toad but she couldn't help it if he looked like one especially since he was bald.

This was probably why he was rarely seen bare-headed. Even when he entered the homes of the sick and was already rolling up his shirt sleeves, his hat was still on his head. In warm weather it was a panama of fine, light straw and when it was cold, a well-shaped fedora in the correct colour for his suit. His hats, like his black bag, were part of his trademark.

Dr Green sped through town and up and down the country roads in the latest model Buick. He thought they were superior to Cadillacs and bought a new car every year, then drove it gleaming from the showroom to the little girl's grandparents house to be admired. But thereafter it was usually covered with the dust of the back roads where so many of the sick lived. The car never looked as good as it could which was a shame, the little girl thought, especially the white-walled tyres. Still, it was a fast car and he drove fast. The little girl and her cousin Bernard used to spend hours imitating the sound of the engine after he had roared past them and the farm. With their bare feet mashing the accelerator and screeching the brakes, they'd run up and down the road pounding the dust as they pretended to drive. Though they didn't admit it, they were both a little afraid of Dr Green. But they knew for a fact that

Dr Green wasn't afraid of anybody. That's what made his car so exciting to drive.

As he got out of the car and walked up the path to the house the little girl thought of slipping behind the hydrangeas, but he had already seen her.

'What you doin sittin there in the dark?' Dr Green stopped on the bottom step, suddenly no longer in a hurry.

'Nothing.' The little girl shrugged her shoulders uneasily. She was relieved when he put his hands in his pockets.

'You're a funny little thing sometimes.'

The little girl tried to look past him as if something on the road had caught her interest.

'Ain't you?' Dr Green persisted.

'No.'

'And you sittin out here in the dark by yourself?'

'I was just thinking.'

He laughed his short, rough laugh. 'What you got to think about.'

'Things.' The little girl couldn't think of anything else to say.

'Things?'

She gave a little nod.

'And you so little to be so serious.' He pulled one hand out of his pocket and dropped a peppermint candy into her lap. When she realized what it was she said thank you.

'Fatten you up some,' he said.

'I was thinking about the night.' She suddenly felt able to explain herself.

He looked around him at the darkness while she unwrapped the candy and put it in her mouth.

'So what you know about the night?' he asked her.

She shrugged her shoulders.

'Muh?'

'Nothing,' she replied, not very proud of her answer and nearly loosing the peppermint drop for her trouble.

'Well you gotta know something if you thinkin about it. Ain't that right?'

She tucked the candy into the corner of her cheek, something

103

she had seen the old woman do innumerable times in church when it was time to sing a hymn. 'Cause it's dark and quiet and you have to guess where everything is.' She sucked the peppermint and swallowed some of its sweetness.

'Well sir.' Dr Green laughed his short laugh. 'Thinkin bout the night. Yeah you funny.'

'No I'm not.'

'Sittin here thinkin about the night. Better think about something else.' He walked on up the steps past her. 'The night can be a bad time. Ain't that so Reve?' he called over to her grandfather as he opened the screen door and stepped on to the front porch. 'Yeah. The night can be a bad time,' he repeated.

The little girl found the old woman sitting on her bed, listening to the radio. A small lamp on the table beside her cast a circle of light in the corner of the room where she sat. And her head, which was half in shadow and half in light, glimmered whenever she nodded in the direction of the radio. She was listening intently to a sermon. The voice of the preacher boomed from another corner where the radio stood, its knobs and dial glowing warmly in the darkness.

The old woman did not see the little girl when she opened the door and peeped inside. The voice on the radio was speaking about the trials and tribulations of life, something the old woman could nod understandingly about. Then as the voice grew louder with excitement, crackling static, the radio seemed to hum in accompaniment to the roused congregation of revivalists. The old woman, caught up in the mood, began to tap her foot on the floor. She called out support and encouragement along with the audience on the radio which was rising to a pitch of excitement and expectation as the preacher warmed up to his sermon. Surrounded now by shouts and foot stomping, the voice ascended in a high, unwavering vibrato, piercing the uproar of the congregation which shouted in admiration at this vocal skill. Then the voice dropped suddenly, and the congregation, hardly able to contain itself, breathed in and hushed to allow the soft sweetness of the voice to tell them about their sadness and suffering.

The old woman lifted her head and swayed from side to side, recognizing in this list of troubles some of her own. In the customary lull before the final crescendo, the little girl stepped deftly inside the room and, without making a sound, closed the door.

'Jesus will save you,' the voice boomed from the radio and the old woman called out, 'Amen.'

'And keep you. Call on Him. He sees your suffering. He knows your enemies. That cause you pain. Why don't you call on Him. Jesus knows. Oh yes He does.'

The congregation chanted in empathy.

'Way in the midnight hour. Waaay in the midnight hour!' The voice rose an octave. 'When your last hope is gone. And you fall down on your knees. And cry.' The voice rose even higher. 'Almighty Father. My Lord.'

The congregation called on the Lord as well.

'Saviour. Sweet Jesus. Why don't you call on Him. Almighty Father. Help me cause I know not what to do. I know not where to turn. When you cry Almighty Jesus, Jeeesus will hear you. Jeeesus will answer your prayer. Oh yes He will. I know He will. He is your comforter. In the midnight hour. And when the darkness has been broken. Broken by the dawn of a new day, the Almighty Father will lift you up and guide you to the Promised Land. Oh yes He will. I know He will.'

The congregation drowned out the voice of the preacher with cries and calls for Jesus to help and save them.

'He will!' The voice emerged over the shouts of the radio audience. 'Come to Him. Come and let Jesus help you. Let Jesus show you the way. Jesus will lift the burden from your shoulders and the heaviness from your heart. Come to Him. Come to Jesus, children. Come to the Father.'

A choir began to sing softly, a background for the soothing invitation from the preacher, which was followed by the sound of chairs scraping as the congregation rose and joined in the song.

'God bless you,' the voice said. 'God bless each and every one of you. Oh how wonderful to see so many come to the Lord.'

The sound of sobbing was picked up by the microphone.

'Yes. Take my hand Precious Lord,' the voice sang along with the choir and congregation. 'Lead me home.'

The old woman joined in, singing softly and humming some of the words. The little girl tiptoed into the room, went over to the foot of the bed and leaned against one of the posters.

'They never gonna finish singing,' the little girl exclaimed.

The old woman glanced at her but didn't say anything.

'Phew!' The little girl leaned against the poster as if she was exhausted as the song ended with a long, drawn-out Amen.

The voice implored the radio audience to be with him next week and for those listening at home to tune in at the same time, then repeated several times the address for sending donations to help the Christian crusade. The singing and the voice gradually faded and the old woman got up from the bed as if to stretch her legs.

'That was that new preacher from Cincinnati that suppose to be so good. I don't know.' She walked over to the radio and turned down the volume.

The little girl climbed on to the bed and gazed up at the ceiling where there was an arc of light. 'He sound just the same as the old one.'

'That's what I was thinking,' the old woman agreed as she went to the window and pulled down the shade, then drew the curtains. 'It was nearly about the same sermon as the last one preached. Think he woulda said something different. Anyway, I'll see what he has to say next week.' She went back to the bed and sat down.

'Maybe he shouldn't do so much hollering.' The little girl continued her criticism of the Evangelist.

'That so those people went to hear him think they getting their money's worth.'

'Grampy said some preachers are always hollering about the same thing cause they don't study the Bible enough.'

'That's true of some of them. Some of them don't know as much as the people they preaching to.' The old woman had begun to sort through some papers she'd picked up from the table beside the bed.

'And Grampy said sometimes they're reading somebody

else's sermon.' The little girl sat up. 'I could write a sermon if I wanted to.'

'Well, I wouldn't put it past you to try.' The old woman picked out a blue sheet of paper and unfolded it. 'But before you do that, how about if you write me a letter first?'

The little girl leaned over and looked at the paper the old woman was holding. 'Who wrote you that letter?'

'This come from my great-niece. All the way from Connecticut.'

She picked up the envelope and read the return address. 'Stanford, Connecticut.' She handed it to the little girl.

'Where is Stanford, Connecticut?' she asked, looking at the envelope with awe.

'Oh, that's way up there past New York.'

'Why does she live way up there?'

'Well her mamma move up there, that's my niece. She's my sister's oldest child. So all her children were born up there.'

'Why did your niece move up there?'

'My niece? Well first she went to New York to study nursing. That's what she wanted to be. My sister only had the one girl. The rest were boys. So they let her go up there to do her training.'

'Is she a nurse?'

'That's right. I believe she did real well at it. Was in charge of something or other.'

'Couldn't she be a nurse down here?'

'Originally that what she was suppose to do. After she was qualified. But she said she couldn't practise down here like she could up there. She wouldna been allowed in the hospital or nothing like that. And she wouldn't get paid nearly as much. I suppose they treat her so much better as well. She just didn't want to come back down here.'

'And she never came back?'

'Well she come back for visits every now and then. She married a man up there. He seemed to be a very nice person and they moved to Connecticut to raise their family and they been up there ever since.'

'Are they my relatives too?'

The old woman nodded. 'Your distant relatives. But y'all is related.'

'I want to go up there and see them.'

The old woman was fingering the letter as if realizing just how far it had come. 'When you get older.'

'I'm going to go to Connecticut though. It sounds nice.'

'Well before you go I want you to write this letter for me so I can send it to them.'

'How come she wrote to you?'

'To tell me my niece been taken ill. They not expecting her to live much longer and they wanted to let the family know.'

'Cause she's going to die?'

'That's what it say in the letter.'

They sat in a ladened silence while the old woman looked over the letter, trying to find the relevant part.

'I suppose they plan to bury her up there. It don't say.'

'In Connecticut?'

'I suppose so. Though she don't say. But if they was planning to bring her back down here she would have said something about it. Oh well.'

'Are you sad cause she's going to die?'

'She's not that old.' The old woman refolded the letter. 'But if she's in misery, then she'll be release from it. I believe her husband is still living.' She looked down at the folded paper. 'So if you can write it when you come home from school tomorrow, then they'll know I got the letter.'

'What was her name?'

'My niece? Laura Mae. But they all called her Mae.'

'How old was she?'

'No more than about sixty-five or so.'

'I know somebody else who's going to die.'

'Who's that? Somebody else done take sick?' The old woman had put the letter back in its envelope and was studying the handwriting on the front of it.

'James Chandler.'

'James Chandler? Where you know him from? James Chandler.' The old woman repeated the name, trying to bring some face to mind. She shook her head. No she didn't know anybody of that name, she told herself.

108

'I don't know him,' the little girl said, surprised that the old woman should expect her to. 'I just heard that he was going to die because these men took him away.'

Puzzled, the old woman turned towards the little girl. 'What did you say?'

'I said I know he's going to die.'

'Then what's the matter with him?'

'Some men are going to hang him.'

'Hang him? Where did you hear this from? Sound like you got hold of the wrong end of the stick again.' The old woman decided that's what had happened as she put the letter back on the table and moved her pillow aside to get her nightgown.

'No I didn't,' the little girl said once she realized what the old woman had implied. 'Dr Green said it on the front porch just now. I heard him telling Grampy.'

'Heard him tell what?' She was looking for the scarf she tied around her head that should have been with her nightgown.

'He said they were going to hang this boy name James Chandler.'

The old woman stopped looking for the scarf. 'Say what? Say they was going to hang a boy?'

The little girl nodded solemnly.

'I didn't hear nothing bout this,' the old woman said, more to herself than the little girl.

'He said some men took him from the jailhouse this afternoon and they were going to hang him somewhere. That's what he told Grampy. He was in the jailhouse in Santee and some men took him out and said they were going to hang him.' Repeating the story had agitated the little girl and she began to pull on her hands, frightened by the words that, once spoken, made such terrible images in her head. It was as if they had fallen quietly on her ears as she stood by the front door listening and had remained harmless and without meaning until they fell from her mouth, when each word sprang into a little devil, wrecking the cosy peace of the old woman's room as they leaped about and lurked in the shadows.

Fear, though of a different nature, had taken hold of the old woman and she was unaware of the change in the little girl beside her.

'Why are they going to hang him?' she asked the old woman.

'Child I don't know. I don't even know if you heard this thing right.'

'I did hear it right. Dr Green said his mamma said he couldna done nothing to hurt nobody and he wasn't nothing but a boy cause he was only eighteen. Are they going to hang him cause he hurt a woman?'

'Now why you asking me that?'

'Is that why they hang you, if you hurt a woman?'

The old woman shook her head as if to shake the question out of it rather than because she didn't know the answer.

'His mamma said he never even touch that white woman. Dr Green said his mamma was screaming that they were going to kill her child and he didn't do nothing.'

'All right,' the old woman said, which was her way of asking the little girl to stop. 'I don't think you better say no more about it. It's not something you should a heard anyway. I told you about listening to grown people conversation. See?' She pointed her finger accusingly at the little girl, implying that this was what happened to eavesdroppers. Then she dropped her finger and her eyes to hide what was going on in her mind. 'Now you know why I tell you these things. That's nothing for no child to be knowing about.'

The little girl had stopped listening to the old woman's reproval which didn't have much conviction anyway. She had been snared by the fact that James Chandler had a mother, and the image of an inconsolable woman rose before her. She felt herself to be in the space between James Chandler and his mother, within the force that had pulled them apart. She stared into space, remembering a time when a hawk had swooped down into the farmyard and grabbed a young chick and how afterwards its mother had run around in circles, cackling over and over again her distress. The little girl had thought about how the chick had been taken somewhere where the mother hen could never get to it. She imagined the hen must be wishing more than anything that it could fly so that she could rescue her chick from the hawk. But it couldn't fly. The little girl slouched on the bed, still staring into space as her thoughts took her into another world and the reality of what she imagined entranced her.

The old woman pulled herself up from the bed, then needed to steady herself against the table. 'I done got too tired,' she said wearily. 'Things been on my mind one way and another all day.' Once she was able, she began to pull back the bed covers. 'Come on,' she told the little girl who was still sitting on the bed, 'cause it's way past your bedtime.'

The little girl looked up and stared into the old woman's face, but did not really see her. 'I bet she's so mad at those men for taking her son away.' She had started to get up and then forgot. 'I bet if she had a shotgun, she'd find them and shoot them all and take her son away from them.' She had a deepening scowl between her brows. 'I would shoot them so fast before they could even move. Cause they're mean and they shouldn't have done that. Should they?' She focused her attention on the old woman, whose only answer, which had been her reaction to the little girl's imagined reprisals, was to shake her head.

'You go on in the bathroom and get washed first,' the old woman suggested.

The little girl got up from the bed. 'I would go and find those men and beat them up and get him back. I would beat them up so bad for doing that. I wouldn't let him get hanged.'

'Well I don't know that anybody can do much if they got him.' The old woman sat down heavily on the unmade bed. She spotted the scarf and reached over for it. 'That's just one thing coloured people always got to put up with in this life. It's in the Lord's hands now.' She spread the scarf out on her lap, smoothing it to the edges. 'Go on. Do what I say.'

The little girl left the room reluctantly. She was still scowling with anger and also because she thought her solution to saving James Chandler should be carried out even if there was no one she could tell it to. She couldn't bear to think that nothing could be done except what the old woman had suggested. Suppose God didn't do anything?

Dr Green had gone and her grandfather stood alone on the front lawn. She could smell the cigar smoke from the front door. Her grandfather had already smoked his cigar and she wondered at his smoking another. After a while, he sat down on one of the stone benches, still looking out over the road.

Beyond the house, it was pitch-black. The little girl pressed her face against the screen door and peered into the darkness. No forms or shadows were discernible. Her grandfather must be thinking again, she decided.

It was past the time when cars would drive by. The last one she had heard was Dr Green's when he drove away. Many of the houses had all their lights out and their occupants had gone to bed. The little girl had heard the light switch go off in the old woman's room just before she tiptoed past it, drawn back to the conversation between her grandfather and Dr Green.

They had talked for a long time, occasionally slipping into a heavy silence to ponder something one of them had said. As Dr Green was preparing to leave, the little girl overheard him say for the second time that evening that none of it made any sense. Then he went on to say the woman was always trying to get coloured boys to stop and talk to her. Both coloured and white knew it. No coloured person would go near her.

'Yet,' Dr Green went on, having to face the truth of what had happened, 'she go walk into the sheriff's office and tell him this boy try to rape her. Walk in off the street. Like she just been to town shopping and decide to go in and see the sheriff. And he gone out to the boy's mamma's house, like the fool I always take him for, and pick him up for that. And he know,' Dr Green paused for emphasis, 'if he put that boy in jail cause of something to do with some white woman, some of the Klan bound to get him. And he know they go hang him. And for what? For what?' Dr Green got up and so did her grandfather. Still talking, they walked off the front porch.

'Well if they want an excuse to lynch a coloured man, then they got it. If they want to see some coloured blood.' Dr Green took a long breath. 'The sacrifice for the heathen. Yeah.' He lifted his head and stared up at the sky as if searching for a forecast of what was to come. 'Yeah,' he finally repeated. 'The sacrifice for the heathen. Wanting the stench of blood in their nose. And to foul the air with the smell of the coloured man's fear. So they can stand around and breath it in and be satisfied. Then go on home. What you go do with the heathen, Reve?

When you got to live among them? What you go do?' Dr Green didn't expect an answer and the little girl's grandfather didn't offer one. They walked down the steps together, slow and pensive in their stride.

'Lemee go and see,' she heard Dr Green say as they stepped on to the path. 'Maybe one person can say something to them. I believe I know who all of em are anyway. They know that boy ain't done nothing. See if I can talk some sense into them.'

He drove off slowly and was halfway down the road before he remembered to turn on his headlights.

The hammering on the front door seemed to go on for a long time before her grandfather put on the light and went to see who it was. The little girl lay in her bed wondering what had happened. Once before somebody had come to the door in the middle of the night asking for her grandfather. He had been called to the bedside of a woman who had been stabbed in the chest and was dying. She had wanted him to pray for her before she died.

The little girl sat up. She could hear the murmur of voices but couldn't understand what was being said. After a short time, she heard her grandfather returning to his room where she could hear him getting dressed as he talked to her grandmother. Further along, in the front of the house, she could hear someone else's voice. She got out of bed and stood near the door.

The voice coming from the living room spoke continuously, without pausing, in a low tone, and even though the words were inaudible, the tremors of sound and the breathless agitation carried through to the little girl. She hesitantly put one foot in front of the other as she crept down the hall, needing to know what was happening even though her chest had begun to shiver.

Sitting near the shaft of light from the hallway was a young man and on the other side of the room from him Dr Green stood by the window, peering through a small parting in the curtains.

The young man sat barely on the edge of the chair. He appeared more to be crouched over it, his body hunched as if to contain some pain. From where she was standing, the little girl thought that he was not breathing. Only his eyes moved, shifting in jerks, but never resting on one thing long enough to see it. His eyes were strained and unblinking and would stretch wide open as if he were using them for hearing. He seemed to be hiding, the side of his face was covered by his hand which trembled under the weight of holding his head in place. At times, the trembling would spread to his head and he clamped down on his jaws and for a moment made his small face rigid. His hair was matted and stuck out in peaks. Bits of straw and clay dirt clung to his clothes which were stained and smelled of urine. His feet were bare and caked in dried, grey mud.

Dr Green turned from the window and towards the young man who took his hand away from his face in a gesture of respect. His arms and shoulders began to shake violently and he pressed his hands together as he sat up. Since he had seen everything in one glance, Dr Green looked past him as though the young man was of no particular interest to him. He returned his attention to the window and adjusted a fold in the curtain. Unobserved again, the young man squeezed his eyes shut but the shaking continued.

The silence had lasted too long for either of them. It had caused time to stand still and already the room had filled with the hum of interminableness. Yet they knew that any sound, other than their own, could mean disaster.

Dr Green shifted his weight restlessly but remained by the window. He was looking around at nothing in particular when he spoke again. 'You ought to be over in North Carolina just after daybreak.'

Continuing to press his hands together, but with his eyes opened, the young man nodded.

'Go on and get it out,' Dr Green said almost harshly. 'Nobody go get you now. Go on and get it out. We got you safe.'

The young man gave up the effort of trying to keep his body from trembling. Only his head was spared the uncontrollable convulsion that had taken over the rest of his body. He dropped his head over his chest from where a long howl rose as he covered his face and wept.

Dr Green parted the curtains and peered between them.

'Yeah, get it out now. You don't want to take nothing like that with you. Get it out and leave it here. You can't come back no how. They ain't go let you come back.' He closed the curtain but remained as he was. 'You can't come back so this can't be your home no more. And you ain't got no mamma neither cause she can't do nothing for you no more.' His eyes dropped to the floor and he stepped forward then back to hide his thoughts. 'You on your own from now on. You got to be a man whether you ready or not. The old life is gone. Everything you know since you come into this world. That's all gone. So don't spend too much time thinking bout it cause you can't have it no more. You got to understand that right from the start. Otherwise you not go make it.' Dr Green straightened his shoulders, while glancing quickly at the young man. 'Go on up there and do like I say. Get in the army. They ain go treat you bad. No more than you already know. They ain go treat you good neither, but you get along. Leastways you won't starve. You got to keep out of trouble.' Dr Green paused, the seriousness of this piece of advice had to be appreciated. 'Keep away from trouble. It go be everywhere you turn. Stay away from it and you'll be all right.' He parted the curtains with his fingers as he continued to talk. 'I don't know. I don't know, one of these days things might start to change. I ain't go see it that's for sure. I ain go never vote for nobody or nothing. Maybe if you live long enough to get to my age, they might let you vote. My daddy said that to me. Anyway. You got your life. It got to mean something to you now. You got to do something with it. You hear what I'm saying? Cause a whole lot a coloured men didn't get the chance you got. You got your life. You hear what I'm saying?' Dr Green didn't look for an answer. He dropped the curtain back in place and walked over to a picture and began to study it.

The young man's voice was muffled now. But Dr Green reckoned that every time Chandler thought about it, no matter how many years had passed, he would have to make some kind of sound in order to release himself from its clutches.

After the little girl went back to her room she heard other voices. These were louder. She could hear them talking about gasoline and clothes and money and the best way to get to Chicago on the bus from North Carolina. When they had all left, she heard her grandfather moving round the house, walking in one room and then the next. Finally she heard the sounds of him returning to his bed and the last light was turned off.

She fell asleep and awoke at daybreak. The house and the world outside were so still she could clearly hear the ticking of the clock in the living room. It chimed at the quarter hour. In the half-darkness it was a pretty sound and the little girl was so glad to hear it. She pulled the covers around her and waited for it to sound again. The room began to lighten and a few birds began to chirp outside in the garden. She leaned over and pulled the curtains back. The sun had not yet risen but there was a band of grey light on the edge of the fields. The air coming through the partly opened window was chilly and moist. The little girl snuggled deeper under the covers.

She wondered if James Chandler was in North Carolina. She wondered how far Chicago was from Connecticut. Then she wondered if God knew that Dr Green had got James Chandler away from those men. She wanted to remember to tell the old woman what had happened. She would tell her that God hadn't saved James Chandler even though they had both prayed to him. Dr Green had. The little girl heard the chimes as she drifted back to sleep; she remembered that she was going to write a letter to Connecticut. She liked the idea of knowing that a letter she wrote was going to a place where coloured people were treated nice. She pulled the covers over her head and went to sleep.

Marcella

As the weather grew warm, the old woman began to sit out in the garden again. Once the morning breeze had dropped, she had her chair placed by the side of the house which was sheltered from the drifts of cool air that sometimes accompanied the spring sunshine. There she would sit, her face partly uplifted and her hands spread open on her lap, while the warmth from the sun gradually soothed and loosened her fingers.

The old woman sat on her own. She preferred solitude and the quiet of the back garden where she could slowly settle into the day. Later, perhaps in the afternoon, she would agree to sit out front where she would nod or call back greetings to those who happened to pass by. But first, she wanted to sit, undisturbed, and be warmed by the sun. And with her thoughts for company, the old woman, once the sun's rays had taken away the stiffness and cold, would gratefully fold her hands and look out over the garden.

The trees were covered with bright green leaves, still soft enough to flutter about in the fresh breezes as the old woman gazed up at them. They reminded her of the palm leaves they used to sway back and forth in church the Sunday before Easter. As the sun, filtering through the trees, caught the old woman's eyes, it made her think also of Easter lilies, the white Easter lilies laid out on the altar before daybreak so they could shine in the light coming down from the windows at Sunrise Service. She remembered the Easter lilies glowing, visualizing them now as she watched the light coming through the trees.

And there were all the other flowers. A glory of sweet-smelling flowers, all the scents mingling, there to greet them as they opened the old pine door to enter the church on Easter morning. The flowers had been arranged so beautifully,

117

brought in the night before by the older Sisters, who would decorate the church for the celebration of Easter.

The old woman nodded slowly, the beginning of a smile on her face as she saw again the flowers encircling the altar and pulpit. Then after the service the older women would go over to one and then another, praising each other's work in the flower arrangements. Always saying something real nice so everbody could smile and feel good.

The old woman looked around her daughter's garden, deciding which flowers she would be taking this year. That was the one thing she didn't want to miss doing, contributing flowers for the altar. Her mother had done it before her and Tateta had, for as long as she was able. It was something she had always looked forward to because for some reason which she knew she shared with her mother and her sister and all the other women dedicated to the church, this ceremony renewed the hope in their lives. It was like a blessing, enabling them to carry on, to meet whatever adversity there was bound to be waiting for them somewhere in the future. It was the one time when they knew and accepted the hardships of life because somehow they were made bearable, and they had enough strength left over, despite what had happened and would happen, to be glad to be alive.

The old woman started to feel the spirit that would possess them. Everybody would be ready for spring. Be waiting. Then on Easter Sunday, seem like something would take hold of us. Bring us all together. Everybody would feel the same. It would be a communion. She nodded at these recollections and swayed gently with the leaves.

The voices of children playing had drifted to within hearing distance of the old woman's place in the sun. She listened to this for a moment, her head inclined to one side as she tried to imagine what was going on. There were some children in the garden, that she could tell, and they were laughing and running about. She decided they were playing somewhere at the front of the house. The old woman sat up then said to herself, 'At least they know it's spring.' Otherwise it all happened so quietly now. People didn't get affected so much these days as they used to. No. She shook her head a little sadly. Nowadays they were just looking for better weather so they could get on with doing things. She supposed that's what it was. They had too much else on their minds. The old woman looked up once again at the deepening blue sky. It continued to warm her and she rubbed her hands over the arms of her chair to massage her palms.

It just wasn't the weather though, she was thinking. It was something that came along with the weather. She stopped rubbing her hands to think about it. Something that would just happen one day. And it could be any time, the old woman remembered. One minute you'd be doing something, not thinking about much in particular, then seem like something would touch you. Make you stand up and look round. And when you stood up, you could see how everything had changed. One thing here, something else over yonder, dotted and sprouting all around you. It would just be there, like it was waiting for you to look up and see it. See what had happened. Wherever you turned, things had changed.

And the next thing you know, you'd be breathing it in. Almost make you want to laugh out loud. Then sometimes, it would just get a hold of you and make you feel all wild inside. Make you want to run like a crazy person. Just strike out and run somewhere. 'That's what springtime used to be able to do to you,' the old woman told herself. She chuckled and smiled a long smile that covered her entire face. 'Yeah,' she mumbled softly, 'made you want to get up and run and do all kinda crazy things.' She leaned back in her chair and rocked for a few moments. 'Didn't worry about nothing. Didn't think about nothing. Not for a little while, anyway.' She rocked in silence, sobering, reluctantly, as she realized where she was. 'Well anyway,' she said quietly, 'least I'll see the Easter lilies.'

By the time the sun had reached the middle of the sky, the heat was radiating off the side of the house where the old woman was and she decided to move to where she'd be partly protected by the shade. She resettled herself across from a row of trees that grew along the fence and almost in the driveway that went from the front to the back of the house. Here she could hear even more clearly the playful voices of the children. It sounded

119

like there were a good many of them running around, shouting and excited. As she listened, she suddenly remembered they were there for the Easter egg hunt. She nodded her head now that she knew what was going on. That was what all the commotion was about.

The old woman sat back in her chair, smiling as she listened to their laughter. It was something that she had always enjoyed hearing. She hoped there were plenty of Easter eggs hidden about so that all the children would have a chance to find some. She wished now that she had asked to have her chair taken instead to the front of the house so that she could watch the children as they searched for the eggs. She thought that perhaps she might walk around there later on when they were having their refreshments and see how successful they had been at finding the hidden Easter eggs.

Their laughter was so carefree that it did your heart good just to hear it, the old woman told herself, as she sat peacefully content with her life at the moment.

A while later, some small movement by the trees caught her eye and she looked over and saw a child standing alone. She could see that it was a girl. Can't be looking for no eggs over there, the old woman thought. She was just wondering if she should call over to the child, who maybe felt left out, when she realized she was standing on the other side of the fence. Hidden from the other children by the trees, she was watching them, her small face intense with concentration but expressionless while her eyes seemed lost to all else as they followed the children around the garden. Then without making a move, the child shifted her gaze to the old woman, proving that she had not forgotten to keep guard. For one moment they stared at each other, then the child moved away from the fence, stepping back so quickly that she tripped and nearly fell over an exposed root. She steadied herself against the tree and, without looking either at the old woman or back at the children in the front garden, the girl turned and walked away. By the time the old woman had got up and over to the fence she was gone from view. The old woman stood there, puzzled first by the child's quick disappearance, then wondering how long she had stood there watching and unnoticed.

When she sat down again, the old woman began to think about what had happened with the child. Finally, she shook her head, unable to make any sense of it. 'Don't know who she might be,' she said to herself. 'Must come from one of those houses up there by Sunnyside. But then why was she down here?' She shook her head again, but continued to see in her mind the child's eyes as she stood by the fence staring at the other children.

'What was it she had seen in them?' the old woman asked herself over and over again. The child was looking at the other children and she was looking at them in a way that said she had never seen this before. And yet she recognized what she saw and it held her attention. But then only her eyes had been allowed to be a part of something that she had immediately understood. Her eyes held all the sensation of being with the other children, of doing something the rest of her body would never know.

Something about the look in the child's eyes had shamed the old woman even more than it had disturbed her. Maybe it was because the child was already aware that only her eyes would know certain things. But the old woman then wondered how they could seem so naïve, when they showed so much knowledge, knowledge of other things, unchild-like things. Yet in their innocence they showed no longing, no jealousy, no excitement, no imagining; just a wide-eyed look of seeing and not knowing anything about the other children, but knowing what they saw. What else was like that in her little life? The old woman closed her mind to wondering about such things.

The voices in the front garden had quietened. The hunt must be over. The old woman leaned back in her chair hearing the collective hum of the children talking. She no longer wanted to go to the front of the house and be with them. But she couldn't sit in her chair any longer, haunted as she was by the child who had stood by the fence. The old woman got up, picked up her stick from beside her chair and went for a walk in the back garden.

★

'Grandma said to tell you it's nearly time for dinner.' The little girl waited a moment then lightly nudged the old woman on the shoulder. 'It's nearly time for dinner,' she said again.

The old woman slowly raised her head and began to wonder, as she so often did, where she was.

'I kept on calling you but you didn't answer me. You been asleep.' The little girl felt some responsibility for reorientating the old woman who often seemed at a loss when she was awakened from one of her naps. 'Out here in the garden,' she added, as the old woman began to look around her. She tried to reach down for her walking stick and the little girl picked it up and handed it to her.

'That's right,' the old woman managed to say in gratitude. She took hold of the stick as if it helped her adjust to being awake again. 'Y'all finish your Easter egg hunt?'

The little girl nodded. 'Guess how many eggs I found?'

'Oh, it must a been a plenty. How many?' the old woman asked.

'Nine.'

'Nine! Well that is something. You must a got more than all the rest of them put together.'

'Tommy got eleven,' the little girl said with some regret.

'Still you done real well.'

'I coulda got more but Tommy kept on running in front of me.'

'Well there must a been a lot of eggs for y'all to find so many.'

'I had next to the most eggs,' the little girl told the old woman.

'Well that's wonderful.'

'Guess what?' the little girl said, and began to hop around the old woman's chair with excitement.

'I don't know. What?' The old woman smoothed down her dress and prepared to get up.

'No. Guess,' the little girl demanded, still hopping about the chair.

'Guess what?' The old woman pulled herself up from the chair.

'Guess where I'm going after we eat dinner?'

'Must be somewhere good to get you hopping around so.'

They began to walk towards the house.

'I'm going to get my Easter outfit,' the little girl announced.

'Well that's real nice.'

'Grampy's going to drive me and Grandma to town as soon as we finish eating. And guess what else?'

'What else?'

'I might get a hat too.'

'Well you sure will be dressed up.'

'I know,' the little girl agreed, and then skipped on ahead. 'Maybe I'll see a beautiful purple dress and get some purple socks and then get a beautiful purple hat with ribbons on it.'

'You not go buy no purple shoes?'

'Grandma said she don't think they make purple shoes.'

'Well all the same, I expect you be something to look at.'

The little girl skipped up the steps and held the door open for the old woman as she slowly climbed up.

'Bertie Ruth's going to get her Easter outfit this afternoon too,' the little girl said. 'Her mamma's taking her and her big sister to town and her big sister's going to get a hat and Bertie Ruth might get a hat.'

'Then all a y'all be looking real pretty for Easter.'

'I know,' the little girl said. 'Bertie Ruth's my best friend in the whole wide world and Anne's my next-best friend.'

'Y'all mighty lucky little children,' the old woman said as the two of them went through the house to the dining room. Even though she'd had a nap after her walk, the old woman still felt tired. She hoped that her appetite would come back when she sat down to the table for dinner.

The Monday after Easter, the children at the little girl's school were allowed to wear their Easter outfits for a parade in the afternoon. The little girl rushed home from school and changed into the lavender print frock and the little straw hat with its lavender band which had been sewn on especially to match her dress. Her outfit, like most of the other children's, was slightly soiled after the long day full of Easter celebrations, but her shoes had been polished and she wore clean white socks for the

123

assembly in front of the principal and invited parents and friends.

The little girl hurried back to school in order to show off her clothes to her friends. Her grandmother would be coming along later and like all the other invited guests would also be dressed for the occasion. She had taken care over the outfit that had been sent from New York, fussing with the fox fur which she wanted to look casually draped over the shoulders of her tailored suit. The little girl's grandmother strolled, unhurried, to the school, accepting the compliments and respectful glances she had come to expect as her due as the wife of a prominent and prosperous member of the coloured community. When she arrived at the school, the principal, as dignified as any diplomat, was waiting on the front steps to greet her.

The old woman told them how nice they looked as they were leaving. She said, no, she wasn't up to a visit to the school even when the little girl's grandfather offered to drive her there. She said thanks all the same but told them she was still tired out after sitting in church all day Sunday, listening to those long sermons. She thought she might lie down on the bed for a short nap and then later when she was rested, she'd hear all about the fine clothes everybody was wearing.

While supper was being prepared the little girl sat on the bed in the old woman's room, describing in detail the outfits that had been part of the Easter parade. The old woman had done as she'd said and caught up on her sleep that afternoon. But now as she sat in her chair by the window, nodding as she was expected to do while the little girl chatted on about everyone's clothes, she was wondering what was nagging her. She decided it must have been something she'd dreamt and so she tried but couldn't remember having dreamt anything.

'And Mr Johnson said he was very proud of all of us cause we behave like little ladies and gentlemen all afternoon.' The little girl was smoothing down her very soiled dress with obvious self-satisfaction when the old woman returned her attention to her rambling monologue about the Easter parade. 'And he said we looked so beautiful in our clothes, especially the girls, and that our mammas and daddies should feel proud of themselves for dressing us up so fine.' The little girl paused and took a deep breath while thinking what else to say.

'That sure is nice.' The old woman's few words fell in the middle of the silence. She wanted to listen to what the little girl had to say, but as she began to rock back and forth, trying in herself to understand what they all had experienced, she felt that probably her own life had been too different for her ever to know what they were feeling. And so, she sat nodding at nothing, her senses void of stimulation, and although she continued to hear the words of description and detail, there was no image in her head to accompany them.

The old woman looked over at the little girl who had finally exhausted her recollections of the afternoon. 'Y'all children are very blessed,' the old woman said quietly. 'So blessed to be able to get new clothes specially for Easter. That's something to be thankful for. We didn't even dream of nothing like that when I was growing up. Not even your grandmamma.'

'Grandma always wears a new Easter outfit,' the little girl said, slightly puzzled.

'When she was a child like you nobody never bought no new clothes. We just never had things like that. Children today is very fortunate and you don't even know how blessed you are. Do you?'

The little girl shook her head, not so much because she agreed, more because she didn't understand what the old woman meant.

'All y'all got a school to go to and teachers teaching you things. Even when your daddy was growing up, your gran-daddy and those had to send for a teacher to come down to Eautawville to teach the children. Paid for it themselves, board and lodgings for the teachers, all the books and what not. Everything. Otherwise they wouldna had no learning. It was just the one teacher for everybody and there wasn't nothing like no blackboard or no desk.'

The little girl began to fidget and openly yawned. She had had a long, exciting day and normally she would be interested in how her family lived in the old times, but listening now to the old woman's reminiscences was tiring.

'Most of the children went to school barefoot.' The old

woman laid this fact between them when she began to lose the little girl's attention. 'And clothes with patches on them.'

'We're not allowed to go to school barefoot. Mr Johnson'll send you back home.'

'And that's right too,' the old woman agreed. 'You suppose to show respect for learning. Be clean and neat so people'll know you serious about getting education. Then they'll respect you.' The old woman nodded as she finished. 'That's the chance y'all got now, but it wasn't always like that.'

'And you shouldn't wear holey shoes neither,' the little girl added, 'and smelly clothes to school.'

'No. Always be clean and always behave. That way when folks see you walking with your books and things, they can say how nice you look and know you come from a good family that takes pride in theyselves and care about you getting an education.'

The little girl had lifted her head and was looking without too much interest around the room. 'I know. That's what Mr Johnson keep saying. He said some children don't come to school as clean as they suppose to.' The little girl remembered something. It rekindled her interest. 'Everybody knows exactly who he's talking about. It's always Marcella. Phew! You can smell her in assembly. She smells something terrible.' She used a phrase she had often heard the older children using. 'Phew! Bertie Ruth says it's cause she always wets the bed. Marcella said it's not her wetting the bed but it's her baby sister.' The little girl wrinkled her nose. 'And you know what, Miss Funchess makes her sit at the back of the room. Otherwise we could hardly breathe. And we have to open all the windows even if it's cold outside and Marcella has to sit by herself. She's dumb.'

'No. You not suppose to say that about nobody.' The old woman didn't know what else to say, so much of what the little girl said had shocked her.

'Yes she is dumb too,' the little girl insisted. 'She never knows any answers and she smells. You said we're suppose to have our books and be clean and she's not.'

The old woman shook her head. She was shocked by the little girl's vehement assertions and wondered what had occurred at the school to cause children to openly display hostility and contempt. It was something she had not known existed. 'It's not the child's fault.' A sadness was spreading over the old woman. It weakened her voice and made the little girl wonder for a moment if something was the matter.

'Her mamma oughtn'ta let her come to school like that,' the old woman mumbled. 'Children don't know no better than the parents teach them. If her little sister wet the bed, then her mamma ought to see she wash down every morning.'

'She don't ever wash. That's what Bertie Ruth said. That they probably don't even have any soap. And she wears the same old raggedy clothes too. And one of her shoes, it's got two holes in it. When we walk behind her we can see it. Then she slides her foot on the ground so we can't see those big ole holes. She's silly,' the little girl said as if this was a plain and simple fact of life.

Listening to the circumstances of this unknown child was too uncomfortable for the old woman to stay seated. The faint and sketchy image of her great-grandaughter's life, she knew, was bound to be inaccurate in parts. But she did not understand at all how a child like this Marcella could manage her little life in the face of so many bad opinions about herself. Wasn't the child helpless in defending herself? But then how could she be expected to? The old woman rocked and looked heavenward, for no answer to these questions dwelled within her, she knew. And she knew also that something bad had been laid bare before her. What had been created between children, she asked herself, that so much could separate them and yet keep them close enough together so that their differences became weapons they had learned to use on one another? The old woman shifted in her chair, wanting to get up, but not knowing where to go. She told the Lord she was too old to have to know any more terribleness about the world. It's a terribleness, she thought, like a plague on her mind. She certainly knew no way to combat it. She prayed it would go away and still it hung over her. The old woman wondered, as she continued her plea, if something like this hadn't been bothering her about the Easter egg hunt.

'She doesn't always come to school,' she heard the little girl say. 'Sometimes she does but sometimes she doesn't. She's going to get left behind probably cause she doesn't know as much as the rest of the class. Bertie Ruth said she doesn't even have a daddy. She never had one not even when she was a baby. How come she never had a daddy?' the little girl asked.

'Everybody got a daddy,' the old woman said half-heartedly, knowing that having a father wouldn't really do much for Marcella's reputation. 'I don't think it's nice of Bertie Ruth to be saying things like that and I reckon she don't know what she's talking about anyway.'

'Marcella's daddy doesn't live with them,' the little girl said, confident of her facts. 'Only her mamma lives with her and her sister Carletta who's in the first grade and her baby sister. That's what Marcella said. They sure have funny names. Marcella and Carletta.'

'Well if that's what their mamma want to call them then it's all right.'

'But it doesn't sound like anything.'

'People name their children what they like. Maybe it mean something to the mamma.' The old woman began to wonder if there was anything she could say to the little girl to make her understand that it wasn't right to look down on people, whatever the reason. She would have to think of a way, she told herself.

'They didn't have any Easter outfits either,' the little girl said. 'Miss Funchess said she was glad to see they were cleaned up and had their hair pressed cause the parents were there but they didn't get to parade around with us. Some other children didn't have Easter outfits either,' the little girl added as an afterthought. 'So they had to watch too. One boy named Reginald said he forgot to wear his. He said his daddy bought him a brand-new suit. I bet he never even had a suit. Bertie Ruth told him to wear it tomorrow then. And he said he might if he feels like it. I don't even believe him. He's always saying he's got things when he don't. He said his daddy had a brand-new car once and his daddy can't even drive cause his brother said so.'

'You know what it sound like?' The old woman looked out of the window which was as far away as she could get from the details of the Easter parade. 'It sound to me like y'all don't have the right idea about celebrating Easter. A person don't have to have new clothes just because it's Easter. It may be that some children's parents wasn't able to get them new clothes, specially if they got lots of children. A child's not to blame if their parents don't have the money to get them new clothes just cause other people got them.'

'Well Reginald shouldn't be telling us he got a new suit should he?'

'Maybe y'all made him feel real bad about it. If some children had something you didn't have and they were showing it off in front of you and you know you didn't have whatever it was and that you wasn't going to be able to get it, then you might start to feel real bad too.'

'Then I'd ask if I could have one if I wanted it.'

'And suppose your mamma and daddy couldn't get it for you and you had to watch all the other children? That would make you feel real bad since you want to have the same as they have. Wouldn't it?'

The little girl didn't answer and shrugged, unconvinced, after she'd given it some thought.

Agitated, the old woman got up from her chair by the window. 'I don't know about all this Easter outfit parade. Doesn't sound like it suit everybody. I don't know.'

'Why doesn't it suit everybody,' the little girl asked, slightly defensive.

'Cause it don't sound right.' The old woman slowly walked out of the room. 'No,' she said as she went through the doorway, 'I don't think it sound right a'tall.'

The following day was such a fine one that the old woman decided to return to her sheltered spot after the midday meal. She said it was so warm, she would sit halfway in the shade. So, before going back to school, the little girl helped her to move the rocking chair away from the wall so that she would be out of the direct sunlight. With a lightweight sweater around her shoulders, the old woman sat in her chair and enjoyed watching the day go by. It became warmer, even in the shade, so that eventually the old woman gave in to her drowsiness and, leaning back against the chair, went to sleep.

She thought the twittering of the birds awoke her. They sounded so busy in the tops of the trees, flitting back and forth while a variety of bird calls criss-crossed through the air. The old woman listened with her eyes closed. The sun was shining directly on her and she wondered what time it was. When she heard the voices of the children returning from school, she realized that she must have been asleep for an hour or so. Slowly she opened her eyes, shading them with her hand against the strong sunlight. It had become too warm for her, but she thought it best to wait a while, until she was more alert, before getting up to shift the chair to a cooler spot. She kept her hand over her eyes and looked around her. The voices of the children were nearer. She turned towards the meadow where she could see a group of young girls walking along the path that went beside the fence and across the fields on up to the grey clapboard houses. The girls were coming towards her carrying their school books on their heads, maintaining their balance by staring straight ahead, yet managing to sing a rhyme in chorus.

> I see him in the Springtime
> I see him in the Fall
> I see him downtown Satday night
> Strolling to the ball

The old woman remembered a similar song that they used to sing in her youth. The words were not all the same but she thought it was probably the same rhyme. Smiling a little to herself, she closed her eyes against the sun, continuing to listen to the rhythmic chant of the schoolgirls until it had faded away. It had been such a long time since she had heard anyone singing songs from her youth and as other children walked along the path, she looked at them, curiously observant, wanting to see what else about them might be the same. She decided there were no more similarities that she could recognize. Just the singing she told herself, remembering how they seemed, when she was young, to have a song for every occasion. Washing clothes, working in the fields, walking along the road, sitting down in the evening after supper. Then everybody would have their favourite song and in the darkness that surrounded them and drew them together, they would sing their song or ask someone else to sing it for them. The old woman had forgotten how much she had enjoyed singing. It took your mind off things, she told herself, and left you feeling satisfied, somehow. There was a communal feeling of being relaxed.

As the voices and the noise of the children's movement began to trail off, the gradual return to quiet brought the old woman back to the present. She watched the last few children stroll along on their way home.

Near the end of the last group, she saw the two little girls. One older than the other, huddled so close together, they were nearly walking in each other's footsteps. The older child, holding a copybook to her chest, walked along the path with her head down. The younger one, empty-handed, seemed to be staring away into the distance which she appeared to find preferable to seeing what was around her.

As the group slowed its pace, so did the two little girls and, when one of the other children turned round and looked at them, they both paused and waited. Sensing they would soon have to endure unwanted attention, they watched the group. When nothing happened, the older child, still keeping her eyes on the other children, reached down and picked something, like a stone, out of her shoe. The two of them resumed walking, still close together, but further behind the others. The smaller child returned to staring away ahead, looking neither left nor right, not even acknowledging her sister after the older girl had put her arm round her shoulder.

The old woman and the little girl ate supper alone in the kitchen. For most of the meal they ate in silence. The little girl was hungry and the old woman, who didn't have to wear her teeth, which she found more trouble than they were worth, was eating carefully but with great relish.

When they had begun their slice of apple pie, the little girl, chewing a mouthful, looked up. 'We had apple pie at school today.'

The old woman nodded to let her know she had heard, but continued eating.

'It had icing on top and raisins in the inside. Somebody said they were bugs. But they weren't they were just raisins.'

The old woman didn't say anything, preferring not to think about bugs just then. After a moment in which the little girl did think about them she said, 'They tasted all right. Bertie Ruth didn't eat her pie because she said it just made her sick to think about bugs. But bugs don't taste like raisins, do they?'

The old woman swallowed a mouthful of pie. 'That's not a nice thing to talk about at the table.'

'Why?'

''Cause it might upset a person's digestion.'

'That's what Bertie Ruth said the raisins did to her stomach.'

'Well then, you should know better and talk about something else.'

'What?'

'Well, talk about something that's interesting.'

The little girl stopped eating and thought. 'Something interesting.' She looked up at the ceiling. 'Let me see.'

'Maybe something interesting happen at your school today,' the old woman suggested.

'Something interesting at school?' The little girl shook her head. 'Nope. Nothing interesting. Not today. But something happen to Marcella this morning. After she came to school.'

'What happen to her?' the old woman asked encouragingly.

'Well she was wearing this ole black tam and it had lint all over it and was dirty. And Miss Funchess told her to take it off when we went into the classroom. Cause we're not suppose to wear hats inside the schoolhouse. And she didn't take it off. And when Miss Funchess called on Marcella to read, she said, "Marcella, I thought I told you to take your tam off. You know we don't wear hats inside the school." And she wouldn't take it off. She didn't say nothing. She just sat there, looking at the book, and Miss Funchess said, "Marcella, I'm waiting for you to take that tam off." And she act just like Miss Funchess wasn't talking to her and Miss Funchess said, "Did you hear what I said Marcella? Answer me." She didn't say nothing. Just sat there looking at the book. Then Miss Funchess leaned over her desk and said, "Marcella, I want you to take that tam off your head and put it underneath your desk this minute." Marcella just kept on looking at the book. Then Miss Funchess got up and walked over to Marcella's desk and she bend down over Marcella and she said, "Do you hear me talking to you? Do you?" Marcella nodded her head up and down. Miss Funchess said, "Then take that hat off your head and put it underneath your desk." And Marcella just sat there like she couldn't move. Like she was stiff all over. Then Miss Funchess stood up and put her hands on her hips, like this, and she said, "All right, Miss, you can just go right out of my classroom to Mr Johnson's office." Then Miss Funchess went to her desk and wrote a note to Mr Johnson and told Marcella to take the note with her. Then Marcella went out the room and Miss Funchess told Thomas to read next. And then Charlene was reading and Marcella came back into the classroom and you know what? All her hair was standing up all over her head. She didn't comb it or nothing before she came to school. It was as nappy as could be. She just stood there by the door and Mr Johnson came and told her to take her seat. He said, "Go on and sit down," then he said, "You don't have no shame coming to school looking like that. And your mamma don't have no shame neither, letting you out the house looking like that so you can disgrace the school. That's why white people don't want to be around coloured people when they don't care any more about themselves than that." And he pointed his finger at Marcella's head. His eyes were moving all around the classroom, he was so mad. Everybody was staring at him except Miss Funchess. She was looking down at something on her desk. Then Mr Johnson said, "All right Miss Funchess, you may continue with your teaching." Then he went out the door and Miss Funchess just sat there looking down. She didn't say nothing. Everybody was just sitting there waiting and she kept on looking down and nobody said nothing. It was so quiet. Then she leaned down and wiped her face with a handkerchief and said that we will continue with our reading and that it was Phillip's turn. Marcella didn't get her turn. And all day long Miss Funchess was acting funny. She wouldn't look at nobody. She didn't even make Bertie Ruth eat her pie either.' The little girl picked up the last piece of pie with her hand and then said, just before she ate it, 'Bertie Ruth said she bet Mr Johnson beat Marcella. But she didn't cry.' The little girl put the piece of pie in her mouth and chewed it. 'I can tell if they cry.'

The old woman put her fork down and for a moment gazed reflectively at the table. 'That's the one that got the little sister?'

'Yep,' the little girl nodded, and swallowed. 'They look just the same too. Except Carlotta's real, real small. Marcella's small too. Maybe that's why Mr Johnson didn't beat her. Sometimes he beats you. Sometimes he doesn't.' The little girl was thoughtful for a moment, then added, 'But I know she had to throw her tam away. Cause when we ask her what happen to her tam, she said Mr Johnson made her put it in the trash can.'

When they had finished clearing away the supper dishes, the old woman said she was going to her room, and since they were on their own the little girl decided to join her. The old woman switched on her bedside light, then turned on the radio, keeping the volume low, and afterwards asked the little girl to get her box from under the bed. It was an old hat box that held all her papers, old photographs, cards and the little presents she had been given over the years.

Going through the box with the old woman was one of the little girl's favourite pastimes. So they sat side by side on the bed, slowly sifting through the contents of the box, peering at one item and then another; the little girl asking questions and the old woman explaining how certain things came to be possessions in her life.

The old woman asked for her chair to be moved up beside a juniper tree which was nearby the fence. She said it was getting too hot by the side of the house. And as the afternoon wore on, she moved deeper and deeper into the shade, but not far away from the fence.

She didn't sleep after dinner, but spent most of her time rocking and singing quietly to herself. Twice she rested her chin on her chest but she was not asleep. She was remembering, and could see clearly in her mind another cluster of small clapboard houses, and one in particular where she had sat on countless Saturday afternoons. There in the doorway, looking out over the front yard, she had casually watched whoever it was walking past.

She would sit barefoot, feeling the cool boards underneath her feet, knowing the house was scrubbed and clean. She could smell the lye soap on her hands and on the damp floors inside. And while she waited for the floors to dry, so she could go back inside and cook supper and also the Sunday dinner, she had a little rest in the doorway where she could think about things. She wouldn't actually pray, but she would always begin by thinking about the good things.

She looked around her. The yard was swept. There might be a few flowers in bloom, flowers she had nurtured into growing in the sandy earth, knotted with the roots of pine trees. Then she would notice if the sky was particularly clear, or the air sweet-smelling and she would remember again that the house was cleaned inside and out and it was Saturday afternoon and she didn't have to go to work the next day.

These are my blessings, she would think to herself while listening to her two children playing nearby. Then she would dwell on the three of them. I got my health, she would think gratefully, and can go out to work and support us. I am able to do that. My two girls are safe with me and well. When she reminded herself of these things, her worries didn't seem too bad. And shunning trouble for the moment, she would say almost confidently that she'd find a way because there might be something she could do to solve her problem that she hadn't thought of yet and maybe it would come to mind.

But there were times when she sat in the doorway and knew, despite all she knew, that there was nothing she could do. Sometimes she sat in the doorway hungry, her stomach gnawing in protest as she thought about the little bit of food she had put by for her children. She tried hard to look out over the yard and think about her little blessings. And if they eluded her, then she would draw comfort from the voices of her children. Finally, she would ask God in case He was listening, and to let them both know, for she knew her life could be worse, not to let her children ever know the kind of hunger that she had known.

The old woman opened her eyes, needing to leave her memories behind. She shifted in her chair, brushing imaginary folds out of her dress, then peered over the fence into the field. A gentle breeze blew over the long grass and the old woman inhaled deeply, wishing she was able to feel the grass brush against her legs, a simple pleasure she had always enjoyed and thought she'd taught her children to enjoy as well.

She smiled a sad little smile in resignation. No, she hadn't been able to do everything for them. As hard as she'd tried in the end she had let them down and the time had come when they had known hunger. Despite all her prayers she couldn't keep it from them. She told herself, though in the bitter moment of reconciliation she didn't see it, that the Lord had some reason for letting her children go hungry.

They had cried from it and she had done her best to hush them, mumbling gently some indistinguishable words as they whimpered, unable to understand themselves why being hungry was painful. She had put them to bed but they were too distressed to sleep. Finally she left them, promising there would be some food soon, and had then gone and stood defeated in the doorway, feeling on either side of her the weight of her bare hands that had failed in the end to provide.

She told God He had to give her the strength if she was to carry on. That that was her only hope because she had nowhere else to turn. She stood in the doorway and waited, looking for a sign because she had laid herself open and couldn't move until she had been given some strength from God. Words and feelings choked in her throat and her prayer came out broken and staved by the shaking in her chest. 'Don't let me think it's not worthwhile any more.' She said this to God and herself over and over again, pleading with the both of them. 'Don't never let me doubt or I shall be lost. Don't let me lose hold of myself.' Suddenly she had become terrified of the darkness that took hold of her mind and had cloaked the spirit of her senses as if she had died. She shook her head violently to shatter this darkness that was numbing her. 'Don't let me doubt that my children is a blessing, to bring me joy and to give me hope, whatever else happens. Don't let me pass nothing bad on to my children.' She leaned against the frame of the doorway, her face chilled from the sweat that had broken out over her, relieved at being aware of this small sensation. 'Don't let me stop seeing the blue sky,' she asked, near exhaustion. 'So I don't forget your wondrous gifts, the trees, flowers and other things.'

When the darkness was only on the outside and some clear patch of sky shone light on her surroundings, she had gone inside and got into bed between her sleeping children.

I kept a hold of my self-respect, the old woman said to explain her survival. That the only difference. Somehow, I got the strength to hold on till things changed and got better. Cause if you let go – the old woman paused in her thinking and watched a trail that led down an endless road – she had almost known herself, you were lost forever, she finally said, recognizing with renewed respect this solemn truth. No, she shook her head, you don't come back. Cause things don't seem worth coming back for. No they don't. She rested her arms on her chair, then slowly reached up and brushed her hand over her hair. I seen it happen too many times, to men and to women. Sometimes the women take they children down with them. The image of the road was in front of her again. Take them down and they end up lost too. Sometimes, a woman a just slip away, their minds just slip away, quiet like. Don't say nothing to nobody. And they leave they children. Can't talk to them no more. Can't do nothing for them. Can't show them nothing. And a woman a die like that, away from her children. Never able to even touch them no more. Lord have mercy on they soul, was all the old woman could think to say.

She dropped her head then thoughtfully looked at her hands, which were frail and knotted from the years of scrubbing and cooking in somebody else's kitchen. One of her earliest memories was of standing on a wooden box washing dishes at the big house on the plantation.

Not really wanting to remember, the old woman sighed and folded her hands in her lap. All she had ever been able to do,

137

besides working in the fields, was to work in somebody's house, cleaning up after them.

One time, in her youth, she had dreamed about being a teacher. But after slavery, her people wouldn't let her go to school regularly, not when she could earn a few pennies to help out. She used to dream about being a teacher. Often to help her get through the dreariness of her day she would imagine all the details of how her life would be. She'd have a little house, painted white with a white picket fence in the front and a small flower garden. She would see herself as she walked from her house, her head high and proud, always wearing starched, white blouses and nicely fitting skirts. She'd have polished, soft leather shoes and a fetching little hat, respectable, but fetching. She would be carrying books to and from school and would always smile at and greet her pupils and their parents when she was about town. At school, she would sit behind a large brown desk with a little plant on it and some kind of memento from her past pupils. There would be a dictionary and other books and also a globe so her class would know all about the world. And at the end of the day, before she left, she would neatly arrange all the lesson books on the edge of her desk ready for the next day.

The old woman smiled fondly at her old daydream. How she had longed to be a teacher, even though she rarely went to school. Still, she had always known in her mind how she wanted her life to be. In the end, her dream had faded, because it was beyond her and she knew it. But she had held on to some part of it and passed this on to her children. That was the only difference, she told herself again. Somehow, she had managed to hold on.

It was the boisterous voices of the schoolchildren that caught her attention and brought her back to the present. They were moving alongside the fence with an increased tempo, excited and restless, in a hurry to shake off the inhibiting behaviour of the classroom. They were exaggerating their talk and movements, amusing and teasing each other as they rushed or strolled along, doing whichever expressed their mood but never losing the rhythm of one another's beat.

The old woman reckoned they were just reacting to the heat

which had increased considerably during the day and was probably the start of the hot, humid weather of the long summer. If her guess was right, the old woman told herself as she looked around taking note of the weather, this was the start of a hot spell when for weeks there might not be any let-up from the heat. At least there were plenty of shade trees surrounding the house, the old woman said, grateful for this.

Out beyond the field, on to where the grey clapboard houses stood, there were very few trees. The ground was too hard and infertile for anything to grow from it. And when the houses, which were built low, stood close together, there was no relief from the heat which would become unbearable.

The people who lived there suffered from the heat in silence, rarely remarking upon it, even when it caused them to erupt into violence. If it made them short-tempered, they did not seem to know it.

When the day dawned and the heat rose from the bare ground, it drove some of them out of doors to sit the day out, slumped and undisturbed except by the flies. Others would stay inside. They would delay giving in to the heat. But gradually it would take over their will, slowing them down as they shifted about. Sometimes when any movement was too much effort, they would spread themselves somewhere and sleep and sweat until the day, if not the heat, had gone.

Fights started and ended quickly. No one had enough energy to prolong them unnecessarily. Even crying was short-lived. The children didn't like the eerie quiet that surrounded their whining voices and adults knew that in the end they would have to go somewhere and find a glass of water.

The old woman gazed unblinkingly at the children, again remembering the hot days and stifling nights under a tin roof. She knew all about it. So did these children passing her now. She pressed her lips together and studied them as they went by, understanding the commotion they made. A few of them saw her sitting underneath the juniper tree, and without break-ing their stride or looking too closely at her lush surroundings, nodded or mumbled a greeting to her and she, knowing where they were going, slowly nodded in return.

The old woman saw the two girls and began to get up from

her chair. For a moment she stood, waiting, to make sure of her legs, then with the help of her walking stick went over to the fence.

They came towards her, walking steadily and side by side, the older one with her head down, appearing to need to see where to place her feet. The younger child walked with her head turned slightly to one side, a frown across her brow as if the sunlight were too strong for her eyes. Her steps were long and deliberate, but she kept pace with her sister even while she was looking up into the face of the old woman standing by the fence.

As they went past, the old woman beckoned to her, but she showed no sign of seeing this except by continuing to look back over her shoulder as they walked on. The old woman beckoned again, waving her arm to make sure the child understood she was trying to get their attention. The girl's eyes remained on the old woman as she carried on walking and the expression on her face did not change when she tugged on her sister's arm and pointed back towards the fence where the old woman stood, her arm still raised for them.

She waved for the two girls to come over to her. They watched her, but stayed where they were. Then, without any sign that she would obey, the older child, the one who had stood by the fence watching the children hunt Easter eggs, began to walk back. A step or two behind, her sister followed.

Willing the children to come to her, the old woman waited in silence. They did look alike, she observed as they came towards her: little round-faced girls with big, clear eyes, innocent and wary at the same time. They stopped at the fence and stood before her, faces lowered, staring patiently at something unseen, while she studied them more closely.

The old woman couldn't help smiling down at the two girls, and without having looked at her they seemed to know this. Hesitantly, they glanced up at her. It caused the old woman to forget what she had wanted to say and her smile began to wane as she perceived the remote, sullen expressions set into their faces. Even when they had looked up at her, their mouths remained drawn and firmly shut, resigned already, in their innocent acceptance of fate, to not knowing what to say, to not being allowed to say anything and to not knowing anyone to say anything to. And so, the old woman told herself, they did not have any answers to give in school. To her, their mouths so determinedly shut were even sadder than their eyes. She could feel her own mouth being pulled downwards and the old woman had to struggle within herself to smile again.

She took a step closer to them, forgetting there was the division of the fence. 'How y'all doing?' she asked hoarsely, but with sincerity.

They lowered their eyes and stared into the fence.

'Y'all all right?' the old woman said to encourage them not to be shy.

'Yes'm,' they answered one after the other.

'Well that's nice,' the old woman beamed.

The younger child stole a glance at her then looked for safety at the fence.

'Y'all coming home from school?' the old woman asked, the encouragement for them to talk still in her voice.

They nodded.

'Y'all go to Dunton School?'

They both nodded again, their eyes shifting from one spot on the fence to another.

'Well that's real good.'

In the short silence that followed, the younger child lifted her head again and peered for longer at the old woman. For a moment they looked into each other's eyes, the old woman searching for some sign of light, the child staring into the aged, strange face.

'And what your name?' the old woman asked, a little saddened.

'Carletta,' the child whispered, her head even lower.

'And what your last name, Carletta?'

'Davis.'

'So you call Carletta Davis.' The old woman fitted the two names together as if they brought Carletta to life.

The younger child nodded and said softly, 'Yes m'am.' Not sure why she was pleased with herself, Carletta glanced towards her sister to sense her reaction to this peculiar meeting.

141

'And this here your sister?' the old woman asked, seeing her glance sideways.

Carletta nodded.

'What's your name?' The old woman had to wait for the older girl's reply.

'Marcella.' The child's voice sounded rough as she tossed her name out without caring.

'Yes,' the old woman murmured. Her voice picked up. 'So you Carletta Davis and Marcella Davis.'

They both nodded, heads down again. Carletta had taken her cue from her sister.

'Y'all got real nice names. Real nice,' the old woman said quietly, with conviction.

They both looked up at her and she nodded to reaffirm her statement, then seemed to be trying to absorb what she had told them as the old woman continued.

'Sometimes I see y'all walking back from school. When I'm sitting over there.' The old woman turned slowly and pointed towards the side of the house. 'Right back there. And I see y'all walking together.' She indicated where. 'Look like y'all mindful of each other and that's nice to see.'

Carletta dropped her head to one side and looked up at the old woman, her face puzzled as she listened to the account of their journeys to and from school. She shifted her eyes to her sister who seemed to be studying something on the ground and not hearing the old woman talk.

'And y'all seem like well-mannered little girls.' The old woman tried to hug them with her words. 'I guess y'all to be nice from the way you act when I see you coming along here.'

Carletta looked up at the old woman and then the line of her mouth curled upwards as she smiled briefly. Again she looked at her older sister, holding on to a little of the pleasure of the smile, even though her sister gave her no sign of what she was thinking.

'It's so nice,' the old woman continued, more grateful than she had been since she came to this house to see the child's smile, 'to see young children that's so well behaved. Y'all always be so quiet walking by here. And always walking together, looking after one another.'

142

The older girl, Marcella, looked doubtful, as if the old woman had mistakenly described two other children.

'And your mamma sure must be proud of you,' the old woman continued, believing that the older child's expression was a sign of modesty. 'I bet she's real proud of the way y'all be together.'

The two girls exchanged glances, signalling each other, a practised habit, to join forces. Carletta, still wanting to like the old woman, risked peering up at her. The old woman was nodding harmlessly as she talked and the younger child looked sideways at her sister in order to pass this on to her. Marcella, however, had dropped her head and, frowning, she stared at the ground.

The old woman did not miss the reaction her comment had caused. She had disturbed the two girls and was now lost for words in her regret. She lifted her head and looked over into the field, following the path to Sunnyside.

'Well,' the old woman started, not knowing what else she was going to say but, realizing that the only hold she had on the two little children was her voice, had to say something. 'Your mamma got herself two very nice little girls and I know she must be proud, though she might not say so. And both a y'all going to school and getting a good education. That's wonderful. Anybody be glad for their children getting all that learning.' The old woman nodded confirmation, while still looking out over the field, but wondering if the children had been reassured.

There followed a silence which eased their stance and relaxed their facial expressions.

'What grade you in Marcella?' the old woman asked in a high inquiring voice, that was also soft and delicate.

Marcella raised her head to look at the fence again. 'Third,' she said in her hoarse whisper.

'Third grade!' the old woman repeated. 'Why ain't you doing fine.'

For a moment, Marcella was affected as Carletta had been earlier when a little bubble of pleasure touched her chest and the tightness around her mouth faded briefly.

'And what grade you in Carletta?' The old woman felt she

knew the younger child better and leaned over the fence towards her.

'First grade,' Carletta answered in a rush, then shied away because of her outburst. She then added, her hand covering her mouth, 'I got left back.' She looked up at the old woman to see her reaction.

'Well, sometimes it takes longer to learn some things. But that's all right. Long as you learn in the end. That's all right,' she said reassuringly. 'I bet Marcella'll be able to help you with your school work.'

'She do help,' Carletta told her. She took a step forwards and then back again.

'Well there!' the old woman exclaimed, as if that made all the difference in the world. 'Then y'all both gonna be fine. Cause if you help one another, you'll do all right. And that's what you must always do.' The old woman paused and thought about this herself. 'Sometimes Marcella'll help you,' she told Carletta. 'Other times, you'll be able to help her. Ain't that right?'

'Yes m'am,' Carletta answered, not so much because she understood what the old woman had told her, but because the way she'd said it made her feel good.

The old woman looked at Marcella, waiting for an answer, and Carletta willed her to respond.

'Yes'm,' the older child said obediently.

'That's right,' the old woman said approvingly. 'And I bet y'all love to play together. I know when my daughters was little, about the same age as you, they were always playing together. They couldn't wait to finish the chores and get outside and play something or other.'

Both children were watching the old woman, wondering about her having two girls.

'We had a little house,' the old woman continued, remembering when her daughters were very young, 'one big room in the front and a little tiny room in the back where we used to sleep. And when it was too cold outside or raining they used to sit on the floor, by the stove in the front room, and play for hours. I can still see them like that, playing together on the floor. Then when they were older, they used to walk to school together, like y'all do.' For a while the old woman was lost in memories.

'That there your house?' Carletta pointed through the fence, unable to contain the curiosity that had been building up while the old woman was talking.

'That's my daughter's house,' the old woman told her after she'd turned to look at the house along with Carletta. 'I live there now, with my daughter,' she added.

'That a big ole house.' The younger child peeped unashamedly through the fence at the house and the garden around it. 'They pretty flowers.' She leaned against the fence and smiled at the garden.

Marcella looked at the house, then lowered her gaze and stared at a nearby tree.

'When my daughters was little,' the old woman told her, 'we used to plant a few flowers round our house. They used to cheer us up. We would all tend to the flowers. Sometimes when they were in bloom, we had a few indoors, for decoration, so it look nice.'

'I'm going to grow me some flowers,' Carletta announced, still looking at the garden through the fence.

'That's right,' the old woman said, inspired by Carletta's announcement. 'And maybe Marcella can help you tend to them so you'll have nice pretty flowers round your house.'

'I like flowers,' Carletta admitted softly.

'Well then.' The old woman stepped right up to the fence and leaned over. 'Here,' she said, reaching into the pocket of her dress. 'Here, this for you, Carletta. You take this and buy some flower seeds and plant them all round your house.' The old woman put fifty cents in the child's hand. 'And this for you Marcella. For you to get something that you want to have. Here.'

Marcella looked at the old woman's outstretched hand.

The old woman leaned as far as she could over the fence. 'I know you can find something to get for yourself. You go on and get something nice, you want.'

Marcella raised her hand up above the fence and the old woman put the coin in her palm and folded the child's hand over it.

'That's just for you.'

Marcella closed her hand even more firmly around the coin and then looked over at her sister. Carletta was holding her hands together and smiling. She grinned as she returned her sister's look.

'Now what y'all go say?' the old woman asked as she stepped back from the fence. They looked at her, too stunned by what had happened to know what she meant.

'You suppose to say thank you,' the old woman reminded them.

'Thank you,' they said in unison.

The old woman nodded, 'And you welcome. Now y'all remember what I said. Y'all always be close to each other. Always try to help one another.' She looked first at one and then the other child. 'Cause no matter what happens to you, you'll always have somebody to share it with, good or bad.' The old woman looked at them again, her belief in what she was saying showing in her eyes. 'Someone that got the same memories that you got and can understand how you might be feeling about a thing can always be a comfort. And then, can't nobody make you feel alone.'

Marcella looked up searchingly into the old woman's face, then stared beyond her into the garden.

The old woman continued, 'And there's something else you must do. If ever somebody says something to try to make one of you feel bad about yourself, then the other one got to say: "That's not true. Don't believe what they saying." Say it over and over till the other one believe it and not the ugly thing somebody else done told them. Cause some people in this world will try to make you feel bad about yourself, like you not good enough to do nothing.' The old woman shook her head as if to rid it of this awful but real fact. 'Specially when it's somebody who want to think they better than other people. When somebody like that try to tell you something about yourself, don't even listen to them. Don't even listen,' the old woman repeated sternly. 'Shake your head and say to yourself. "No, that's not so." And don't pay it no attention. Y'all remember that. You must help one another. Remember what I'm saying to you now.'

The old woman paused, shaken and near tears because of the feelings she had worked up in herself. She had to look over the children and across the meadow again. 'And don't never let nobody make you feel shame. That's the wrongest thing you can feel.'

The three of them stood in silence; the words the old woman spoke hung in the air ringing like bells.

The old woman looked down at the children and spoke quietly. 'Y'all remember what I'm telling you. So you grow up to be proud of yourself. And get all the education you can get, so one day you'll be able to do for yourself.' The old woman nodded as if this was prophecy. 'You'll be able to look after yourself and you'll be able to look after your mamma. Cause there're some things,' the old woman sighed heavily, 'you'll come to understand better when you grown. Y'all be good children. Be good to your mamma.' The old woman stepped back from the fence, needing to lean heavily on her walking stick. 'Go on now and get those flower seeds. When you plant them give them plenty of water. Plenty of water and don't let the ground get too hard round them when they growing up.'

The two children backed away from the fence, still looking up at the old woman.

'Tend to them,' the old woman reminded them. 'So they can grow.'

They both nodded at her. 'Yes'm,' Carletta said, trying to suppress a smile that was spreading over her face.

'All right then. Go on.'

They went back on to the path and, turning, walked down it. The old woman watched them. They walked side by side as close together as when she'd first seen them. She stood by the fence, her eyes on them, until they were out of sight.

Jacob's Dream

One afternoon, near the end of summer, the old woman and the little girl, after dressing themselves very carefully, were sitting on the front porch. They were awaiting the arrival of Eva Mae Hayes. Eva Mae was sister-in-law to the old woman and the great-great-aunt of the little girl who was fidgeting on the edge of her chair, annoyed and impatient with the old woman who had told her to stay seated so she didn't get her dress all messed up and wrinkled.

Throughout the afternoon, while they prepared themselves for the visit and afterwards, when they were ready and sitting on the porch, the little girl had repeatedly asked questions about who was this Great-Aunt Eva. But the old woman had been so distant and vague with her replies, that all the little girl knew was that Eva Mae was as old as the hills and that she had written a letter to the old woman which had come to the house the week before.

When the letter arrived, the old woman had studied it for a good while before deciding to take it to her room. She sat down on the side of the bed and looked at the letter again before making up her mind to open it.

After she had read it, the old woman's reaction was to shake her head in disbelief, then, nearly smiling, she wondered at the irony of life. But as she sat there, drawn to thinking beyond the contents of the letter, reliving old memories that it had disturbed like dust in a disused room, her expression of sad irony changed to one of sufferance as she prepared herself for whatever might be ahead.

The old woman finally put the letter under a little box on her bedside table, which was just the right size to hide it from view, and also, she told herself, to keep it where it was.

That evening, when she and the little girl were in her room

waiting to listen to a radio programme, the old woman took the letter from under the box and without looking at it put it on the bed beside her. Then, as if a thought had just occurred to her, she asked the little girl to get the hat box from under the bed.

'I got a feeling,' she said out loud, though it meant nothing to the little girl, 'there's something in there I want to find out.'

The little girl pulled the box from under the bed and hurriedly dropped it on the old woman's lap, then went to sit in the chair by the radio.

The old woman forgot about the programme as she untied the ribbon and prepared herself to look for a piece of paper she hoped she hadn't, in a pique of anger, thrown out.

'I never heard of anybody called Eva Mae.' The little girl stood over the old woman who was still rummaging through the hat box.

The radio programme had ended and the little girl had become curious as to what was in the hat box that the old woman preferred to one of her favourite radio shows. She peered into the box as if she could see something interesting too. 'And I never heard of anybody called Jacob neither.'

'Sure enough,' the old woman had mumbled without looking up from the box. Beside her on the bed, papers of all shapes and colours had been scattered and more than once she had gone back to them to make certain she had not overlooked the one she was searching for.

'Eva Mae must be somebody I don't know,' the little girl said to prompt the old woman to explain who she was.

'I already told you,' the old woman said with some agitation, 'Eva Mae was your great-grandaddy's sister.'

'I know,' the little girl said as she picked up a letter and looked at it. 'But I don't know who she is.'

Although the little girl hadn't thought she'd noticed, the old woman took the letter from her and put it back on the bed.

'Does she know who I am?' the little girl persisted. She waited for an answer. There was none. 'Does Jacob know who I am?'

The old woman shook her head.

'Are you glad they're coming?' The little girl had gathered that this was no ordinary visit.

The old woman unfolded a piece of paper which contained a letter.

'Is she your friend?' The little girl was determined to get some kind of answer. She waited, then leaned over to see what was in the letter.

'I sure do wish you'd stop asking me all these questions. Can't you go somewhere or sit somewhere else stead of standing over me. You haven't stop talking since that pro-gramme went off. I can't even hear myself think.'

The little girl backed away.

'What time is it anyway?' the old woman asked.

The little girl shrugged her shoulders, staring as silently as she could at the old woman who was beginning to feel she had been too short-tempered.

'You keep on asking me all these questions,' she said to justify her reaction, 'so that I don't know if I'm coming or going.' Her voice quietened as she spoke and she went back to the letter she had just found.

'Could I look at the pictures?' The little girl had crept back to the side of the bed.

'Not just now.' The old woman shooed her away with her hand. 'Now go on off till I get through.'

The little girl went to the foot of the bed and dropped down on it. But the old woman hadn't noticed. She straightened the fold in the letter which was written on several pages of lined paper. It was one of only two letters she had ever received from her sister. This one, though faded with age, had been clearly and carefully written. It had been sent to her in September of 1924.

Dear Ellen,
Trust my letter find all of you in good health. It leaves us well but busy from sun up to sun down in the fields. I don't complain and know I should be thankful for a good crop to see us through the year. I thought and thought about writing you to tell you the news and decided in the end to write since you are bound to hear it by and by and

you might not hear it the way it happen. Charles daughter, Rosaleen, died last week giving birth to a baby boy. I could not believe it myself since I never heard tell she was expecting. Charles came to the house early Monday morning to tell me the news and to ask me to help lay her out since I was the nearest one to family. I did go because poor Rosaleen was not to blame for what her mother and Charles have done. Even though she did the same and died from it. So now the girl and her mother are both dead and Charles is by himself. Eva Mae was in Augusta and did not get home in time for the funeral which was so pitiful with Charles crying like a baby and the baby crying and never going to know its mother. Charles name the baby Jacob. Rev. Browning did not say nothing a'tall about Rosaleen being what she was and anybody that say otherwise is telling a lie. She was buried in the churchyard by her mamma's people. Charles is saying he is going to raise the baby because after all it is his grandson. Everybody know that whether he say it nor not. All the same he is looking poor, coughing from his chest a lot of the time. He ask about you and the girls. I give him what news I had but had to bite my tongue not to say more. How he go raise that baby I don't know. Probably Eva Mae will have something to do with it. She just the same. If I don't get to bed soon I won't feel like getting up in the morning. It's gone past midnight. Love to all. Tateta.

The old woman refolded her sister's letter and carefully put it back inside the paper. That's what she had thought, she told herself, and Tateta's letter had proved it. Eva Mae Hayes was coming here and bringing Charles' illegitimate grandson with her.

'There's no end to what that woman won't do. I declare,' the old woman huffed, allowing the indignation she felt to reflect in her voice. 'If she ain't the most menacing heffer to walk on two feet then I don't know what.'

'What did she do? You mean Eva Mae?' The little girl's face was alive with interest.

The old woman eyed her sharply, wondering why she had

asked such a question, then realized she must have spoken out loud.

'What did she do?' The little girl waited expectantly, her eyes on the old woman so she did not miss any detail of the answer.

'Ain't you suppose to be in bed?' The old woman wasn't going to let on about what she was thinking or repeat what she had inadvertently said out loud. 'Go on and get up from there and get yourself ready for bed. Go on.'

Reluctantly, the little girl got up from the bed. 'Well why were you talking about her then?'

The old woman refused to answer her. 'Go on and do like I say. You know you suppose to done be in bed.'

'All I ask about was Eva Mae.'

'And don't you be calling no grown people by they first name. You know better than that.' The old woman had become cross with the little girl and couldn't help frowning and showing the irritation she felt. 'When you goin to learn some manners?' Somehow she had shifted her sister's letter in with some others and had lost it. When she found it again and put it aside safely, some of her annoyance faded. She looked up to say a more civil good night to the little girl but she had gone and the bedroom door was closed.

The old woman sat back on the bed and, resting her hands in her lap, surveyed the papers scattered around her. She realized that she had allowed Eva Mae to do the same thing to her sense of well-being.

After all these years, she thought, as she caught sight of the envelope that contained her sister-in-law's letter, it's still bothering me to think about her. Even though Charles been dead all this time. She sure can't interfere between us no more, the old woman reminded herself, then sighed heavily, again looking at the confusion of papers surrounding her. She realized she was tired and the thought of gathering up all the things on her bed and putting them back in her box wearied her even more. Still, she told herself as she got up, if she intended to sleep on her bed tonight that's what she had to do.

After she had finished, the old woman made two promises to herself. One was to make up for the way she had talked to the little girl. That she would do in the morning. And the other was on no account to allow Eva Mae to upset her life again.

The car bringing Eva Mae Hayes pulled up to the house without either the old woman or the little girl noticing. A wasp had somehow gotten on to the porch and the little girl was nervously dodging one way and then another as the wasp frantically flew around their heads. The old woman, holding her fan up and plainly irritated by all the commotion, instructed the little girl to keep still long enough for the wasp to calm down so they could open the door and let it out. And it was as the little girl began to ease over to the screen door to let the insect escape that she saw the car. A young man had gotten out and was looking up at the house.

'Just don't stand there looking like a nincompoop!' The old woman's irritation had quickly been replaced by exasperation as the little girl stood in the doorway staring down at the car and the man beside it.

'Go on down to the car,' the old woman ordered. 'You know that's probably them. Go on and stop acting like you simple.'

The little girl tiptoed down the steps.

'Be something else for her to talk about,' the old woman mumbled to herself as she watched the car, not yet prepared to look at the young man next to it.

As the little girl approached the car, the young man opened the back door and began to help Eva Mae to get out. The little girl stopped and waited, having sensed, more because of what the old woman had not said, that the appearance of Eva Mae Hayes would be worth watching.

It was, however, with some difficulty that Eva Mae climbed out from the back seat of the car. Being older and more feeble than she would admit to herself, the journey, which had taken nearly five hours, had almost been too much for her. Still she was determined to emerge looking as spritely and alert as she thought the occasion called for. 'I might not be as young as I used to be,' she told Jacob when he carefully settled her into

153

the back of the car earlier that day, 'but I got plenty of stuffing left yet.'

Jacob smiled and agreed with her. He said if there was one thing she had plenty of, it was stuffing. But during the hot and arduous journey over roads dusty and lumpy from a prolongued dry spell, Eva Mae was feeling, even if she wouldn't admit it, that perhaps she had more stuffing than she needed.

After a few false starts, when finally she allowed Jacob to coordinate her efforts, Eva Mae descended from the car. Then holding on to Jacob's arm to make sure of her footing and using the opportunity to survey her surroundings, Eva Mae prepared herself for the last part of her journey. She took from Jacob a large, black handbag which she put on her arm and pressed against her chest. Then without waiting for Jacob to help her, she made her way on to the paving stones and started up the path.

The little girl had watched with fascination as Eva Mae emerged from the car, showing herself to be not much taller than she had seemed sitting on the back seat. Once, she hadn't been much bigger than the little girl, but through the years her petiteness, which had delighted her and many of her admirers, had spread into a stout and buxom figure, which she now fitted snugly but expensively in black. She had remained vain about her tiny feet and was wearing a pair of beautifully embroidered slippers. Some years back Eva Mae had taken to wearing dark glasses. She had noticed how effectively they contrasted with her thick silver hair which she wore braided and pinned at the back. Her state of presence, which she had never allowed her size or pale colouring to detract from, was firmly intact as she continued up the walkway to the house. The little girl, as she stood watching her, joined the ranks of so many before her in wondering, upon seeing Eva Mae move with a sense of purpose, who she was.

Timid with awe the little girl stepped to one side as Eva Mae approached her, and it was at this point that Eva Mae paused and professed to see for the first time the little girl standing in front of her.

'Well, well, well.' Delight spread across Eva Mae's face. 'And who is this here?' Her voice had a slow, sing-song rhythm and was rich for a woman of her size. 'And what a pretty little thing. Come here darling. Come here and give me some sugar. Yes.'

The little girl walked demurely towards her Great-Aunt Eva Mae and was embraced in powdered softness.

'Aren't you a little dollbaby? What a pretty little thing,' Eva Mae murmured. 'Let me look at you.' She held the little girl at arm's length, even more delighted at what she saw. 'Oh this is wonderful. And you one of the little grans. Must be one of Ellen's great-grandchildren.'

The little girl nodded into the smiling face.

'I bet you don't know who this is. You don't know who I am do you?' Eva Mae's voice rose almost childishly.

'Great-Aunt Eva Mae,' the little girl piped up almost before Eva Mae had finished speaking.

'That's right,' Eva Mae sang. 'Aren't you a smart little girl. Oh this is so wonderful.' She pulled the little girl to her bosom again but this time Jacob was there to steady her as she wavered slightly and had to rest her weight momentarily against the little girl. She took hold of his arm again as though she did so to speak to him.

'Jacob. Isn't this wonderful. The Lord has answered my prayers. I'm so glad.' She looked towards the little girl again. 'This my Jacob. That's who he is.' Slowly she walked between Jacob and the little girl, continuing to talk as if their company was all that concerned her. 'Isn't he something handsome? My Jacob. Handsome just like his grandaddy. Oh the Lord is good. Yes He is. The Lord is good.' Her voice had become stronger and carried a good way ahead of her.

The little girl stole a glance at Jacob, who had his head down either in respectful submission to his great-aunt's voice or because he was thinking of something else. He didn't look at all like Great-Aunt Eva, the little girl decided. He was tall and lanky in his slow stride. He was also much darker than his aunt who looked as though she had been made out of bread flour. Jacob had golden brown skin, smooth and like the colour of honey. But like Eva Mae, the little girl did think he was handsome. She was very aware of him walking on the other side of her great-aunt.

'That's right,' Eva Mae said when Jacob paused to give her time to catch her breath. 'I'm going to get there,' she said lightly, smiling a golden-tooth smile at the little girl. 'I come all this way to see that lady and that's what I'm going to do. That's certainly what I'm going to do. Now where's that Ellen? Where is she?'

'Up there,' the little girl pointed. 'Sitting on the front porch.'

'Is that where she is? Well that's who I come to see. After all these years. Yes Lord. I come to see her after all these years.'

They had nearly reached the house while Eva Mae was talking and as they came to the steps that led up to the screen porch, the door opened and the old woman stood there. She paused for only a moment, then with the help of her walking stick, taking one step then another, she went down to meet Eva Mae Hayes.

Eva Mae stopped then clasped her hands together as she saw the old woman. And when she set foot on the bottom step, Eva Mae, in silent slow motion, reached out with wide-open arms.

'Oh Ellen,' she cried, and walked forward to embrace the old woman. 'My, my, my. Isn't this something? Thank the Lord. Thank the Lord. How you doing Ellen?' Eva Mae kept one arm around the old woman as she peered with great concern over her. 'Oh you looking fine. Don't you look fine.'

'You not doing so bad yourself.' The old woman allowed herself to be hugged again.

'Oh I prayed for this moment,' Eva Mae said between squeezes. 'I was determined to get here.' She stepped back and looked up at the house. 'I was determined to get here. Praise the Lord.'

'Well, I see you still getting round. Just like you always did.' The old woman seemed to be looking politely askance of Eva Mae, who was still surveying the house, when in fact she was taking in every detail of her old acquaintance. 'I always said,' the old woman paused and looked back at the house along with Eva Mae, 'that you go outlive everybody else.'

Her last remark caught Eva Mae's attention. She pressed her hand to her chest. 'No, no,' Eva Mae denied, as though it was never her intention to live as long as she had. 'You don't know

Ellen, but these old bones is just about worn out.' She patted her chest. 'Just about worn out.' She took the old woman by the arm, a frail grasp this time. 'I just had to see you once more. Once more, that's all.'

After the slightest pause, the old woman said, 'Well you better come on up here and sit down.' She turned to reclimb the steps. 'Though I don't believe nothing go wear you out.'

'Lord have mercy, Ellen.' Eva Mae shook her head in denial again as the two of them slowly moved up the steps.

Jacob had gone ahead and was standing by the open door when they reached the top.

'You know, Ellen,' Eva Mae said, suddenly taking hold of the old woman with both hands. 'My time is nearly out.'

The old woman didn't answer, and despite Eva Mae's tactics to divert her, she stole a glance at Jacob before they shuffled on to the front porch.

'I know one thing,' the old woman said as the familiarity of the young man's face shocked all her senses, 'you didn't come all this way just to tell me that.'

'Oh Ellen,' Eva Mae laughed a little nervously, 'you haven't changed a bit. Not a bit.'

It was while they were all settling into their chairs that the old woman had her longest look at the quiet young man who had seated himself opposite her. For one moment during the shifting of chairs and adjusting of cushions, she opened her eyes wide and looked at him. Then blinking once or twice, she picked up her fan and offered her guests something to drink.

After a long swallow of iced tea, Eva Mae turned her attention to the little girl who was sitting beside her. Jacob leaned towards them, smiling and appearing interested in what the little girl was saying. And delighted to have the attention of all around her including the old woman, the little girl sat up and in her best voice began to chatter about herself.

The old woman wondered, before she could stop herself, how it was he didn't recognize her. She moved her fan back and forth and slowly sipped her tea hoping that these movements and the little girl's voice disguised her agitation. They seemed like the same eyes, she told herself, only now they were gazing calmly at the little girl. And when she had last seen them, they were closing, finally, and this child here had not even been born. It was something only she and Eva Mae knew. They were the only two left who remembered Charles. Moisture from her glass dropped on the old woman's lap and it burned like a tear. She pressed the spot with her handkerchief, then turned and looked outside to find some comfort.

Her eyes fell on the broad base of an old oak tree that grew alongside, shading the front porch. She raised her head to look at the great branches that hung over them, wishing that somehow they could be arms and that she could lean herself against the tree and feel safe. But her eyes were drawn again to the trunk which was gnarled and uneven in its thickness, spreading out into protruding roots that made the path to the side of the house a perilous walk for her. Remaining comfortless, she turned and faced more inner thoughts.

How many years was it? something inside her demanded to know. Many, she answered. Sixty-seven, something told her. Sixty-seven years, she admitted, was when I first looked in his eyes believing everything they said to me. That's how long ago it was.

Why had Eva Mae brought this to her? Anger and despair rose in her chest as more memories slipped out from hidden places. He had these light brown eyes, she admitted, seeing them again, set in his face. Almost hazel colour. Details had begun to uncurl like a freed spring. Shiny eyes. Even when they were bloodshot. Able to look into her. Even when they had turned yellow. Able to know her. Make her stand still. Another drop of moisture fell on to her lap and this time she carefully wrapped her handkerchief around the bottom of the glass. Then absently she rattled the pieces of ice which clinked from side to side, sounding like the distant echo of a bell.

Eva Mae was saying how much better she felt. She chuckled, then said she had thought she was about through when they finally got here, driving all that distance. But she was feeling much better now. Seemed that all she needed was a little rest and a nice cool drink. She smiled at the little girl and playfully pulled one of her plaits.

'Oh how this brings back the old times.' Eva Mae leaned

back in her chair and looked around. 'Yes,' she drawled slowly, pleased with the resonance of her voice. 'Sitting here together. The good old times, Ellen. Sitting here watching the afternoon go by.' Eva Mae took the little girl's plait again, swinging it as she talked. 'Oh if I was young again, I'd want to get up and do something. Do something!' She clapped her hands in delight. 'I'll tell you what,' she leaned towards the little girl as if they were conspirators, 'when me and your great-grandmother were young, we used to be two high-stepping young ladies. Yes sir-ree.' Eva Mae's voice dropped to a base. 'We were the young ladies of the time. Yes. Isn't that right Ellen? Child we were something. Strutting around. Oh we used to have some good times. We had some good times.' She leaned even closer to the little girl. 'What do you say about that? We weren't always old you know. We had our good time. Isn't that right Ellen?'

The old woman had continued to fan herself, appearing not to be taking too much notice of Eva Mae's antics. 'I don't know if your memory serving you all that correct if you asking me. All that about high steppin.'

'Sure we were high stepping,' Eva Mae said, almost before the old woman had finished. She turned to the little girl. 'Why your great-grandmother was something. She was something.' Eva Mae lifted one small foot off the floor and although it didn't go very high, she still gave the impression of repeating what she said she and the old woman had once done.

'The only high steppin I used to do,' the old woman interjected over Eva Mae's chatter, 'was to the cotton field. That's the only place I used to high step it to. You must be getting me mixed up with some of those Williams girls you used to run around with, Eva Mae. Seem to me that your memory done got worse than it used to be.'

'No,' Eva Mae said, more certain of her facts and still feeling light-hearted, 'we all used to do it. Have fun together. That's how it was. All of us having a good time together. We go back a long way.' She looked fondly at the little girl. 'Me and this lady over here go back a long way. I bet you didn't know that, now did you?'

The little girl shook her head as she sensed something weighing down the easy-going words passing in front of her.

And although she didn't know why, she decided not to ask Eva Mae any questions. She did, however, glance over towards the old woman who looked meaningfully back at her. So to make sure no questions slipped out of her mouth, the little girl pressed her lips together. Satisfied that her message had been received, the old woman casually looked off in another direction.

'I know I'm old,' Eva Mae said in defence of herself. 'I know I'm an old lady. But I just haven't forgotten how things used to be. I just didn't forget, that's all.' She picked up her glass of tea and took a long drink.

'And I didn't forget much either, Eva Mae,' the old woman said soberly, then added, 'although there is things I sure do wish I could forget and that's the truth.'

'Oh don't I know,' Eva Mae said in quiet sympathy. 'Child don't I know.'

'On the other hand,' the old woman continued, speaking more to herself than Eva Mae, 'there is no use for anybody to go digging in the past.'

'That's the truth,' Eva Mae was quick to agree. 'No you can't live in the past and not a day goes by I don't say that to myself.' Eva Mae nodded thoughtfully before continuing, 'I don't know though. Seem like every year that goes by, the past seems to be getting closer, till you almost feel like it's sitting there on your shoulder. That's what it seems like.'

'That's your conscience talking to you Eva Mae. That must be what it is.' The old woman was fanning herself deliberately as she made this pronouncement.

'Sometimes it seem as though I can hear people talking to me,' Eva Mae continued as if she were describing an ailment. 'I don't know. I suppose I'm just getting old. That's all it is. I'm just getting old.'

'Getting old?' The old woman chuckled with amusement. 'Eva Mae you is old. About as old as you can get. Just like me. An every so often I get to thinking I done outstayed my welcome and I know one thing for certain, you been here a good bit longer than me. Getting old? Eva Mae you full of stuff.'

'Whatever it is,' Eva Mae raised her hand to show the

seriousness of her testimony, 'I got a feeling about it, a strong feeling, deep in my bones. In these old bones and I got to do something about it.' Eva Mae leaned back against her chair as if her statement had sapped all her strength. 'All I know is this, I got one or two things left I got to do. Yes, if the Lord be willing. I got one or two things left to do.'

'Eva Mae, ever since I know you, you always had one or two things you had to do.' The old woman was shaking her head, refusing to be concerned about Eva Mae's sudden feebleness.

'No, there's no rest for the weary.' Eva Mae appeared to be agreeing with the old woman. 'I can't lay my burdens down, though I had them to carry all my life. But Ellen you got to say this, I never complain. Whatever my troubles, I never complained.'

'No,' the old woman said, not so much because she agreed with Eva Mae, but because she was putting an end to the conversation.

Eva Mae had opened her mouth to carry on then realized she had been cut short. She nodded righteously instead and sat back again, momentarily lost for words.

There was a lull in the conversation and no one knew what to say, so they sat in a half-easy silence which was eventually interrupted by the increasing drone of an aeroplane. The little girl leaned forward to see it and Eva Mae, still replanning her tactics, smiled at her.

'The next time I come here, I'm coming in an airplane.' Eva Mae burst into laughter. Some of her strength had returned. 'That's right,' she said, amused at what she was saying. 'I'm coming in an airplane.'

The little girl looked back at her, trying to imagine Eva Mae sitting inside an aeroplane.

She seemed to guess what the little girl was thinking. 'Wouldn't you like to fly with me? Go all up in the air and fly to somewhere like Paris or London? Fly somewhere nice and have a good time? Go to gay Paree? Wouldn't you like to do that?'

The little girl shrugged, not knowing whether to take Eva Mae seriously or not.

'Jacob here's been on an airplane,' Eva Mae announced, making the probability of her suggestion seem more real.

They all looked at Jacob, who had lowered his head bashfully at the way his aunt had spoken.

'For real?' the little girl asked, instantly impressed with Jacob.

'Sure,' Eva Mae answered nonchalantly before Jacob had a chance to respond. 'He's been on airplanes. I don't know how many times.'

'Twice,' Jacob said, holding up two fingers so that his aunt couldn't misconstrue what he'd said.

'No it was more than that.' She waved aside his fingers. 'You had to change plane and all that. All the way out to Chicago. That was from New York,' she added, as though she were remembering some of the many details of the journey. 'And then all the way back from Chicago to New York again.'

'It was the same flight, Aunt Eva.' Jacob spoke patiently, smiling at his aunt's insistence in trying to make it more than it was.

'Well, it seem like it was more than that,' Eva Mae said to have the last word.

Jacob shook his head and, still smiling, looked up through the screening, trying to see the plane that had circled and was coming back over the house. 'That one's military,' he said to the little girl, then strained to see more of the aircraft. He announced that he was going outside for a better look and, standing up, excused himself from the women's company.

The old woman nodded her consent, noticing that he was certainly well mannered, while trying not to take any more account of his personality or appearance. The little girl was asking her if she could go and see the plane too and the old woman nodded again, reminding her to behave herself and not to get her dress dirty.

The little girl promised that she wouldn't as she hurried off the front porch, just barely saying pardon as she stepped in front of Eva Mae. She had until now found her great-aunt fascinating to watch, but then Jacob had suddenly become more interesting and somehow mysterious. She had become excited about him, not that he had really said much. But the little girl had noticed how both women had become still and

watchful when he talked. Yet they had avoided looking at him
and each other even though the little girl had sensed that Jacob
had their complete attention.

The little girl also liked Jacob's deep, rich voice and the
smoothness of his words, which were spoken slowly as if he
already knew a great many things. When his eyes shone, it was
apparent that he had inherited his aunt's sense of humour but
had made better use of it. But what drew the little girl to feel
close to him was the fact that he had flown in an aeroplane like
her daddy. A plane had taken her father across the sea to
England where he was still. Feelings that were the result of
these things caused her to stand as near as she dared while she
and Jacob studied the sky for signs of the aeroplane.

The old woman looked at Jacob and the little girl standing
together on the lawn, and after watching the old woman, so
did Eva Mae.

'She sure is a sweet little child. And don't she take after her
daddy. I do declare.' Eva Mae nodded approvingly in the
direction of the little girl.

'She favours her mamma a good bit as well,' the old woman
said, as she continued to study Jacob and the little girl.

'That's right,' Eva Mae agreed as if the old woman was
confirming something she had already said. 'Though I don't
believe I know her mamma's people. I didn't get to know that
side of the family. That was after Charles had died.' Eva Mae
sighed as she did every time she mentioned the death of her
brother. 'Lord didn't he leave me with my hands full. At my
age.' She paused, then shook her head when there was no
sympathy forthcoming. 'All that responsibility. Lord, I didn't
know which way to turn first. Ellen, child, you don't know
how blessed you are.' Eva Mae was saying this when the old
woman returned to listening to her.

She had been wondering, as she stared out over the lawn,
what had caused Eva Mae to bring Charles's illegitimate
grandson with her. And then had wondered, even more
wearily, what it was that Eva Mae wanted from her. There
had been no hint at the purpose of her visit in the letter, but
the old woman knew Eva Mae had come because she wanted
something. She only wished she had it in her to ask outright

what she wanted. But such rudeness was beneath her and always had been. And besides, the old woman told herself, at her age, provocations that would have taunted her into action when she was younger were now just a nuisance, wearying, she admitted, but only a nuisance. Eva Mae would tell her by and by. Why else would she have come? So, in the meantime, she would just have to try and not be reminded of Charles. As much as she could see him in that boy, Jacob, she must try and not remember about that.

'You are so blessed,' Eva Mae was repeating with more emphasis. 'And it's wonderful to see.'

'Yes, and I'm grateful for it,' the old woman replied.

'Got all your family around you,' Eva Mae continued. 'That's something I never had. Me and Charles never had any family. And we were both so young when mamma and pappa died. I always thought that was the reason why Charles couldn't ever settle down. That something I couldn't ever persuade him to do.' Eva Mae paused to show her regret. 'And it wasn't but the two of us. Then when he passed, I was on my own in this world. And been left with a child to look after nobody else wanted. Lord have mercy. That was one of the last things Charles said to me. Eva look after my grandson. Promise me that one thing. He begged me. That's what he said, his exact words. He ask me to do that just before he died and left me alone in this world.' Eva Mae crossed her arms over her chest as she leaned back in her chair.

'Well,' the old woman said, giving no sign of how she felt, 'you just have to go ahead and do the best you can. That's all there is to do.'

'Lord have mercy,' Eva Mae said as if to amen the old woman's comment. 'Do the best you can. And that's all anybody can do. Just like you say, Ellen. Go on ahead and do the best you can. And didn't I know that's what you would say. I told myself. Lord I said, I don't have anybody left in this world. But if I had to pick somebody that I could turn to in my hour of need, who would it be? I didn't have to wait for an answer. Because Ellen, a picture of you came before me just like a vision. Like a vision and I said to myself, that's the best person I know. That's what I said because that's the truth and everybody know it and would say the same. That Ellen is a good person. That's what they would say and that's why I came here to see you Ellen. That's why I had to come.'

The old woman rocked back and forth in her chair, but it was an automatic motion, requiring no conscious effort, as was the movement of her fan swaying over her chest while she glanced with a casual eye on no one thing in particular. And although there was nothing about her which suggested what, if anything, held her attention, she was listening to Eva Mae's every word, noting every innuendo and insinuation, knowing Eva Mae was hoping to prod her into making the desired move so that before she knew what had happened, her sister-in-law planned to have her right where she wanted her. With an agreeable expression on her face, the old woman homed in on Eva Mae's voice, listening and waiting so that she would know what it was Eva Mae wanted from her before she came right out and said it. They had known each other a long time, Eva Mae was saying as the old woman thought the same thing.

Jacob and the little girl had seated themselves on a stone bench in the middle of the lawn after the aeroplane, which held their attention for several minutes, had finally disappeared into the distance, although the little girl claimed after they sat down that she could still hear the drone of the engine.

Jacob had explained to her about wings and propellers and had answered all the questions she'd asked so that the little girl had painted in her mind a picture of her father sitting in an aeroplane on his way to England. Afterwards she had told Jacob she couldn't understand why aeroplane windows didn't open. That way she explained, emphatic in the face of disagreement, people could jump out if the plane started to crash. It was the only feature of an aeroplane which bothered her, but she failed to convince Jacob of the sense in what she was saying and he failed to convince her that it would be impossible to fly if every passenger had their windows opened. In the end Jacob decided they had better change the subject and the little girl, unused to his smooth tolerance of her excitable behaviour and all the attention he so willingly gave her, agreed without even hesitating.

She told him instead about her school and best friend Bertie Ruth, who sometimes wasn't her best friend when she made her angry. This was the situation at the moment, but rather than not have a best friend to talk about, the little girl decided to mention her, but with that qualification.

Her dream, she told Jacob, when he asked her what she wanted most in the world, was to go to State College and be the homecoming queen and wear the most beautiful gown in the world, even more beautiful than Cinderella's.

Jacob had smiled at her, but it wasn't the teasing smile she was used to getting when she announced some elaborate plan for herself to whomever might be listening. It was a smile that encouraged something inside her to expand and grow warm and she became lost for words.

Jacob took over the talking, seeming not to notice her new shyness. He had nodded approvingly as if her silence was something they both desired.

'So,' Jacob said slowly, 'after you finish State and been homecoming queen, what are you going to do then?'

The little girl had to think of an answer. She wanted to impress Jacob. 'Probably I'll be a librarian,' she answered very seriously. Then lifted her head upwards as if she was giving her answer more thought. 'Yep. I'm going to be a librarian in the library.'

'Very good,' Jacob nodded, appearing to be impressed.

'Cause librarians get to read all the books they want,' looking upwards had inspired the little girl to comment further.

'True,' Jacob agreed.

'And they have charge of all the books.' She was remembering a time when she and Bertie Ruth had fought over the same book.

'You like books, do you?' Jacob asked inquiringly.

'Yep. Sure,' the little girl answered as if this should have been obvious.

'So do I,' Jacob told her. 'That's something I wish I had more time to do.'

'I've got plenty of books,' the little girl announced. 'In my room. I have a bookcase. Grampy put it in there. And I have a lot of books in it.'

'You're very lucky then,' Jacob told her. 'Not many children get to have books in their room.'

'I know,' the little girl said as if she had heard this several times before. 'But they're not all my books. Some of them are Grampy's because he didn't have anywhere else to put them.'

'But you're still lucky,' Jacob said.

'You didn't have any books?' the little girl asked.

'No, I had a few. My grandfather used to buy me books before he died.'

'When did he die?' the little girl asked with concern.

'It was a long time ago. When I was about your age.'

'Oh,' the little girl said quietly, wondering if her own grandfather would be dying soon. The next moment she asked, 'Did he buy you a lot of storybooks?'

Jacob's smile this time was due to remembering. 'Yeah. Sometimes. But most of them were too hard for me. Mainly he would get me grown-up books. Every time he saw a book and he thought I should know about it, he used to buy it. He was a funny old man.'

'My grandaddy's a old man too,' the little girl told him. 'But I don't think he's funny.'

'He's a preacher, right?' Jacob asked her.

She nodded.

'Well preachers have to be serious, don't they?'

The little girl thought about all the preachers she knew and came to the conclusion that this was true. 'Wasn't your grandfather a preacher?'

'No indeed! In fact I think that's about the last thing he would have been even if anybody would let him.'

'Why?' the little girl asked.

'Well,' Jacob answered slowly, 'let's just say he wasn't cut out to be a preacher. Like I told you, he was a funny old man. Just a funny old man with funny ideas.'

'What funny ideas?'

Jacob looked at her, his even white teeth gleaming for a moment. 'About life,' he answered softly. 'Now go on ahead and ask me some more questions.'

The little girl was puzzled. 'What questions?'

'Never mind,' Jacob said, putting his hand on the top of her head, like Dr Green sometimes did, only he left it there as though he had chosen her head specially to rest his hand on.

The little girl held her head very still, not wanting to disturb his resting hand and perhaps cause him to move it. A moment later he did anyway as he stood up and looked around.

'State College isn't far from here?' he asked as he peered into the distance.

'It's back that way.' The little girl pointed beyond the back of the house. 'Are you going to go there too?'

'I've already been to college,' Jacob told her.

'You did?' The little girl's eyes lit up. 'At State College?'

'No, I went to a college in New York.'

'New York!'

'Yep.'

'Were you living up there?'

'For four years.'

'Goll–lee!' the little girl's voice was rising with excitement. 'Is that where you live now?'

'In a few weeks, I'll be moving to Chicago.'

'Where you've been on the airplane?'

Jacob nodded.

'Goll–lee!' The little girl felt as though she was talking to a celebrity and the fact that Jacob was so unbothered by his fame only heightened the excitement for her. 'Is that where you're going to live?'

'Yep. For about six years if I'm lucky.' Jacob had begun to stroll along the driveway towards the back of the house.

'I wish I could go to Chicago,' the little girl said wistfully. 'The only place I've ever been to is ole Charleston.'

'Charleston is a very nice town,' Jacob told her.

'But you can drive there. Everybody's been to ole Charleston. I wish I could go to Chicago.'

'Well, maybe one day you'll get there. If you really want to go.'

'I really want to,' the little girl said, squeezing her eyes shut with wishing. 'I want to travel all over the world and fly in airplanes and ride on ships, all over the world.'

'Then that's what you should do.'

'I'm going to,' the little girl said, wide-eyed as if she was looking at herself doing these things.

'Well,' Jacob told her as they walked past the screened front porch and on down the path, 'librarians don't get much chance to travel.'

'I'm not going to be a librarian,' the little girl said without hesitation.

Jacob threw back his head and laughed. 'So what are you going to be?' he was finally able to ask her.

'I'm going to be somebody that makes a lot of money so I can travel everywhere.'

'All right then,' Jacob said to hide his amusement. 'You do that.'

'What are you going to be?' the little girl challenged.

'Well,' Jacob said, suddenly serious again. 'If my wish comes true, then I'm going to be a doctor.' He was gazing deeply into the field that lay by the side of the house when the little girl looked up at him.

The sound of Jacob's laughter when he and the little girl walked past the porch startled Eva Mae and for a moment she forgot what she was about to say. It had the same effect on the old woman, who despite herself couldn't take her eyes off the pair of them until they were out of sight.

It was the clarity of his laugh that had unnerved her and yet there was no comparison with Charles whose lungs had become so weak before he died that he could neither cough nor laugh. In his youth, the old woman was remembering, when his health had been better, his laughter had been so weighed down with the contradictions and disappointments of his own existence that there was not much sound to speak of. Eventually it had become a silent laugh. Something had choked off the sounds of his emotion and before they separated she never heard him laugh or cry.

Perhaps, the old woman told herself to pull herself out of the past, it was just the full laughter of a young man that had caught her attention. She wasn't sure, when she thought about it, when she had last heard such a thing.

'Jacob always did like children,' Eva Mae was saying while

she herself collected her thoughts. 'But then again he likes everybody. Always has. Yes.'

'Well that's nice to hear,' the old woman said as she resettled herself in her chair, while hoping that this would dispel the lingering memories from a long time ago.

'Yes,' Eva Mae repeated, as if the word could be of some comfort to both of them. 'You know Jacob plans to be a doctor?'

'Well that is something,' the old woman said.

'Lord, that boy has worked hard to get into that medical school.' Eva Mae had decided it wasn't too early to bring in her great-nephew whom she would have freely admitted, overcome for a while by honest feelings, was like a son to her. Whether it was also the time to admit this to her sister-in-law, she couldn't judge, but she circled closer to the object of her visit as she continued to talk about Jacob.

'I'm not going to say I had anything to do with it. I did just as Charles asked me because I like to think I'm a Christian too, when all is said and done. That was my brother's request and I vowed that if I didn't do another good deed on this earth, I was going to see to it that I kept my promise to him. All these years I've tried to do just that and the boy has worked hard and he's done real well for himself. Lord, when I think of all the things he could have done and all the things he could have turned out to be. Lord knows the trouble some people have trying to bring up children. When I think of all that, then I'm so grateful. You know I'm no spring chicken, Ellen, with a whole lot of time and energy on my hands. I don't believe I could have managed what with all the rest of it as well. If that boy had been troublesome I wouldn't have been able. But not one day, not one day, did he give me cause for concern. Now that's something.'

'Well that sure is good to hear.' The old woman's reply was guarded, but she felt it would be mean of her not to show some regard for what Eva Mae had said.

'And Lord, Ellen,' Eva Mae continued, having taken encouragement from the small concession given to her by the old woman, 'one day, I think he must have been about eleven, no older than that, he came into the kitchen where I was busy doing something. I can't remember what, but I know I had my hands full and he just said as plain as anything, "Aunt Eva I've decided I'm going to be a doctor." Well, the way he said it caught hold of me and I stopped what I was doing to listen. "What's that you said, Jacob?" I wanted to hear him say it again. "I'm going to heal people when I grow up. Maybe I can even stop people from dying." "People got to die, Jacob," I said, "you can't stop people from dying." "But they don't have to die because nobody can help them. Do they, Aunt Eva?" Child, I didn't know what to say. A chill came all over me and I said to myself, somebody else is talking through that child. It made me start to shake. I had to turn around and look at him good. "I'm going to be a doctor." Jacob was looking right at me and all I could see when I look back was this child's face and hear this child's voice. "Then that's what you'll do." I told him that. "I'm going to see to it. Cause that's what your grandaddy would want and it's what I want and what you want. So, I'm going to see to it." That was ten years ago when Jacob said that and he went right ahead and now he's got into this medical school in Chicago just like he said he was going to.'

'Well that sure is something to be proud of, sure is,' the old woman said as she rocked thoughtfully.

Eva Mae was nodding quietly, which surprised the old woman who was waiting for her to continue. She had guessed that if it wasn't the next sentence, then it would be the one after that when Eva Mae got round to revealing why it was she had come there.

Eva Mae took a deep breath to speak, which momentarily satisfied the old woman.

'I didn't have any idea schooling could cost so much money. Oooh Ellen, it would take your breath away. When Jacob told me how much he needed, all I could say was, how much! I'm going to have to dig deep for all that, I said it to myself. But I reckoned if I got all my business affairs in order, we could just about manage. That's what I've been doing these past few weeks and when I wrote you that letter.'

Eva Mae paused and the old woman nodded. Her guess wasn't quite right, but near enough.

'Well,' Eva Mae said, then leaned over. She reached down and picked up her handbag. 'All that digging and searching and what not.' She slowly opened the bag. 'Lo and behold if I didn't come across this here.' She reached into the handbag and pulled out a small, square leather box, fastened with a little brass clasp. 'Here Ellen. This is suppose to be yours and I want you to have it.'

The old woman had stopped rocking and if Eva Mae noticed this she give no sign that she did.

'I don't know if you know what this is.' Eva Mae stretched over towards the old woman.

'Yes,' the old woman said without looking at either the box or Eva Mae. 'I know what it is.'

'Then you know you should have it.' Eva Mae continued to offer the box to the old woman.

'Is that why you came all this way, Eva Mae? To give me that?'

'I want you to have it.'

'Maybe you didn't know it, but I give that back.'

'I do know it, but I also know it belongs to you.'

'Eva Mae, I'm too old to be worrying about things like that.'

'Well I'm old too and I want to stop worrying about them. Here Ellen, take this and pass it down to your children. That's how it's suppose to be. It belong to my mother. My father gave it to her when they married. It went to Charles when my mother died. After that Charles gave it to you and you suppose to hand it down to one of your children.'

The old woman didn't say anything or in any way acknowledge that she had heard what Eva Mae said or knew that she had put the box on the table between them.

'I got something to ask you,' Eva Mae said as she sat back in her chair and settled her handbag in her lap. The old woman lowered her head to hide the look on her face. Eva Mae, the old woman said to herself, you might be old as the hills, but nobody but the devil himself can out-trick you. Then on the other hand, the old woman tried to console herself, you had a lifetime of getting what you want for yourself. While I struggle through my youth to put food in the mouth of my children, you had no such worry or preoccupation. All you had to do was tend to your immediate needs whatever they might be and as far as I know, you never give a moment's thought to the future or to anybody else but yourself. So, the old woman thought as she lifted her head, I'm not too surprised by what you done. She sat back in her chair and consoled herself with another thought: whatever it was Eva Mae was going to ask of her, she still had the power to say as loudly and as firmly as she wished, no.

'I'm asking you,' Eva Mae began her request, 'to ask Reverend Mosely if he would be the legal guardian of Jacob. That's why I come all this way myself. Because I need to know before too long that there's somebody I can trust looking after my boy's affairs. Looking after his welfare. Jacob's going to be away for six years. That's a long time Ellen.' Eva Mae laughed a little uncomfortably. 'And if there's one thing I know for certain, six years from now, my toes will be curled up for sure. That's one thing I do know, for sure. And I got to know he's going to get through medical school. So I can rest in peace. That's what I want. So I can go and rest in peace.' Eva Mae was finished. To signal this, she reached for her iced tea but the glass was empty. 'I sure wouldn't mind another glass of tea.' She leaned back with the empty glass in her hand. 'Ooh, I'm just about talked out.' Eva Mae looked neither left nor right after her request had been made.

Grunting as she got up from her chair, the old woman turned towards the table and picked up the empty pitcher. 'I believe there's some more tea in the house.'

While Eva Mae continued to stare in front of her, the old woman shuffled across her path of vision and on towards the screen door.

'Do you know Dr Green?' the little girl asked Jacob as they continued to walk through the back garden.

'Dr Green? Nope.'

'He's a doctor. He makes sick people better. And one time there was a boy who was going to get hanged and Dr Green went and got him and saved him.'

Jacob looked at the little girl with increased interest.

173

'It's true,' the little girl said, nodding vehemently in case Jacob was doubting what she'd told him. 'He did. I know. You can ask Grampy. They were going to hang him and Dr Green went and got him and they came here and another man drove him all the way to North Carolina. It's true.' The little girl began to nod again.

Jacob stopped walking and folded his arms across his chest.

'You can ask Grampy,' the little girl offered as proof that she was telling the truth. When she'd told Bertie Ruth, her best friend refused to believe her and accused her of making it up. Bertie Ruth reminded her that she was always making up stories and said she didn't believe anything she said anyway. This had resulted in tears of frustration and the little girl had finally taken a swipe at Bertie Ruth, whose mother had telephoned and related the whole incident, from Bertie Ruth's point of view, to her grandmother.

No one except the little girl thought Bertie Ruth was as much to blame as she was, an opinion she still maintained even though she had been made to apologize, and the two of them had become friends again. And because her grandfather had forbidden her to talk about the hanging, she had continued to feel her side of the story, which would have vindicated her and justified her action, had gone untold. But since Jacob had proved, several times in her eyes, to be extraordinary, the little girl had no hesitation in telling him about the boy who was saved from hanging. She also felt that if Jacob confronted her grandfather about it, they would be meeting on equal terms, and her grandfather would no doubt discuss the entire incident, man to man, giving it all the flavour and colour that made him as respected a storyteller as he was a preacher.

'I believe you,' Jacob said almost soothingly, having noticed the earnest plea in the little girl's eyes. He watched the relief spread over her face, and as they resumed walking, he asked calmly, 'So they saved his life?'

'Yes,' the little girl answered animatedly. 'They saved his life, but he had to go away and never come back. Not ever. That's what Dr Green told him and then the other man and Grampy told him again.'

'Well I hope he's gone somewhere safe to live.'

The little girl nodded. 'He's gone to the war. In the Pacific.' She was eager to give Jacob more details to add credibility to her story. 'I know cause he wrote Dr Green a letter and he told Grampy and I heard them talking about it.'

Jacob was shaking his head regretfully.

'He's all right,' the little girl reassured him. 'They can't get him there. It's far away and he's saving the country. My Uncle James is in the Pacific too. In Hawaii and he might get a medal because he's very brave.'

'Mmmm. I see,' Jacob said. He had stopped walking again and was looking at the carefully tended orchard that was the pride of the little girl's grandfather.

'That's Grampy's,' the little girl volunteered when she saw where Jacob was looking.

'Very nice,' Jacob observed. 'Very peaceful.'

'I go in there all the time,' the little girl told him. 'Sometimes I climb the trees and you can see all around up there.'

Jacob nodded and smiled down at her.

'You can see everything,' she said, as though only she had discovered the tops of trees. 'All the way over to State College.' She pointed towards the end of the trees. 'And all the way over to Sunnyside.' She swung her arm round in the opposite direction.

Looking through to the back of the orchard, Jacob had spotted a small wooden building with a chimney. 'And what's that over there?' He nodded in the direction of the building. 'Is that a house?'

'No, that's Grampy's. But it's like a house,' the little girl went on to explain, 'only it's just got one room. And a outhouse at the back. But you can't see it from here.'

Jacob was staring at the building with fascination, so the little girl continued to describe it to him while wondering what it was about that run-down old shed that interested him. Her grandmother was bothered by it, especially the outhouse at the back, and missed no opportunity to express her feelings about it. And while the little girl herself had not given the building much thought, having gotten used to her grandmother's habitual disparagement every time she was reminded of its existence and her grandfather's utter disregard of what her grandmother thought of it, she was curious that Jacob was the only other person who found it worthy of notice. She was looking at the building too, as she told Jacob what there was inside. But none of what she said made it sound any more interesting.

'It's got a little stove and there's some wood in a box in the corner, and a cot and some blankets on it. But I don't think Grampy sleeps on it. And some chairs and two tables, a big one and a little one. And the big table's got a typewriter on it.' She paused, thinking this might be worth noting, then added, 'And some more books. I know how to type on the typewriter,' she told Jacob when he failed to comment on the contents of the little building.

Jacob nodded thoughtfully, but said nothing.

'Do you want to go look inside it?' the little girl offered. At this point she would do anything to please Jacob, and so they carried on down through the orchard towards the shed even though she knew it was strictly off limits to her and everybody else.

Saying no wasn't as simple a sound to make as the old woman had imagined. Because somehow, and later that evening, after Eva Mae and Jacob were gone and she had the time and was alone in her bedroom, then, the old woman told herself, she would piece this thing together. Because somehow, Eva Mae had succeeded in removing from around them the circumstances whereby she could have uttered: no; or words to that effect. Such words no longer seemed fitting, and would have in a way been an incomplete answer and would therefore have forced her to attempt to explain what she meant. And since the old woman was now uncertain of where Eva Mae would move from next, she felt she was bound to be trapped by her words, saying something that Eva Mae would interpret, as easily as she pleased, while claiming good will between them, as consent to her request. And the old woman would be left to listen helplessly less she give Eva Mae even more grounds for saying whatever suited her, or worse, expose herself to appearing unable to make sense, which she knew Eva Mae would openly regard as a reflection on her old age and incompetence.

The old woman sat back, too preoccupied to rock, wondering

as her mind rushed forwards and backwards over the events up to then where, if anywhere, lay Eva Mae's weakness. Feeling something akin to defeat, she reckoned all those years of hardship had left her too weary to meet this late challenge and she regretted for a moment that she had not learned to be more like the Eva Maes of the world.

'What makes you think the boy can't tend to his own affairs? Not a boy even. A grown man.' She rocked once or twice, then waited for Eva Mae to speak.

'Oh he can. He can,' Eva Mae said reassuringly. 'Sure. He does it now. Sure. You know he's already lived in New York for four years. And Lord knows if you can live in New York, you ought to be able to live anyplace. No, I wasn't talking about that.'

'No?' the old woman asked after a significant pause between Eva Mae and herself.

'No,' Eva Mae repeated, making the word long and definite. 'You know, I got to thinking about what it's like if you don't have any family. None a t'all. None. That's what I got to thinking about.'

'I see,' the old woman muttered to let Eva Mae know she had some more explaining to do.

'It's one thing when you old like me. And everybody's died out. You got to expect that. It's bound to happen and you going to be alone. And that's a different thing altogether.'

The old woman declined to take advantage of Eva Mae's offer for comment. So before the silence got too long she continued.

'Probably that's not even something you give much thought to. Lord, how many grans and great-grans you got?' Eva Mae had leaned forward to look inquiringly in the direction of the old woman.

'Plenty,' the old woman answered.

'And everyone a blessing to you and to each other. A big family is a blessing. That's the truth Ellen. You got to be like me and Jacob to appreciate something like that. That's the truth.'

'I know what you talking about,' the old woman said to tell Eva Mae to get on with it.

'Yes,' Eva Mae said, accepting the old woman's remark as sympathy for her situation. 'Ellen, I know you not the kind of person to blame somebody for what their parents have done. You'd be the first one to stand up and side with somebody so being blamed. I know you would. Stand up in the face of opposition least the innocent be wronged. Am I speaking the truth?'

The old woman dared not answer the question. At least not right away, not before she had time to think all round her answer. She wanted first though to draw back from what Eva Mae was showing her about herself, knowing better than to trust this perspective with its hidden motive. She did not deny the general truth of what Eva Mae had said, but since her sister-in-law was waiting to make a specific point once she had concurred, she had to somehow in her reply, in the same instance, agree with and deny what Eva Mae had said about her.

She rocked in her chair to let Eva Mae know she was not refusing to answer, otherwise Eva Mae might be prompted into saying more. No, the old woman wanted her to halt right where she was waiting for an answer.

'Yes,' the old woman said, nodding her head as she rocked. 'I agree. I'm go stand up for what is right and I'm go stand beside the innocent and those that been wronged and I do that Eva Mae cause I stand up for myself first. A person got to know when to do that. Got to know when to do it throughout they life. Otherwise you can't do nothing else that's any good and you ain't go be no good to nobodys else. Since you ask me, I'm a tell it like it is. I'm a tell it just like I see it and believe down through the years.'

Some of Eva Mae's size and colour seemed gone when the old woman looked over at her. And that evening, in her room, looking back on that particular moment, the old woman could see that Eva Mae was sick. This caused her to wonder, as she had always been prone to do when life, in the shape of somebody's actions, presented a puzzle to her. Was it divine justice that had sent Eva Mae to her door so that she could now see that the countless times her sister-in-law had indifferently or even callously caused her sadness and pain had been accounted for? Because Eva Mae had come in the end to care about somebody too and now stood facing something much worse than poverty as time ran out and left her to wonder what would become of Jacob.

After the little girl had shown Jacob how well she could type, he wandered around the little room, taking in all its detail. Eventually, after having selected a book from a shelf, he sat down on the cot and browsed through it.

'What's that?' the little girl asked, without much interest.

Jacob didn't answer for a minute. 'It's a book about prominent Negro men.'

'Oh.' The little girl was even less interested.

'I've never seen this before,' Jacob murmured as he leaned over the book reading here and there.

'Grampy's got lots of books,' the little girl said, as if that explained Jacob's discovery.

'I'd like to borrow it. When will your grandfather be back?'

She nearly said he was away for a long time, but didn't want to tell Jacob a fib. On the other hand, she didn't want to be punished either. 'I'll ask him for you,' she offered too anxiously for Jacob not to suspect something.

He turned away from her and looked around the room again, guessing that it was private, and then returned his gaze to the little girl. She couldn't meet his eyes. Without saying anything, Jacob got up and put the book back where he had found it, then, taking the little girl by the shoulder, led her towards the door. 'All right,' he said finally, 'you ask him for me. Will you do that?'

The little girl nodded and meant it. She would find a way for Jacob to borrow the book.

'Promise?' he asked her.

'Yes,' she answered, looking him squarely in the face.

'Right,' he said and stepped outside.

Jacob and the little girl strolled towards the fence at the back of the orchard. It was a place the little girl knew well. Often, when her grandfather was in his little house writing and did not want to be disturbed, she would wander around here and sometimes, especially in the late afternoon, ended up sitting on top of the fence watching the sun set on the horizon. It was slipping down to there now, spreading a gold-and-red light on the trees and on her and Jacob as they walked towards the fence.

The little girl climbed quickly to the top and sat not far from where Jacob stood, resting his arms, as he gazed out over the field.

'My grandaddy had a shed we used to go to,' he said, his eyes thoughtful and clear in the direct sunlight. 'After I started to get older, he put a little stove in it and I helped him. We used to go in there a lot, even after he got sick.' Jacob nodded, appreciating anew the effort his grandfather had made as his health failed him. 'I always wanted to go there,' Jacob needed to verbalize his appreciation, 'because I used to like him so much when he was there. I don't know why.' Jacob paused and decided to figure out why this was so. 'I think probably because he used to be more like I thought he ought to be. There used to be more of him.' Jacob thought back over what he had just said, then nodded in agreement with it. 'I used to wish he could be like that all the time. He would start to smile and be easy, like the shed was magic or something. I could always tell how he was thinking and feeling. I could just look at him and see it.' Jacob paused for a moment to laugh at himself. 'I had this little thing I would do. I used to pray real, real hard when we were in there, real hard that grandaddy would stay the same all the time and be happy. Be like that all the time.' Jacob laughed again. 'I used to pray with my whole body, like some of those deacons used to do, get stiff from head to toe, I wanted it so bad for grandaddy. And for me. I used to dream about how we'd be walking down the street, feeling like we did inside the shed. That was all I wanted to do. Just walk down the street beside grandaddy.' Jacob raised his eyes a little when he stopped to imagine once more his childish dream. 'The only thing I know that would be like it is flying. Just being able to move and float and turn and just stay still in the air. That's how my dream used to make me feel inside.' Jacob slowly shook his head. 'I dreamed about it and dreamed about it. I used to imagine we went everywhere together feeling like we did in the little shed. Just being glad about things and every time we got ready to leave, I would start to get so tight inside and wondering if this time it would happen and he would stay the way he was. I used to make a deal with myself: if I could make him stay that way for a hour, he would be like that forever. But it would just go away from him. I used to watch it slip off and I would try to say and do all kind of things to keep it. It was like trying to hold on to daylight when night was coming. Slipped away. Gone. And he'd be back to his usual self. He would try to hold on too. I could tell he didn't want to change back. But it was too much for him to do. I understand.' Jacob smiled sadly and wistfully. 'Like trying to hold air in your fist.' He grabbed out then knotted his hand into a fist and released it, exposing its emptiness. Soberly he looked into the sunset. 'I dreamed about it, seeing it in my head, us walking together, till he died and was covered up in the ground. Poor grandaddy.'

The little girl sat quietly on top of the fence, imagining even more vividly than Jacob the happiness he and his grandfather would have shared if his wish had come true. She looked around her, trying to think of something that might still make Jacob have his dream. She wondered if she could offer him her grandfather. She began to fidget with the thought of it but eventually told herself it was one of those ideas of hers that made everybody stare at her in amazement. She didn't want Jacob to do this and so, slumping a little as she let the idea float away, she too turned and stared at the coloured sky.

'Sometimes,' Jacob told her, deciding to speak again after a long silence, 'we would take one of the books he'd bought me and after we'd made a fire and it was burning good, we used to cook on that stove . . . red-eyed peas and rice . . . and while they were cooking, gosh, I can smell them now, I used to read out of the book while he sat there, rolling cigarettes and listening. "That's right," he used to say, nodding through the smoke. "Go ahead and read some more. Don't matter if you don't understand all of it. Read it anyway." And I'd read it. Read till those peas and rice were done.' Jacob dropped his head and laughed. 'Boy we had some good times. We really had some good times.'

The little girl watched him as he lifted his head and, wide-eyed again, gazed into the field.

'Were you sad when he died?' she asked, wondering how she would feel if someone she loved died. She imagined the old woman dying, but this frightened her and she pushed the thought away. She went back to thinking about Jacob's grandfather who was already dead. 'Were you?' she asked again.

'Very, very sad,' he told her. 'Very sad because he was very special. Fine and special.'

'I thought you said he was a funny old man?'

Jacob looked at her and smiled at the expression of doubt that was suddenly on her face. 'He was a funny old man too. He was both.'

'Did he make you laugh?'

'No not like that,' Jacob tried to explain. 'I mean he could be funny. He could make you laugh if he wanted to. No,' Jacob became thoughtful as he talked. 'He had these ideas about things. Opinions he'd worked out for himself. A kind of philosophy.'

'What's that?' The little girl had screwed up her face.

Jacob had to suppress a smile. 'Well, it's sort of trying to explain why life is the way it is. Why things happen and don't happen. Philosophy is something like that.'

'Phil-los-to-fee,' the little girl said slowly, trying to make the word have meaning.

'Phi-los-o-phy,' Jacob corrected.

'When you ask why?' the little girl asked.

Jacob nodded. 'And it's the reason for things. It's how you explain the reason why.' He looked at the little girl to see if she understood what he was saying.

She had screwed up her face again with the effort of trying to follow his words. A moment later her face was clear and she asked, 'What did he do about phi-los-o-phy?'

Jacob nodded at her correct pronunciation, noting that she was pleased with herself. 'Well, he didn't do anything. You don't do anything with philosophy. You think and speak about it. Your ideas.'

'Like what?'

Jacob rubbed his hands over his face to help him explain.

'Well one time, I remember he said . . . well, he ask me did I know why coloured people laugh so much. What happened was we'd seen this coloured man when we were walking down the street one day who was being arrested by a policeman and there were about four or five other coloured men standing around watching. And all of a sudden, when the policeman was about to put him in the car, the man just burst out laughing. He was laughing so hard you could hear him up and down the street. He was buckled over and the policeman had to struggle to get him in the back of the car. When he started laughing like that, all the other men watching started laughing too as if they didn't mind what was happening. and they were laughing with him. That's when grandaddy asked me why do coloured people laugh so much. I said I didn't know, we just did when something was funny. And he said, no, that's not so. Coloured people laugh to keep from going crazy, that they had to laugh at things that were bothering them because there wasn't anything they could do about it. So they had to laugh it off like they don't care. That was why. Do you understand?'

The little girl shook her head, but something that Jacob had said had made her feel very serious inside even though he was talking about laughing. Later on she would ask other people to explain what Jacob and his grandaddy meant, others including the old woman, who dismissed the question so quickly and with so much irritation the little girl knew better than to pursue it or repeat the other things Jacob had told her, though she was never to forget them.

'According to grandaddy,' – Jacob continued to impart his early teachings to her – 'he said laughing also stopped coloured people from choking, otherwise they might strangle on life. He said some people did strangle and nothing the undertakers could do make them look any other way but strangled. Laughing on the other hand loosened up the knots of life so you could breathe but there was nothing you could do about untying yourself. That ignorance had you bind up. Ignorance was waiting to wrap round you the minite you were born. That's how grandaddy used to see things. That's what he believed when he died.'

The little girl thought for a long time about what to say. 'He's probably in heaven now,' she said, imitating the comforting assurance she had so often heard her grandfather use to fill grieving silences.

Jacob looked at her and, hiding his own feelings, nodded his thanks.

Feeling noble and somehow proud that she had carried on in herself something of her grandfather's way, the little girl thought of what else she might say. Jacob, watching her out of the corner of his eye, wondered what kind of woman she would grow into being. He wondered what part of her childhood would influence her most. She would probably be attractive he guessed. Men would look at her and she would know it since already she showed a sexual awareness of herself. She was also bright and quick. He wondered if she had too much imagination. He wondered whether she would be sharp-tongued or coy since it was obvious she would get what she wanted. Then he wondered if either of them had much chance of loosening the ropes his grandfather could see. For a moment he pictured her determined efforts and it caused him to laugh.

'What did you say you were going to be when you grow up?' he asked, still smiling at his imaginary picture of her.

The little girl couldn't remember what she had told Jacob but thought quickly. 'I'm going to write books,' she answered, as if it were the repetition of her earlier reply.

Impressed, Jacob raised his eyebrows. 'Write books!'

'Yes.' Now she was embarrassed by her answer and turned to face the glare from the lowering sun. It blinded her and gave Jacob a chance to study her further.

'Promise me you'll do that,' he asked softly, sending a feeling of sensation through her.

She didn't know what to answer and so shielded her eyes as though watching the sun deafened her to his voice.

'I'll be waiting to read the first one, okay?'

The little girl took a deep breath but couldn't stop herself from shaking.

When the sun had gone down and long shadows had spread across and dimmed the light in the orchard, Jacob and the little girl started to walk back to the house.

'One of these days I want you to write me a letter.' Jacob was a little way ahead as he spoke.

'Why?' The little girl caught up with him and waited for his answer.

'To tell me how you're getting on.'

'Why?' she asked again, wanting a more substantial answer.

'Well, because a lot of people when they grow up end up making a mess out of their lives. Things get them down. I just want to know if you made it.'

'Made what?'

'Made a life for yourself doing what you want.'

'Why do you want to know that?'

'Oh, I don't know. Because of something my grandaddy said one time. He said if life ever got easier for the coloured woman, maybe she be easier on the coloured man.'

'But I'm going to write books,' the little girl reminded him and then skipped on ahead of him. 'And I'm going to travel everywhere in the world,' she called back to him, remembering her earlier ambition. After a while she stopped skipping and waited for him. 'Are you really going to be a doctor?' the little girl asked.

'If I can make it.'

'Will you write and tell me if you become a doctor?'

Jacob stopped walking and looked down at the little girl. It was his turn to wonder. 'All right. If you want me to.'

'Goody,' the little girl said, and began skipping again.

'Why?' Jacob called after her. 'Why do you want to know?'

'Because,' the little girl answered as she continued skipping, 'you can come here and be the doctor instead of ole Dr Green.'

'Where you been to all this time?' the old woman asked as Jacob and the little girl came back on to the front porch.

'In the orchard,' the little girl answered for both of them.

'Well, it's time we started to get ready to go. We got to be getting on back,' Eva Mae said with some effort, and with Jacob's help, pulled herself up from the chair. 'Goodness, I been sitting here a long time.' She laughed as she steadied herself.

Eva Mae was just as effusive in making her departure. The

little girl was smothered to her chest several times and had firmly planted in her hand a silver dollar. She was elated and expressed eternal gratitude to her great-great-aunt.

The old woman remained on the top step from where she waved while the little girl, waving frantically with one hand and holding on to her coin with the other, stood by the side of the road where the car had been. She waved until Eva Mae and Jacob had driven out of sight.

As they were going back inside the house, the old woman asked the little girl to go and get the little leather box off the table on the front porch.

'What is it?' the little girl asked, examining the box closely while she stood by the table.

'Just bring it on here,' the old woman told her. 'And pick up that envelope off my chair. I thought I had it in my pocket.'

The little girl got the envelope and looked at it as well. 'It's got Grampy's name on it.'

'If you not the nosiest somebody I ever come across. Hand it here.'

'What's in the box?'

'Nothing for you to worry about none t'all.' The old woman took the box and the envelope and put them both in her pocket.

'I like Jacob,' the little girl announced. 'And Aunt Eva,' she added, remembering the silver dollar. 'I really like Jacob though.'

'Sure enough,' the old woman said uninterestedly.

'He was telling me about his grandfather and he had a phi-los-o-phy and he knew all about life. That's what a philosophy is.'

'Oh yeah,' the old woman mumbled.

'Yep,' the little girl nodded her head. 'Do you want to know what he said about the coloured man and working at mean jobs?'

'Not at all.'

'Don't you want to know what he said?'

'I reckon I done already heard it. Many a time.' The old woman opened the door to the living room and headed towards her bedroom.

186

'But you just met Jacob,' the little girl trailed after her.

'That's true,' the old woman said, still refusing to be drawn into conversation, but she couldn't help adding, 'Life always got one or two surprises in store for you, even when you get to my age.'

'That's not what Jacob's grandaddy said,' the little girl told her, misunderstanding her last comment.

'Well, when your grandaddy get home,' the old woman looked with relief at her own door, 'ask him to come see me please.'

The little girl nodded, her mind already on something else as she continued to follow behind the old woman. 'Guess what. I'm going to be a writer and write books.'

'Oh yeah, and what you go write books about?'

'About life,' the little girl answered as if this should have been obvious.

The old woman eased herself down on her bed and after a moment looked up at the little girl. 'I don't know if they go believe you.' And before the little girl had a chance to answer she asked her to go and see if her grandmother wouldn't come and loosen her stays. 'I don't know why they feeling so uncomfortable. Must be from having to look at Eva Mae wrapped up so tight in that corset. No wonder she could hardly get up and down and doing all that laughing. One time I thought she was going to bust wide open. That's one person that won't never change.'

The little girl began to tell her what Jacob's grandfather had said about coloured people being bound up, but the old woman shooed her off before she could explain. Unbothered by the old woman's impatience, the little girl went off humming and was already thinking about spending her silver dollar. First, though, she would show it to Bertie Ruth and tell her, describing every detail, about Jacob.

The Spirit Man

Sonny was the first to return from the war. One evening, when the little girl and her grandmother were in the living room listening to a music programme on the radio, someone hammered on the glass pane of the front door and then walked in. It took them a moment to realize the man in the army uniform was Sonny. Then, crying out his name, they rushed up to him and grabbed him as he stood by the door unloading the gear he had carried all the way back from Europe.

They both hugged him at the same time, exclaiming that they didn't know it was him and how different he looked. The little girl's grandmother said she couldn't get over how he had changed so in the two years he was overseas, that his face was fuller and he had a moustache. She said he had grown into a man.

When Sonny, finally free of his bags, was able in turn to put an arm around each of them while they continued to look him over, thrilled and overjoyed at the sight of him, they saw that more in him had changed than just the physical maturings of a young man grown into a man. It created a shyness between them which they tried to pretend did not matter. Perhaps it was the uniform, hard and crackling against their skin. It seemed to hide a part of the Sonny they knew or maybe it was showing them a part of the Sonny they did not know. They made no mention of it as Sonny pulled the two of them closer to him, squeezing them as hard as he had so many times imagined he would if he lived to see any of his family again. He had been in the war, they suddenly remembered, and their feelings for him were flooded with tenderness and tinged with emotions akin to grief for the something that was lost, and they ended their embraces of him making fluttering, consoling touches with their fingertips.

The old woman called from the bedroom, asking what all the fuss was about, but in their excitement no one had heard her. She listened to the voices, trying to make out what was going on, and eventually got herself up from her chair and, leaning heavily on her walking stick, shuffled slowly into the living room.

Sonny was the first to see her as she entered the room and, folding his arms over his chest, appeared to stare in disbelief.

'Gran, that you? Don't tell me you still here. That must be a ghost I see over there. You still hangin on? I don't believe it.'

'Course I'm still here. What do you think? Making all this racket out here. Be enough to wake up the dead anyway.'

The old woman stood squarely and with her feet wide apart, her walking stick by her side. She studied Sonny unblinkingly as he walked over to her.

'Yeah, I'm still here,' she said again more quietly as he slowly embraced her. 'Had to make sure all the children get back safe from that war.'

Sonny continued to hold her, dropping his head on her shoulder.

'Go on,' she said, after she'd touched the back of his head, 'and quit squeezing the life out a me.'

Sonny stepped back and looked down at her.

'I come back safe,' he told her.

'You in one piece then?' She looked him up and down as if to make sure.

'Yeah, I'm in one piece. I wasn't go let nobody put no holes through me. No sir!'

'Well I thank the Lord for that.'

'The Lord! I was the one doing the ducking.'

'Go on and hush up now.'

'And there was some close calls out there. If the Lord had any sense He wasn't no way around.'

'Go on now, before I take this stick to you, talking like that. I might be getting old, but I can still swing this stick when I want to.' She lifted it to show him.

'Yes m'am,' Sonny said with mock subservience. 'Cause I didn't go all that way and got shot at to come back here and get killed with your stick.'

'Well then you better behave yourself, specially since you say you in one piece.'

Sonny stepped up to her again and kissed her loudly on the top of her head.

'Didn't you hear me? Go on and stop all this foolishness.' She tried not to smile as she pointed to an armchair in the corner of the room and slowly, more slowly than Sonny remembered, he walked her over to it.

They stayed up late listening to Sonny talk about the war, though in fact he talked more about the countries they'd gone through rather than the fighting, describing some of the people he'd met, the rapturous reception they were given. Both coloured and white alike, Sonny said, astonishing them, were treated the same by white people over there. He told them they even invited them into their houses.

The little girl sat spellbound listening to Sonny describe his experiences in one country and then another. To her, they had just been coloured shapes on the globe in her classroom, but now, her mind was full of her own imaginings as she pictured from what her cousin said the people who lived overseas.

She didn't know she was asleep, nor did anyone else, until she nearly fell off her chair. She tried to convince them that she was still awake as she was led away to her bedroom because they were still talking, her grandfather, sitting composedly and erect in a corner of the sofa and Sonny, his hands deep in his pockets, shifting from one foot to the other in front of the mantelpiece. She wanted to say good night to him but he wouldn't have heard her anyway, he was so preoccupied by what they were talking about. Suddenly he interrupted the little girl's grandfather.

'This is where I disagree,' Sonny shook his head adamantly. 'The coloured soldier's not go put up with it. Not any more. He's not going back. No! Not to be treated that way. Wait for what? What for?' Sonny shook his head again. 'It go be different. Got to be. They owe it to us. No siree we not waiting. No siree.'

Undressing in her bedroom, the little girl wanted to know what they were talking about. It upset her that Sonny, who had been smiling and saying wonderful things a little while before, seemed angry about something. She was told not to worry about it and to get into bed and go to sleep, which she couldn't help doing, despite her concern for her cousin.

Sonny had a few weeks remaining in the army and reported to a camp just outside Columbia to finish off his time before being discharged from the army. When he could, however, he would hitchhike to Orangeburg and spend a few hours there since his own home was too far away.

They all knew how he was longing to return to his family and take up the farming he had reluctantly left when he was drafted, upon turning eighteen, in the middle of the war. His older brother had been called up earlier and was sent to the Pacific. They had not seen each other for four years. So it was of his family and his home that he talked. He told the little girl – who was always a loyal and willing audience, allowing him, as he needed to, to think out loud about his youth which he now realized was behind him forever – about the good times he and his brother and her father used to have before they had to go away to the war. The little girl loved to hear him talk about their exploits and adventures. It helped her to imagine what her father was like. She didn't remember him very well, though she loved him desperately, perhaps even more than before, especially when she sat before the photograph of him in his uniform. But she couldn't remember much about him. Before he left to go back to Columbia, Sonny would always tell her that her father would be home soon, but she couldn't remember what their home used to be like.

She would try to picture it and would wish fervently each day that that was the day her father would return. And sometimes, hopeful about the next day, she would lie awake at night describing to herself their reunion. She planned it a dozen different ways particularly how she would greet her father. She wanted very much to show him how grown-up she had become. But she also wanted to run up to him as fast as she could as soon as she saw him and this overwhelming desire always caused her plans to get all muddled in the end.

The thought of seeing her father after three years would

send a rash of goose pimples over her and sometimes, for hardly any reason at all, she would burst into tears and couldn't explain to anybody what the matter was. Her grandmother and the old woman would be left wondering what had come over her when she ran away from them.

Alone and hurting for something she couldn't even explain to herself, the little girl cried big, hot tears that would drop out of her eyes no matter how hard she tried to stop them and no matter how tightly she held her eyes closed. It made her want to hide away from everything, though somehow she always ended up sitting on the back steps and, blurry-eyed, would stare out over the bare, dry field of early autumn. She would sit, hardly breathing, trying to blend in with the total stillness of the landscape that seemed more flat and empty as each day drew them closer to winter. Sitting there, she would begin to accept that one more day was passing without her father and without her mother and their home because she could see what she was feeling inside spreading over the fields. It helped to soothe the confusion within her until it was as though the more still and quiet the fields became, the more they waited with her. And she told herself that whatever it was that dried the fields in the wake of winter also knew when it was she would see her father again.

'I believe you must be gettin a few growin pains. That must be what it is,' the old woman said, eyeing the little girl as she gloomily and without purpose wandered one way and then another in the bedroom.

'You think that's what it is got you so grumpy round here?' she asked when the little girl made no comment.

She had her back to the old woman and had stopped to study the glass dial on the face of the radio, slowly turning the knobs as if she might tune in an answer to the old woman's questions.

'Whatever it is,' the old woman continued, 'sure done make you touchy.' She waited a moment longer then spoke again. 'Seem to me everybody have to go through changes. Sometimes they don't always understand what is happening to them and it makes them kinda impatient-actin. But in the end it's nothing but a few growin pains. That's all it is. Otherwise,' the old woman paused and scrutinized the little girl very carefully, 'otherwise if it is something else, then they ought to tell somebody about it and get it off their chest.'

The little girl sighed heavily as if the old woman's words were weighing her down. Then, still not saying anything, she walked over to the dresser which was her favourite place in the room unless the old woman allowed her to take the box out from under the bed. And since she didn't feel amenable enough to ask for the box she would have to play with the little china figures and hope that everything else around her would go away.

The little girl leaned her arms on the dressing table and looked closely at the delicately painted little figures that decorated the table top. The old woman hadn't ever paid them much attention, but the little girl would now spend hours standing at the dresser pretending that the figures were real people. She knew the details of everyone of them but as she looked at them now, trying very hard, she couldn't make them become real people. Even when she picked one of them up and swirled it around, it was still cold, a hard little thing in her hands with a painted face that didn't resemble people at all. It made a hollow sound when she reluctantly set it back down on the dresser. She stood there staring forlornly at their little reflections in the mirror.

'Anyway,' she said almost belligerently, 'what are growing pains?' The little girl was looking at the old woman in the mirror, her arms still folded on top of the dresser.

'What did you say?' The old woman had turned away a while ago and was lost in her own thoughts. Slowly she focused her eyes on the little girl.

'What's growing pains?' Now she was staring at herself in the mirror.

'Well,' the old woman pursed her lips and thought. 'Everybody gets different kinds of growin pains. Depends on what's growin. Say for instance it's your legs, getting long and skinny. Something like that. Then they might keep getting all tangled up together and always be bumping you into things. Other times, it might be that you just starting to think different about one thing and another. When things don't seem to look the

193

same any more. You might start to get all absent-minded and not hear people when they talking to you. Because you so busy thinking. Then you have growing pains inside where nobody can see what's going on. It's private like.'

'But how do you know I got growing pains?'

'Cause I seen it a heap of times. In your grandmamma, in your daddy and now I'm pretty certain that's what I see in you.'

'Well, when is it going to go away?' Allowing frustration to rise, the little girl walked away from the mirror and over to the foot of the bed. She stood there, not knowing what to do with herself.

'Oh it don't last too long,' the old woman told her in a tone that suggested she shouldn't be too bothered by it. 'It all depends. One day you got it. The next day you get up and it's gone.'

The little girl was staring up at the picture of her great-grandfather. Although her grandmother had put the picture there when she was preparing the old woman's room, it had rarely been acknowledged and he was not often talked about. The old woman watched her as she looked with new interest at the picture, remembering to finish her explanation.

'Cause you be through growing into whatever it was you had to grow into. Everybody's got to go through things,' the old woman continued, though her voice was fading as her attention was caught by the picture on the wall. 'All through life,' she added. 'It's not something you can pretend don't happen. Whatever it is, you got to face up to it.' The old woman nodded, more to herself than the little girl.

'Did my great-grandfather love his children?' the little girl asked suddenly, causing the old woman to wonder if she had heard correctly.

'I believe so,' she finally answered. 'Yes, in his own way, I believe he did.' She wasn't sure if this was the answer the little girl was looking for but she felt it was the closest to the truth.

'Then why did he go away and leave them? If he loved them?'

'Well that's not to say he didn't love them. You sure are

194

asking a bunch of strange questions,' the old woman said, hoping this would provoke an explanation from the little girl.

'Well I don't like him,' the little girl announced, looking straight at the picture as if it could hear her.

The old woman didn't know what to say. 'Well, it seem to me,' she began, though still puzzled by what the little girl had said, 'that since you didn't never know your great-grandaddy and don't know all that much about him, that's a strange thing to say.'

'No it isn't,' the little girl snapped.

'Well whether you bothered by something or not is no reason to start blaming people and getting cross no matter what it is . . .'

'He wasn't nice so I don't care.'

'Now just hold on a minute. You just hold on one minute cause if you go on acting the way you are and treating people like you don't have no respect for them, then you go turn into a nasty person and nobody like a nasty person.' The old woman pointed her finger towards the little girl and continued, 'And furthermore nobody go want to be around you. Now you just stop and think about how you been acting around here lately and see if you can't do better.'

'I don't like him,' the little girl cried out before she could stop herself. 'I don't like him at all.' She was stone-faced in her admission but her voice had become shaky. She pressed her mouth inwards and held it tight and without another word turned on her heels and walked out of the old woman's room. Staring straight ahead, determined to ignore everything, she stepped past her grandparents and went out of the house.

'Well sir!' the old woman muttered when she could find her tongue. 'What in the world done come over her?' She shook her head, amazed at the outburst. 'I declare if I know.'

The old woman sat for a long time trying to make sense out of the little girl's behaviour. Thinking back over their conversation, she searched for some sign of the trouble because she knew now that the little girl was deeply troubled. The old woman shook her head, baffled and unable to come up with any explanation. It was as if something had happened to her and for the first time since the old woman had come to know her, nothing she said or they talked about had led them to the problem. It was wearying, the old woman told herself, admitting that these days she was feeling about as dried out as the leaves tumbling down from the trees outside and no more able than they were to make any difference to what was going on around her.

She shook her head once again and finally blamed it all on the war. 'Things done got so different,' she murmured. 'Everything's changing so fast. All the time. A person can't keep up with it no more.' The old woman watched through the window as some bright yellow leaves fluttered slowly down to the ground. She just wasn't able any more to understand all the things going on around her. If she tried to think about it, it only made her confused. Anyway, it didn't seem worth the trouble. 'Course I never did expect to live to see some of what I done see,' she said out loud, needing to release from her mind some of the weighty thoughts that were gathering there. And also the sound of her own voice, familiar and unchanged, gave her some comfort. 'No wonder all of it don't make no sense,' she rationalized. 'Besides a person's not meant to understand things that going to go on after them. Not unless they some kind a prophet who suppose to warn people. Otherwise you not suppose to understand or know what's go happen. All these things like atom bombs dropping and people turning into smoke. Nothing left of them but smoke! And all those Jewish people. How a person suppose to make sense out a something like that? I sure don't know what to make of it. Seem like everybody done gone crazy. Even my own kin. There's Sonny, just grown into a man. Ain had time to know much about nothing and he out there say he demanding they give the coloured man the vote or else. And saying coloured children ought to be going to white schools and things like that. What go happen to him, he out there talking like that so any white person can hear all this crazy talk? Lord he sure don't know what he doing and I don't know for him. What is things coming to? No, I don't know. It tires you out. That's all I know, it tires you out and you still don't know nothing a t'all. The troubles of the world. Lord, the troubles of the world.'

The old woman shut her eyes tight for a moment, but

whether to stop thinking these disturbing thoughts or to seek solace from God, she did not know. Opening her eyes again, she stared deeply into the distance, stretching her eyesight as though she needed to see further than she had ever seen before until, sightless, her vision merged into eternity where she saw nothing and everything and her room around her was just an illusion.

When eventually she leaned back into her chair and looked again at the garden, blinking occasionally at the sunlight, she reckoned that this was one of the richest autumns she could remember.

The little girl had marched herself away from the house and stopped only when she came upon the fence that divided the garden from the field, and with the orchard between her and the house she felt well hidden from view.

By the time she had arrived at the fence, where she stood wondering what to do, the little girl had transferred her anger from the picture on the wall to the old woman who was mean enough to blame her and to say she wasn't nice. The worst part of it, the little girl was thinking, and it made her indecisive about what to do with herself, was that the old woman had said people wouldn't like her and didn't want to be around her. Well, maybe nobody liked her either, the little girl retaliated, and wished she had said this to the old woman's face. 'Shut up, you old lady, you mean old lady. You boonkie.' The little girl called the old woman the worst name she could think of, her mouth tight and her hands balled into fists. She kicked the fence wishing she could punch it with her hand as well.

She thinks she knows so much – the little girl had turned her back to the fence and in agitation was pressing against it while continuously digging her heel into the ground. She doesn't know about anything. So how could she know people didn't want to be around her. 'I bet my daddy would be so mad if I told him. Boy, he would be so angry at her for saying that. I'm going to tell him what she said as soon as he gets back so he can go and shout at her. She doesn't know anything.' The little girl's voice had caught in her throat on a lump that had begun to ache. She put her hand around her neck and swallowed but the lump only hurt more. 'As soon as my daddy gets back, I'm going to tell him everything.' She was speaking to herself again, struggling to stop the lump from getting any larger. Her eyesight blurred and she turned towards the fence and pressed her head against it. When she did so, she thought of Jacob, and between him and her father and the unkind words, the lump finally got too large and, still talking to herself, she started to cry. 'I'm gonna tell my daddy everything. Soon as I tell him about the dog, he's gonna go get his gun and go shoot that dog, till he's dead. He'll be so mad and he might even shoot the man too. He'll be so angry.'

The little girl stopped crying and imagined her father getting his gun down from over the mantelpiece and standing before the dog. And when it got up and started to growl, her daddy would aim the gun right at the dog and shoot it down. And she would watched the dog lying on the ground, howling and whining cause it was shot.

Sniffling, her crying abated since she told herself what would happen once her father returned, the little girl began to recall the scene each morning, walking to school and past the house of a white man who would sometimes be waiting in the doorway behind the screen and tell his dog to go chase her. She would stand, paralysed with fear, once she heard the dog barking as it ran out of the yard towards her. Crying out against whatever might happen, she stood with her legs pressed together, holding her books over her chest as the dog, growling, encircled her. She knew if she ran, it would chase her, snapping at her legs. She could feel him on her heels, ready to tear a piece of flesh from her. And so she stood, frozen, squashing herself together, as the dog, obeying the calls from its master, moved around her, daring her to run.

Again she imagined her father aiming at and shooting the dog as it ran towards her. Then it wouldn't snap at her legs any more and hound her any more, showing her its teeth and the red inside its mouth. He would just be lying there, twitching, about to die. She had seen a dead dog before. Someone had shot one of the bird dogs by mistake when they'd gone hunting with her father in the woods behind the farm. And later in the day she had gone with one of the farm hands who had to dig a grave and bury it. The dog's mouth was partly open and a little bit of blood had dribbled out of the side of it. Its eyes were half-open, staring and as still as anything she had ever seen. When she had looked closely into them she could tell that they couldn't see anything and the dog was just the same when they dragged it off and buried it. Only its head moved to one side when they pushed it into the grave. That's how dead she wanted her father to shoot that white man's dog. Then it wouldn't matter how many times he told it to go get her, it would just lie there. No matter what the white man said, that dog wouldn't be able to move or do anything.

It was only her morning walk to school that the little girl had come to dread. The dog didn't bother her in the afternoon because the man had gone to work. He worked in the liquor store on the way into town and, when he was gone, the gate to the yard was closed and often the dog was nowhere around.

Sometimes, when the little girl was walking home, she spied the wife of the liquor store man and she would have a little boy with her. The little boy had started to learn to walk and the wife would stand him up somewhere in the yard and then step back and, holding out her arms, would call for him to come to her. Often the liquor store man's wife would kneel on the ground clapping for the little boy's attention when he wanted to play or look at something else. Once as she walked by, the little boy had seen her and instead of going to his mother had toddled over to the fence. He grabbed hold of the fence, pleased with himself, and, smiling, lifted his face, showing her a few teeth when she looked over at him. He garbled something at her, but she had already looked away because the liquor store man's wife was yelling at him to come back from the fence that minute.

The little girl supposed that the liquor store man's wife must have told him because the next morning the gate was open and the dog met her even before she could pass the house. This time, as terrified as she was, she looked over at the man, seeing the outline of his white undershirt against the screening, and felt spawned inside her a round, hard hatred for the liquor store man. It kept her panic at bay as she waited for the dog to be called off her and watched it, tail wagging and satisfied, go back to its master. She walked on to school thinking about the round, hard little ball she could feel as definitely as if she were rolling it around in her hand. It was as hard as a stone and she wondered what she would do with it. There was only one thing she didn't like about it: she wished it wasn't so heavy.

For days afterwards, she imagined what, if she could toss the steel ball back and forth in her hands, she should do to the dog and the liquor store man. She wanted to do something terrible, more terrible than shooting, and one afternoon when she heard her grandmother telling someone how an unfortunate woman had badly burned her hands and arms with lye while making soap, she decided what she would do. It would fix that ole liquor store man and teach him to sic his dog on her.

The little girl had spent the rest of the afternoon looking for the bottle of lye which she knew was kept somewhere around the house. After searching everywhere that she could think of, she asked her grandmother, prepared with an excuse about wanting to know where it was so she didn't accidently get a hold of it and burn herself. Her grandmother said there was no danger of that because it was locked up in a cupboard in the shed.

After checking to make sure the cupboard was locked, the little girl accepted that she would have to delay her plan. But once she had gotten hold of the lye, she would keep the bottle in her school bag and the next time the little boy came to the fence, she would take it out and pour it on his face.

She felt the hard, round ball weighing against something inside her as she imagined what she was going to do. It seemed to her that it was growing larger, taking up more space. In a way it was like the lump that caught in her throat. Both had pushed against and squeezed something out of the way, leaving no room for the something to be whatever it had been, making her feel sad about losing from herself whatever the something was.

The lump and the heavy ball weighed down on her so that her shoulders were making it hard for her to breathe. She pressed her head into the fence again, as if this might relieve some of the tightness within her. But when she tried to take a deep breath, her chest heaved and shook as though she had been crying for a long, long time, like the night after her mother had boarded the train for Philadelphia.

She shut her eyes and tried to think of her father again. 'He's gonna get that man,' the little girl mumbled, and was unconvinced by the tone of her voice because she was remembering how her father had said she was grown-up enough to look after herself. And knowing what was expected of her, she had nodded. That was what he had wanted her to do, look after herself and be like him. And she remembered how she had been embarrassed at how close she had come to grabbing hold of him while he was saying goodbye. She had caught herself just in time and instead had nodded at what he had said while hiding from him and her grandparents the feelings that had nearly surfaced in front of all of them.

'All right then,' he had told her. 'You can take care of yourself. That's what you go do any?'

She had nodded again, her mouth pressed together, and would have burst wide open rather than let the lump escape with the sound of her voice. She had stayed like that while her father had swung himself into the car, pressed his foot down on the accelerator and was gone.

She was supposed to look after herself, she told the fence, but the man in the liquor store had caused her to fail because she didn't know what to do about him. The fear of the dog running and barking towards her took hold of her imagination and frightened her hatred into impotence, leaving her as vulnerable as before. Her last defence had left her. Maybe the liquor store man would still send the dog after her even if she threw the lye on his son because maybe he didn't like his son and wouldn't care.

No matter what, the little girl told herself as she knotted her entire body against the fence, she wasn't going to tell her father. She wasn't going to tell anybody.

The cold weather had come earlier than usual that year. People asked themselves and each other when was the last time they had had frost before the end of October. And while the collard greens and other winter vegetables were ready for cooking earlier than they would have been, it was a hard chore getting in the last of the cotton with cold, stiff hands and backs straining to keep warm and weighed down with damp cotton.

They decided to go ahead with the butchering which had originally been planned to take place after the little girl's father returned from overseas. But an air of uncertainty, whether brought on by the early frost or some other unknown force, had spread over the house and although no one spoke to the little girl about what had caused it, she knew eventually that it had to do with more than the cold. Nor could the feeling of alarm that was growing in her be blamed on growing pains.

Saturday, the day of the butchering, dawned frosty and bright. The sky was blue enough for them to comment on as the little girl's grandparents sat down to a light breakfast, after completing chores and finishing off last-minute details before leaving the house for the long day in the country.

The little girl had become increasingly excited as she waited for them to finish eating so they could be on their way. There was a lot to look forward to and she consciously pushed aside her worries, at least to some place in the back of her mind, in her desire to enjoy the day. She was especially looking forward to playing with her cousins since they would be able to do pretty much as they liked. She knew from past times that the grown-ups would be too busy preparing the meat and having a good time themselves to take much notice of what the children were doing. There would be many of her relatives there and friends and neighbours would come by and visit. And of course there would be a lot of food, prepared with great care during the previous days: sweet potato pie and potato salad and biscuits. There would also be collard greens cooked with the remainder of last year's smoked bacon and rice to be eaten along with the pieces of fresh pork that would be barbequed outside throughout the day. And inside would be a big pot of chitlins, bubbling its aroma everywhere and steaming up the kitchen where the little girl had her earliest memories.

The day's events would stretch well into the night, where amid the smoke and glowing red ashes of the deserted fires, the children would chase each other and play spooky games that were only scary enough to thrill in the early darkness of autumn evenings.

★

202

The old woman was slow to get up and the little girl's grandmother had been in her room twice to see about her. Finally, she came out to tell them that her mother was too unwell to make the journey to Bowman.

The little girl slumped with disappointment. Why did she have to get sick today, she asked herself, greatly annoyed with the old woman. She sat dejectedly in the kitchen while they went into the bedroom to discuss what should be done.

They concluded that the old woman had just taken a chill because of the sudden cold weather. It had made her listless and slow in her movements and so, she said, she just wasn't up to her usual self. But that was all; otherwise, she was all right.

In the end, they decided to telephone Miss Pelzer, a friend of the little girl's grandmother, who had been a nurse until she had retired to look after her own mother before she'd died. Miss Pelzer readily agreed to come over and to spend the day with the old woman and attend to her needs. The little girl was so relieved that she rushed up to greet Miss Pelzer when she marched through the front door.

They moved around the house quietly as they put on coats and gathered together the things they were taking to the country. Just before they were about to leave, the little girl tiptoed to the old woman's room and very carefully pushed open the door and poked her head inside. She had suddenly felt in a forgiving mood and was prepared to renew her old relationship with the old woman. Several days had passed since her outburst and she had had few words for the old woman. In the busy and slightly confused air leading up to Thanksgiving and the hoped-for arrival of her father, she had slipped the notice of the grown-ups and had spent most of her time outside the house doing as she pleased. But because she had something to look forward to again, she felt generous towards the old woman as she pushed the door further and stepped inside.

The old woman was lying under several more quilts and seemed to be sleeping. The little girl glanced around the room which she had never seen purposely darkened during the day-time. It seemed quieter than usual, even with the sound of the old woman's breathing. Feeling a little disappointed, but knowing that she shouldn't awaken the old woman, the little girl slowly closed the door and walked away.

The sun had risen above the woods that bordered the back of the farm and was sparkling through the tops of the trees and down on to the crusty ground as the men, prepared for the day's work, headed towards the pigsty. By mid-morning, the sun had warmed everything and the smell of the singed animals, fresh blood and meat mingled with the smoke from the fires and the heady moisture of autumn mould. The day was going according to plan and, with the hardest work just about over, the men were in a good mood. Their laughter and shouts to each other were high-spirited and the children, sensing the mood of well-being, ran about with even greater enthusiasm and frolicking behaviour.

The little girl played nonstop with her cousins. They ran and chased each other and were soon down to their shirt sleeves and barefoot. They hadn't been given much to do because they were too excited to pay attention and in the end, it was easier to keep them out of the way. They were ordered, several times, to put their jackets and shoes back on, but they didn't.

Once when they paused to catch their breath, the little girl was shown a new litter of puppies which had been born underneath the house. She and her cousin, Sam, crawled up to them and watched for a long time as they curled and squirmed around their mother, sucking then dozing, one on top the other.

The little girl's cousin told her that another puppy had been born blind and had been drowned. She was sad when he told her this. Her cousin said he had been sad too and had asked his father not to drown it. They both looked on in silence at the remaining puppies.

Having thought about it philosophically, Sam explained to her that a bird dog wasn't any good if it was blind. He repeated what he'd heard his father say. 'You can't train it and it's no use to you.'

Feeling highly moral as she disputed the remarks of a grown-up the little girl turned to her cousin. 'But they don't drown people if they're blind, do they?'

'I don't know that,' her cousin responded matter-of-factly as he nudged up closer to the puppies and rested his chin on his hands. 'Maybe they do and maybe they don't.' They both thought about this, trying to remember if they'd ever heard anything about what had been done to a blind person. They both remembered Mr Bamburger at the same time. But he was only blind in one eye and went around painting houses so he didn't count.

'Maybe they do drown em,' her cousin finally concluded.

'Probably right,' the little girl concurred.

The little girl told her cousin about the liquor store man. Sitting underneath the house in semi-darkness, she didn't feel as though she was letting her father down.

Her cousin said he thought her father would get his shotgun down and go straight out and shoot that nasty ole dog. He said that's what he would do. Go right out and shoot it. With his BB rifle he added.

The little girl said she didn't know he had a BB rifle and he told her he had a brand-new one from Sears and Roebuck. He'd picked it out of the catalogue. They crawled out from under the house to go and see the rifle.

Later in the day, the little girl's cousin shot a sparrow with his new gun. It had been perched on the telegraph line near the pole out by the road. They had moved very cautiously up to it and her cousin had taken aim, fired and the sparrow fell to the ground, almost at their feet.

They had tried to pluck and gut it, but it was so skinny and the feathers were so hard to pull out that in the end Sam had hurled the bird across the road and into one of the fields.

For some reason, and she didn't know why, the little girl felt very guilty about the sparrow. The grown-ups had been amused by their efforts to cook it over one of the open fires, but had also been pleased that her cousin's aim had been so accurate. Her cousin had been quite proud of himself and bragged about what he would shoot the next time.

Throughout the remainder of the day, the little girl would picture the sparrow sitting on the telegraph line, chirping unsuspectingly as they approached it. She knew, within herself, that if the old woman had been there, she could have told them they had done wrong to kill the sparrow, no matter what the grown-ups had said. She would have called them over to her and quietly explained to them why they shouldn't have done it.

The little girl knew they shouldn't have shot the sparrow, but she didn't know why and although she didn't understand the disturbing feeling she was left with, she knew that if the old woman had talked to her about what they had done, the disturbing feeling would have gone away. She didn't want any of these feelings inside her today because they weighed her down and stopped her from being aware of what was going on around her. It was as if something separated her from her cousins and only she knew about it. In desperation, she began to run about again, shouting louder and playing harder than the others, trying to outplay the heavy feeling that had slipped almost automatically inside her stomach.

The sense of separation stayed with her and prevented the day from being like the other special days she could remember. She wished for a while that the old woman had come and was sitting in a corner of the kitchen enjoying the warmth from the stove, and as the day drew to an end she became anxious to get back to Orangeburg and see how her great-grandmother was. At one time, when she heard some of the grown-ups discussing how warm the day had turned out to be, she wondered if Miss Pelzer would know to put the old woman's chair outside so she could sit in the sun for a little while.

Late that night they returned from the country. The little girl had slept in the back of the car and felt cold and tired when they got out. There were things to unload from the car and she stumbled back and forth to the house trying to help until she was sent off to bed. She climbed in without even washing and fell asleep instantly.

The following morning she was awakened by the sound of voices which was unusual because Sunday mornings were always quiet. It was a time when her grandfather would be thinking about his sermon and didn't have much to say to anybody and her grandmother would be carefully dressing herself for church.

The little girl sat up in bed and listened. She could hear her grandmother's voice, but could not make out the others. She got out of bed and walked down the hallway and stood at the entrance to the living room. Her grandmother, in a house-dress which she never wore on Sundays, was talking to Miss Pelzer, who had returned and this time was wearing her uniform. The little girl heard footsteps behind her and turned to see Dr Green.

'Hey there, Blackie.' Dr Green called her by his nickname for her which normally would have annoyed her. But the little girl stood looking at him uncomprehendingly.

'What's the matter. The cat got your tongue?'

She shook her head.

'What in the world you got on your face?' He lifted her chin up and studied it. 'Look like dirt. You been in bed sleepin with all that dirt on your face?' He stepped back and looked at her from head to foot. 'Could start a farm with all the dirt on you.'

Before the little girl could think of something to say, Dr Green had walked past her and into the room.

'Everybody decide to get sick on Sunday morning. I got to get on over to St Matthews, one of the Pearson's gone down with something or nother.'

'Who that is, old Mr Pearson?' Miss Pelzer asked with interest. 'I saw his son last week and he said he wasn't feeling too good.'

'Well it's the daughter.' Dr Green dropped his hat on his head.

'Wonder what could be ailin her?' Miss Pelzer's interest had heightened.

'Keep her comfortable,' Dr Green addressed the little girl's grandmother. 'That's about it. Try and keep her drinking. Broth and whatnot. She not go eat too much. When your time come, it come. Ain't that right?'

Nobody answered him. The little girl wanted to ask him, when what time had come, but he was out of the door before she could think how to phrase her question. She asked her grandmother instead as she sat down wearily in a chair, but Miss Pelzer, who had sat on the chair's arm, was saying how blessed that dear old lady was to be here and with her own people to look after her where it was peaceful and quiet.

Neither one of them heard the little girl. Miss Pelzer was patting her grandmother's arm as she continued talking.

'And she's not in no pain. Now that's another blessing. That's what you got to do. Count your blessings. Thank the Lord he see fit to do things this way. Cause that's something to give you strength. When you think of some of the suffering I seen. Lord have mercy. Now, now, now.' She patted her grandmother's arm again and got up. 'Let me go and see about making you some hot tea. Then you can go right to your room and get yourself some rest. Cause that's what you need right now, some rest. You can't be running yourself down, not at a time like this. No. That's what I'm here for.'

'What's the matter?' The little girl had begun to tremble as she stood in the cold room listening to Miss Pelzer.

Surprised to hear a voice, her grandmother's friend looked over towards her. 'Hello there. How you this morning? Now you go promise me not to bother your grandmother cause she been up all night and she about to drop from tiredness. You go be a good little girl ain't you?' Miss Pelzer smiled a big smile and went smartly into the kitchen.

The little girl walked over to her grandmother who was still sitting in the chair, her arms folded over her chest and seemingly lost in thought.

The little girl leaned towards her and nearly whispered, 'What's the matter?' The shivering had gotten worse and she held her arms over her body.

'Mamma's not doing too well,' her grandmother answered from a distance.

'Is she sick?'

'I'm afraid so.'

'Is she going to die?'

'She's not doing well a'tall.'

The little girl stood beside her grandmother, not knowing what else to say and feeling even more the chill that was on the house.

'Where's Grampy?' she suddenly thought to ask. Maybe he could do something she had begun to think. Sometimes when people who were sick asked him to pray for them, they got better and afterwards in church they said his prayers had made them well again. Maybe he would help her great-grandmother.

'Where's Grampy?' she asked again because her grandmother had not heard her.

'I believe he's gone out to his shed.'

Miss Pelzer came back into the room and took charge. She reminded the little girl again that she must be good and quiet and sent her off to wash herself.

The old woman's door was halfway open and although the curtains had been drawn back and the blind was up, the little lamp on the table beside the bed was lit. The lamp shade had been tilted at an angle which caused the light to shine down along the patterned quilt on the old woman's bed, brightening the colours on the quilt while the old woman's head and shoulders were dimmed by the long shadow of the shade.

She lay with her face towards the wall and her hands, partly visible underneath the long-sleeved gown, were resting on top of the covers. As the little girl walked towards her, she slowly turned her head and looked down the bed at her. She watched her for a few moments then, as if tired, closed her eyes.

Without making a sound, the little girl stepped up to the bed and looked down at the old woman who was lying so still and looked so different. It seemed to the little girl as if she had become smaller and her face was tiny against all the pillows that had been placed around her head.

The little girl was stunned by the transformation which did not seem possible. She continued to look at the old woman, trying to make her appear the way she used to be. For a moment she wondered if the woman in the bed was really her great-grandmother or if they'd made a mistake and put somebody else in her place. Then she thought that if the old woman would get out of bed then she would look like herself again.

'What's the matter?' she finally asked because she needed to know. Her voice was hoarse and she cleared her throat which seemed too loud a noise in the silence of the room.

The old woman did not answer her.

She put one hand on the edge of the cover and leaned over

slightly. 'What's the matter?' she asked in a loud, hopeful whisper. 'Are you sick?' She was prepared to believe whatever the old woman said to her. She wanted her to say something so she could hear her voice. She wanted her to explain what was bothering her and say that it would probably go away in a little while. This was what she would say when she had aches and pains before and she and the little girl would wait until whatever it was had gone and she was beginning to feel a little better.

'Are you sick?' the little girl asked in a louder, less considerate voice that shook a little at the edges.

The old woman opened her eyes and looked at her. The little girl watched her face and waited for her to say something.

'Come over here.' The old woman's voice was barely audible but the little girl heard it clearly and leaned further over the bed.

'I'm here,' the little girl told her in case she didn't know where she was. She moved even closer to her to make sure she could see her.

The old woman looked into her face, her eyes moving from one part of it to another while the little girl held herself absolutely still, waiting for the old woman to speak again.

'What's that you got all over your face?'

The little girl put her hand to her face as if to find out what it was.

'What you done got?'

'Nothing,' the little girl answered, but wondered if she had caught some disease somehow associated with her great-grandmother. She rubbed her face for clues.

'You got it on your hands.' The old woman was looking at her hand as it moved over her face.

The little girl looked at her hands.

'That's nothing,' she said, no longer worried. 'That's just some dirt. I just got some dirt on me. I was playing,' she explained, ready to tell the old woman all about the day before now that they were talking to each other.

'Oh,' the old woman said slowly. 'That's what it is.' She lifted her hand up from the cover and dropped it down softly on the little girl's. 'Mmmm.' Very lightly, the old woman stroked the little girl's hand and then closed her eyes.

'How come they lettin you play in your nightgown.'

The little girl looked down at herself. 'I just got up. I been in the bed sleeping. It's morning time,' she explained. 'I wasn't playing in my nightgown. I just got up.'

'Oh I see,' the old woman stroked her hand again. 'You better not let your grandmamma see you. Go on now. Get yourself washed up. You go get dress for Sunday School?'

The little girl hadn't thought about Sunday School and so she didn't answer.

The old woman took hold of her hand. 'I want you to do something for me.' She paused. 'You listening?'

The little girl nodded and the old woman sensed this with her eyes closed; she continued. 'When you get to church, go up to Miss Green.' She paused again. 'Tell her for me that I'm sorry not to be there to read the Sunday School verse.' She paused, then continued. 'But I prepared my lesson just the same. Can you remember all that.'

Again the little girl nodded.

'All right now. You go on and get washed up and dressed.'

The little girl started to go out of the room. She had wanted to talk more to the old woman. She meant to ask her how long it would be before she was better, but instead she was doing what the old woman had told her because maybe that was all part of what had to be done to make her well. She would go to church and tell Miss Green what her great-grandmother had said and maybe she would come back with a message for the old woman. She walked out of the room unsatisfied, but despite that doing for the first time what she had been told, without making any comments.

'That's right,' the old woman said as she left the room.

Her grandfather never talked in the car when they were driving to church on Sunday mornings because he would still be thinking about his sermon and preparing himself to preach. The little girl's grandmother had long ago got into the habit of carrying on a conversation by herself with the little girl occasionally supplying a missing word or phrase or even a missing piece of information omitted from her grandmother's commentary. Usually when she tried to add more than a few words to the conversation she was given a disapproving stare by the old woman who sat on the back seat beside her. The little girl resented being made to hush up but the old woman compensated by passing her a peppermint sweet from an old brown paper bag she kept in the corner of her handbag, which she would periodically replenish with peppermints specifically for eating in church. It had made the inside of her handbag and her handkerchief, which she would also pass to the little girl to blow her nose with, smell strongly of peppermint. The little girl thought of this, realizing that there would be no candy and no gossipy conversation for her to listen to as she sat silently beside her grandfather, who in a world of his own was cruising down the road to Eautawville.

The little girl looked out of the window as she passed field after field of harvested crops. Here and there at the corners of the cotton field, she could see stalks with tufts of white cotton hanging on them. It was cotton that had been planted later in the season than usual, and the pickers were slow gathering it in because of the cold weather. The little girl looked out of the window, trying to amuse herself since she suspected that her grandfather had forgotten she was in the car.

He would often forget she was present if he was concentrating on something. Sometimes he would look up and stare at her as if she were a stranger then look down again. Other times when he had no one else to talk to but wanted to expound some theory, he spoke to her as if she were an adult, able to understand biblical philosophy. Occasionally he would allow her to ask questions but she didn't often impress him with her curiosity and he didn't spend much time answering or trying to explain things to her. She had concluded that the best thing she could do in his company was to keep quiet.

Her grandfather caused her to jump by calling her name. While he was waiting for her to acknowledge him, she was wondering whether she had imagined she heard him speak. She decided he had spoken, though he was still driving and behaving the same as before, and she was wondering if she was expected to answer him. She was about to say, yes sir, which was how everyone else answered him, when, whether impatient for her reply or because he had not expected one, he began to talk to her.

The little girl was so startled that she didn't understand the beginning of what he was saying to her. She had never heard him speak in the car on Sunday mornings and was starting to believe that something had come over him, the way she had heard of this happening to other people. It was the sort of thing her grandmother would talk about just now. How a woman who barely uttered a word to anybody had started talking and nobody could shut her up and they had ended up throwing water on her.

The little girl's mind had wandered off in this direction as she tried to explain to herself why her grandfather had suddenly started talking.

She realized though that he was talking to her. He was telling her that she would be going up north.

'I'm going to live up north?' she asked him, thinking she must have misheard him.

Since that was what he had said, the little girl's grandfather saw no reason to repeat himself and he carried on saying what he had to say. Her father was up there and already had a job and had found an apartment for them to move into. Her father had decided he couldn't live in the south any more and he didn't want her going to segregated schools.

'What segregated schools?' The little girl was trying very hard to imagine what was happening so she could begin to understand what her grandfather meant.

He didn't explain what segregated schools were. He said it was because the schools were better and the little girl said, oh. He told her white and coloured children went to school together and she would be learning a lot more and would have more opportunities that she wouldn't have down here.

His sentences flew past the little girl without her grasping very much of what he was saying. He mentioned Philadelphia and the little girl understood that was where her parents were, but she could not imagine where Philadelphia was as she tried to superimpose it over the flat, reddish land on either side of the road. She knew it was a big city and that her aunt and uncle lived there and so she imagined her parents and her aunt and uncle standing together in a big building. The little girl asked her grandfather what an apartment was. He told her it was a few rooms inside a big building. That a lot of people lived in a few rooms inside this building, one on top of the other.

The little girl decided not to ask any more questions. She just listened to her grandfather as he continued to talk. He said her aunt and uncle would be coming south for Thanksgiving and would take her back with them.

She forgot she was supposed to give Miss Green the message from her great-grandmother because Miss Green had rushed up to her as soon as she'd set eyes on the little girl saying how exciting it was going to be moving all the way to Philadelphia and wasn't she a lucky little thing.

Later in the morning, when she did remember what she had been asked to do, the little girl went up to Miss Green with the message. But Miss Green didn't seem to be listening when she repeated word for word what the old woman had said. Miss Green kept smiling down at her saying she thought it was so wonderful, that it was wonderful news and couldn't she come with her. She told the little girl that she had nearly gone north once to study music.

It seemed to the little girl that everybody in church wanted to talk about her moving to Philadelphia. They seemed in awe of the word. Although some of the girls who sat beside her in Sunday School looked at her darkly and said she probably thought she was better than anybody else since she was going up north, and they stayed away from her, staring after her as if she were already too different from them for them to talk to.

As though every person in the congregation didn't already know, her grandfather announced from the pulpit that she was leaving South Carolina for good. Once he'd said that, they gave him their undivided attention in case he imparted a few more details about his son's decision to live up north. But her grandfather was spare with any information he might have and chose instead to liken his son's migration to that of the children of Israel leaving the land of Egypt, while at the same time declaring he would be left to mourn the loss of his son and his son's family. Then, after pausing so they could all reflect on his loss, he asked the congregation in a heavy voice if the circle would be unbroken.

Before he had finished his question some of the older women were calling out in support of his sorrow, but appearing not to hear their words of comfort or being too moved by his speech to pause and acknowledge them, he spoke over their voices asking God how much longer would the coloured man be driven from his home by the white man's staff of prejudice. He said he must pray Mighty and ask the Heavenly Father to watch over my son and his children and if it was His will, then send a wind of change through the south and soften the unfeeling hearts of the white man, send a wind of change that would blow down the wall of hatred that divided His children, one from the other.

The congregation called out to the little girl's grandfather, telling him he was already preaching and they urged him to carry on. But he became silent as if he had become too full of his own emotions to speak further. And they understood this silence and nodded as he cleared his throat and opened the Bible to the text of his sermon.

By the time the little girl's aunt and uncle had arrived the old woman was permanently confined to bed. They would go in individually or in twos for a few minutes at a time and sit silently or talk quietly to each other about nothing in particular as their eyes moved from the bed to some other object in the room. And when some kind of end to their visit had been reached by a final and prolonged sigh, a signal by one or another of them, they got up from a chair, adjusted something in the room and halfway closed the door behind them.

Miss Pelzer came over every day to help tend to the old woman and also to sit with her when they all wanted to go out. Sometimes the little girl was left with Miss Pelzer also, when her aunt and uncle along with her grandparents went off to procure some southern delicacy to take back north with them.

The little girl would linger near the old woman's door,

wanting to see her great-grandmother, believing that if some-how they were alone again, the old woman would speak to her. But she disliked Miss Pelzer's presence so much that she wouldn't go in the room.

What was even worse for the little girl was that the room had been changed so much that it no longer seemed like the old woman's. The chifforobe, with all the old woman's clothes, had been removed and in its place was a large table covered with a white cloth and stacked with linens and towels, a wash basin and soap. The radio had been covered as well and sitting on top of it were large brown bottles of liquid and another stack of white cloths. The blinds were always half drawn, which was something the old woman never did. She raised her blind first thing in the morning and did not pull it again until she was getting herself ready for bed. Instead of sunlight shining in the room, a bright overhead light shone down on everything and there were no more half-hidden corners for the little girl to slip into and feel safe. During the times when the light was turned out the room took on a vagueness which only the white pieces of cloth stood out against.

So the little girl would mill about, somewhere near the door. A few times she stepped inside, almost as if by accident, and received a glance but no word from Miss Pelzer, who had established herself in the old woman's rocking chair, and was busy crocheting some circular object the name of which the little girl had immediately forgotten when Miss Pelzer told her.

After a forlorn look around the room, she would peer over at the bed where the old woman lay, barely visible under her patchwork quilt.

Travelling with her aunt and uncle this time, the little girl and her grandparents went down to the country for Thanksgiving. Again the children were allowed to run about and do as they pleased, and only once did they have to assemble quietly when the little girl's grandfather offered grace over the Thanksgiving dinner. It was a long prayer, but the children were used to long prayers and there were a few coughs and shuffles, most of which were timed to coincide with a 'Yes Lord' or a 'Do Jesus' amen from one of the grown-ups.

After grace, they were herded into the kitchen where they ate their meal on their own, and despite visits and threats from the dining room, it was a riotous affair. They were enjoying being off school and the specialness of Thanksgiving, but their minds were already on Christmas, and they talked and grew excited describing what they wanted and might be getting under the Christmas tree.

The little girl had tried but couldn't imagine what Christmas would be like in Philadelphia. Her cousin Sam said he didn't know what it would be like either. But he told her he knew it snowed there so probably there would be snow all over the ground and everywhere, the same as on the Christmas pictures. Then, professing to know what snow looked like, he slipped off to the parlour and returned with a box of Christmas cards which he said proved he was right.

Together they pored over the box of cards which the little girl couldn't stop rubbing her hands over because of the glitter that covered them. They imagined streets with horse-drawn sleighs, streetlamps lit with candles glowing yellow and houses decorated with holly and bunches of rosy-cheeked children singing under windows, and people in long dresses and waist-coats and top hats carting loads of beautifully wrapped gifts all over Philadelphia.

They concluded that she ought to have a real good time at Christmas. Privately the little girl thought she would have a good time but it didn't make her want to leave her home and go there. She didn't tell her cousin this since he seemed to think that out of the two Christmases, she would have the better one.

The puppies had come out from under the house. Two of them had been given away. The other they had decided to keep to replace Mirrow who was getting old and couldn't track as well as he used to. They played with old Mirrow who'd been around since both of them could remember. They also played with the puppy which had been named Sparky, but he wasn't as obedient and patient as old Mirrow.

It was nearly dark when they sat down on the back steps and

stared into the stableyard where a cow was slowly licking a salt block. Every time it occurred to the little girl that she was going away, she would shake her head before a feeling of sadness could settle upon her. She imagined she was shaking up the little glass box with the little house and flakes of snow that used to be on the old woman's dresser and before the snow flakes could start to settle she would shake again as she had done so many times standing in front of the dresser.

The little girl and her cousin didn't know how to say good-bye to each other. Neither of them had ever gone away for a long time. They hadn't thought about the fact that they might not see each other for years, but they were aware though that time was slipping away and there were only a few hours left and when time was up they could in no way influence what came after. They were aware of this and so they used the remainder of their time together to talk of other things, taking care to agree with each other, which was what they had heard their parents do when saying farewell to someone going far away whom they wouldn't see again for some unknown period of time. It made them feel like grown-ups to hear themselves repeating these adult phrases and it pleased them to realize they knew them well enough to be spontaneous in their replies. They began to realize that doing this was the same as saying goodbye.

'That's one thing,' her cousin said after there had been a thoughtful silence between them. 'There won't be no ole white man up there with dogs to sic on you. Boy, they'd put him in jail so fast. They not allowed to do that in Philadelphia. Policemen a come and take you right off to jail. Yes siree, if they try and sic a dog on you.' He made it sound like the most certain way of being put in jail. 'Be there in a minute with his sireen and he'll take out his gun so fast. He might even shoot him.' He was nodding as if this were a near certainty.

The little girl nodded with him.

'And I know one other thing,' her cousin continued, 'sure would shoot that dog.' He pulled an imaginary gun from his hip and fired it several times at the ground in front of them.

'That ole liquor store man.' The little girl was shaking her head as she looked at the spot where she imagined the dog would have been shot. 'I wish he would come up north,' she said as a dare. 'I bet they would put him in jail as soon as he got up there cause I would go right,' she thumped her knee with her fist, 'right to the police and tell them so they would lock him up in the jailhouse.' Now that they were talking out in the open about the liquor store man, something that had been made possible because of her imminent departure, she was free to show her feelings which were more evident in her voice than what she said.

'Yep, they sure would,' her cousin agreed, feeling anger for her.

There was another thoughtful silence while they both imagined in their own way the liquor store man being apprehended and hauled off to jail by policemen who would show him no mercy. Even if there had been no justice for them and the liquor store man remained free to choose his next victim, at least they had limited the realm of his terror.

'Spirits,' her cousin said, puzzling over the word. 'That's what they called liquor in the north.' He was remembering his uncle talking about tasting the spirit when the men passed around a bottle of whiskey concealed in a brown paper bag. 'Spirits,' he repeated the word.

'The spirit man,' the little girl said. 'The Spirit Man.' It make him sound like something akin to the devil. 'They don't have any spirit man up north cause they not allowed.'

'Nope,' her cousin said in agreement, then after a while he added, 'Up north they got different names for a lot of things.'

He and the little girl nodded wisely.

The dawn when they left was the coldest. As they stirred, a line of light had parted the land from the sky, but both remained black even into the distance. If a rooster hadn't flown up to the top of the chicken coop, there would have been no other sign that a new day had begun.

Their footsteps crunched on the frozen gravel as they packed into the trunk of the car their suitcases and a lunchbox, then checked the car over once more, making sure it was ready for the long drive.

They went into the house for the last time and stood around

the kitchen table studying the map, not because they didn't know the way, but to make note of the places where the highway patrol were known to harass coloured drivers. They repeated stories they had heard, forgetting to drink the coffee the little girl's grandmother had made to warm them up.

The little girl's uncle said, to finalize the discussion, that once they got as far as Washington, D.C. it wouldn't be too bad from there on to Philadelphia. They then discussed filling stations where it was safe to stop and her uncle said maybe they would meet up with another coloured family and they would drive one behind the other which made it less likely that the highway patrol would pull them over.

While they were talking, the little girl walked through the dining room and through to the living room, both of which were in darkness, except for the light shining from the kitchen, and then down the hall which was brightly lit. She went to her room and stood in the doorway. The blankets and sheets had been stripped from her bed and folded as neatly as the little girl could manage on the hope chest at the foot of the bed. The spread had been pulled over to cover the mattress and the pillows. The flatness of the bed made it look odd.

The little girl looked up at the picture of the man and his wife, she had always thought they were husband and wife, standing in the middle of a field of harvested wheat. The picture had hung over the bed for a long time and once, when the little girl had taken it down, she discovered that the wall behind it was a different shade. She had looked at the square patch for a long time as if it might be a picture in itself, then put back the one that hung there. And during the time she had lived there, she had seen as much in that picture as she had through the window. There were times when she felt as though she were walking over the stubbly wheat field seeing a new light in a different sky. She wondered if she would find another picture she could look into as deeply as that one.

The old woman's door was closed. The little girl opened it carefully. Twice before she had stood by the old woman's bed and told her that she was going to live up north in Philadelphia. But the old woman had never opened her eyes or in any way shown that she had heard what the little girl was saying to her.

The little girl tiptoed into the room. Only the lamp beside her bed was on and the old woman's head and shoulders were hidden from her until she walked up to the bed and looked down at her. She called out her name very quietly then waited. She called her once more, her eyes searching the old woman's face. Very slowly and gently she reached over and lifted up the old woman's hand and held it.

Her grandparents stood on the front lawn and watched as their car backed out of the driveway and on to the street. The little girl didn't take her eyes off them until their shapes had disappeared into the darkness. Then she lifted her eyes from where they would still be standing and looked after the light that was shining from the window, until it suddenly went out when the car turned the corner.

Epilogue

She was finally resting herself on the front porch, in time for the early evening air to refresh her, and she was so grateful for the feeling of peace that was settling over her, easing away all the tiredness so that it was hardly worth thinking about. She rocked slowly in her chair, feeling a soft wind on her face, and hearing the sound of the wind brushing against the pines, she hummed an equally soft tune deep in her throat until she heard her mother's voice speaking. She paused for a moment then knew that she could hum and hear her mother's voice at the same time. Like resting at the end of a hard day, she had looked forward to her mother who was company to her, like the wind in the trees.

'I know,' she heard herself say as her mother spoke through the both of them, because she understood all that her mother was and all that she was. So a great love flowed through her as her mother continued to speak.

'Love kin bring you out yourself.' Her mother's voice was full of the strength that she had known in the peak of her life, when nothing could bend her determination or break her spirit. And she saw all that had stood before her mother and all that she had already met and passed and she saw every shade of experience that had shaped her mind and her body and she understood herself when she said, 'I know.'

Their voices embraced them both. Her mother's words caressed her. They were strong, long fingers at the sides of her head brushing away all the sorrow and pain, pulling from her head all the obstacles that stood between them knowing each other. Talking about blame wasn't even necessary.

'Y'all was my children and a love grow inside me as y'all grow inside me. Life suppose to let love grow.'

'I know,' she said again, and the world vibrated through the

222

air like five hundred birds flying out from the trees and she smiled knowing her words had spread so far. She laughed and her voice blended with Tateta's.

'Well sir,' she said and Tateta nodded and together they sat looking down the long rows of cotton they had walked. She wondered if she'd finished but Tateta told her someone else would carry on, that she had picked her rows. She wondered if she could not have done more. Tateta said it was time to enjoy the evening.

She nodded her head and didn't need to speak again. They were one and had gone beyond talking. She pressed her foot against the softness of her sister's back and Tateta took hold of it and she understood how they were all one and that no work had been left undone, that another one would take her place as they had passed down to them and through them all the things that they were, and it would be their turn to uncover and behold the love that was meant to continue growing once life separated and began on its own. They could see all this in their oneness because in their time they had held it, shrouded but alive, burning in them sometimes. It glowed between them like the sunset. It warmed them and spread through their bodies in the late evening but they had to leave it to someone else, to spread its warmth on to others, in time.

The old woman reached out as far as she could and held on to a hand to pass on some of the warmth from her sunset. She wondered if it would be known. Tateta said love would always be known. She took a deep sigh and held on to her mother's hand and let go of the other. She glimpsed the rows of cotton that lay ahead and saw someone moving towards it as twilight set on the day.